**"You seem taken aback
that I should praise you, Miss Mortimer. . . ."**

"I confess I am, Sir Greville," she replied, deciding that honesty was the best policy.

"Would you like me to revoke my words?" He smiled a little. It wasn't exactly a warm smile, but neither was it cold. Just somewhere in between. "Perhaps I will be able to convince you of my sincerity when I escort you to the ball tonight. I vow I will show you every attention."

The ball! After the excitement of the night, she had quite forgotten it!

Coming next month

THE NOTORIOUS WIDOW
by Allison Lane

When a scoundrel tries to tarnish a young widow's reputation, a valiant earl tries to repair the damage—and mend her broken heart as well.

"**A formidable talent.**" —*Romantic Times*

☐ 0-451-20166-3 / $4.99

THE PRODIGAL HERO
by Nancy Butler

MacHeath, a former sailor, regains his honor by rescuing the daughter of his former employer. But he never imagined that he'd also rescue her heart.

"**A writer not to be missed.**" —*Mary Balogh*

☐ 0-451-20172-8 / $4.99

A GRAND DESIGN
by Emma Jensen

A marquess requires the services of an architect, but is completely unprepared for the audacious charms of the architect's niece.

"**One of my favorites.**" —*Barbara Metzger*

☐ 0-451-20121-3 / $4.99

Mistletoe Mischief

Sandra Heath

A SIGNET BOOK

SIGNET
Published by New American Library, a division of
Penguin Putnam Inc., 375 Hudson Street,
New York, New York 10014, U.S.A.
Penguin Books Ltd, 27 Wrights Lane,
London W8 5TZ, England
Penguin Books Australia Ltd, Ringwood,
Victoria, Australia
Penguin Books Canada Ltd, 10 Alcorn Avenue,
Toronto, Ontario, Canada M4V 3B2
Penguin Books (N.Z.) Ltd, 182–190 Wairau Road,
Auckland 10, New Zealand

Penguin Books Ltd, Registered Offices:
Harmondsworth, Middlesex, England

First published by Signet, an imprint of New American Library,
a division of Penguin Putnam Inc.

First Printing, October 2000
10 9 8 7 6 5 4 3 2 1

 REGISTERED TRADEMARK—MARCA REGISTRADA

Printed in the United States of America

PUBLISHER'S NOTE
This is a work of fiction. Names, characters, places, and incidents either are the
product of the author's imagination or are used fictitiously, and any resemblance
to actual persons, living or dead, business establishments, events, or locales is
entirely coincidental.

BOOKS ARE AVAILABLE AT QUANTITY DISCOUNTS WHEN USED TO PROMOTE PROD-
UCTS OR SERVICES. FOR INFORMATION PLEASE WRITE TO PREMIUM MARKETING DIVI-
SION, PENGUIN PUTNAM INC., 375 HUDSON STREET, NEW YORK, NEW YORK 10014.

Chapter 1

Lady Evangeline Radcliffe was not in the mood to brook argument. Oh, indeed not. The trials of being a certain age were irksome enough already without having an insolent lodging keeper to deal with as well. She had just journeyed twenty uncomfortable miles from Bath, enduring flushes that required an open carriage window regardless of the freezing December temperature, and she had no intention of being fobbed off by Mr. Tully Ramsbotham, a pompous carrot-topped fellow who was built like an outhouse and had the manners to match!

The plumes on her fashionable brown velvet hat trembled as she confronted him in the chilly hallway of his three-story kingdom in the market square of Wells. His stubborn effrontery was the only obstacle between her and the young woman she had been secretly seeking for eight years, so she glared up at him from her diminutive five feet one inch.

"Don't make the mistake of trifling with me, Mr. Ramsbotham, for I am not one of your unfortunate servants. Besides, this is supposed to be the season of goodwill, or had that escaped your attention? Now, then, I have been given to understand that a Miss Mortimer is newly staying here, and I wish to see her immediately." With a peremptory flick of her fur-lined traveling cloak, she marched into his cozy low-beamed parlor, where a maid was attaching a garland of Christmas greenery to the mantelshelf.

It was the sixteenth of December, a Tuesday, and pale afternoon sunlight shone coldly through the small uneven panes of the bow window. It was a far cry from the previous day, when a terrible storm had lashed the land. Now it was calm and peaceful again, and outside, the crowded square of the little cathedral city in Somerset was cluttered with stalls as seasonal preparations got under way. The magnificent towers of the nearby cathedral soared above the rooftops, and the air was so still that smoke rose vertically from chimneys. Icicles hung from eaves, everyone's breath stood out in clouds, and roast chestnuts were much in demand. The sound of street calls and fiddle music drifted into the room, and a dog set up a clamor as a stagecoach departed from the town's principal inn, where only moments before Evangeline had secured the only tolerable rooms, and where her elderly French maid, Annie, was at that moment making everything as comfortable as she could.

Mr. Ramsbotham, a former blacksmith who could easily have picked Evangeline up in one fist, was momentarily too startled to do anything, but then he saw red. Fists clenched, he pursued his unwelcome caller into the parlor. "You can't come in here as if you own the place, my lady! This is *my* property!"

"I am aware of whose property it is, sirrah."

"So grand lady or not, you're trespassing, and I want you out of here right now!" he shouted. The maid's eyes widened, and she abandoned her holly, ivy, and mistletoe to hurry out.

Evangeline wasn't intimidated. "Oh, stuff and nonsense, Mr. Ramsbotham," she declared. "Such a fuss about so little! Just bring Miss Mortimer, and all will be swiftly accomplished. Well, don't just stand there, man, go to it!" She waved him away as if he were an irritating fly.

He was sorely tempted to bundle her off the premises, fancy plumes and all, but then discretion belatedly achieved victory over valor; after all, she *was* titled, and heaven alone knew what hornets' nest she could stir up for him if the mood took her. A nerve twitched at his temple as he bit back his anger. "Very well, my lady. I will see that Miss Mortimer is informed of your presence."

She gave him an infuriatingly gracious nod. "That was all you needed to say in the first place."

He scowled and went out, but the moment the door closed behind him, Evangeline's hazel eyes became less certain. Was she making a monumental error of judgment by coming here? With a sigh she placed her reticule and sable muff on a table. Beneath her cloak she wore a fawn merino pelisse and matching gown, and on her feet there were neat brown ankle boots that laced at the back. Everything about her was *à la mode,* as might be expected from someone who resided in the most prestigious area of Brighton, and whose forays to London were for the sole purpose of visiting a preeminent dressmaker.

Removing her gloves, she went to hold her cold hands out to the welcome warmth of the fire. Then she glanced critically at her reflection in the faded mirror on the chimney breast. Maybe she was a little embonpoint now, which was to be expected in her fifty-first year, but thankfully she still retained some of the looks that had once made her the toast of the capital. Her hair was now liberally sprinkled with gray, and these days she was obliged to employ Chinese cosmetic papers on her cheeks to lessen the too healthy bloom resulting from years of Brighton's incomparable sea air. But the paper, powder, or cream had not yet been invented that could conceal the mortifying flushes she had been beset by for the past six months or so. Her mother used to say that such things were a sign of being "past it," but Evangeline didn't feel past anything, in fact, having never married, she didn't feel she had even reached it yet!

However, this December of 1806 her life had certainly reached a turning point, for not only had she finally bowed to royal pressure and agreed to sell her beloved home in Brighton to the Prince of Wales—a fact she had yet to impart to her relatives—but she could no longer stand by and allow those same relatives to fritter away their chances of happiness. The time had come to act, but she would have to wait until New Year's Eve before she could really start.

The forthcoming sale of Radcliffe House was almost the least of her problems, and had only come about because Prinny was determined to further enlarge his precious Marine Pavilion. Both properties stood side by side overlooking Brighton's famous Steine, and in recent years the Pavilion had been extended so much that it was practically cheek by jowl with Radcliffe House. This had created a rather jarring effect because Radcliffe House was a square four stories built of redbrick, whereas the Pavilion was a long, low two stories covered with cream tiles. From the moment Prinny got it into his head to raze both Radcliffe House and the upper portion of Great East Street to the ground in order to improve his own property, she had known no peace. Not that the matter was anything other than amicable, for she and the prince were good friends and he was paying far more than her property was worth; but right now it was just another irritation.

Far more imminent and problematical was the matter of sorting out people's private lives. She had silly heads to knock together, desired matches to bring about, scoundrels to see off, and orphans to rescue. And that was without the added vexation of the Tully Ramsbothams of this world, and the Rollo Witherspoons of the next! She knew Rollo was somewhere in the room with her now, because she had not only heard his footsteps accompanying her, but also his ghostly "tut" at the lodging keeper's insolence. Mr. Ramsbotham and the maid heard nothing of course; but then they wouldn't. Nobody else did. It was most frustrating, but she could hardly admit to the world that she went everywhere with the persistent spirit of a Restoration actor at her heels! She knew those around her feared she was a little mad, but it couldn't be helped, for when one was being haunted, there was very little one could do about it. Besides, Rollo could be quite agreeable company when he chose.

As if he knew her thoughts, Rollo began to address

her from somewhere over her left shoulder. "Mistress, I think—"

"Not now, if you please, Master Witherspoon, for I have things of my own to think about."

"As thou wishest, mistress."

Evangeline gazed into the mirror, her twenty-six-year-old favorite nephew and chosen heir, Lord Rupert Radcliffe, uppermost in her mind. He had dismayed everyone when he foolishly spurned Chloe, the daughter of Evangeline's oldest and dearest friend in Brighton, Admiral Sir Jocelyn Holcroft. Chloe was adorable, with short golden hair, big blue eyes, and a dainty figure. Enchantingly scatterbrained, impulsive, and kindhearted, Chloe was the perfect bride for Rupert, who was the youngest son of Evangeline's brother, the Duke of Dencaster. But he had bungled his opportunity, and now a certain Oliver March was slyly insinuating himself into her affections. The latest whisper suggested an announcement on St. Valentine's Day, which wouldn't do at all! Mr. March should be given his congé, and Rupert's ears should be soundly boxed.

Evangeline gave her reflection a long-suffering look, for her other nephew, Sir Greville Seton, presented as great a problem. Greville wasn't strictly her nephew, more a third or fourth cousin one removed, or some such convoluted thing, but whatever the connection, she called him nephew. He was handsome, dashing, charming, wealthy, and sought after; but he was also complex and—occasionally—downright difficult. At thirty-four he should have been married long since, but there was no sign of a bride. That had to be rectified, for if ever a man was in need of a wife, it was Greville.

Finally, in Miss Megan Mortimer, Evangeline had the orphan in need of rescue; provided she was the right Megan Mortimer, of course. Oh, surely there could not be another who apparently fitted the bill so completely? This Megan's age and background was right, so she *must* be the right one. It was a great pity that she was a companion, because Greville would dislike her on principle, but it couldn't be helped. Whatever his opinion on the matter, his aunt was determined to gather the young lady safely into her protection. And to think that if the customary Christmas arrangements had not gone wrong this year, Megan might never have been discovered at all.

It had started several weeks ago, when she realized that her usual yuletide guests could not come until New Year's Eve because of prior commitments of one sort or another. Then had come an invitation to stay in Bath with her old friend Lady Jane Strickland, with whom she had almost lost all contact. Yesterday she had arrived in Bath to find Jane's loathsome son and daughter-in-law, Ralph and Sophia, on the point of leaving for London, having cut short the first visit they had made to Bath after a long family rift. The rift was apparently in danger of resumption because Sophia, elder daughter of Lord and Lady Garsington of Brighton and every bit as objectionable as her parents, had discovered Ralph in shocking circumstances with the young woman employed as his mother's companion. Ralph claimed to have been the innocent victim of shameless advances, and Sophia had demanded the companion's immediate dismissal without a reference.

Jane had rather reprehensibly complied, for it was apparent to everyone that if any shameless advances had taken place, they had been of Ralph's lecherous doing. But Jane's compliance had not been swift enough for Sophia, who had never wished to mend the rift in the first place; hence the precipitate departure for the capital.

The ill-used companion, Miss Megan Mortimer, had already packed and departed when Evangeline arrived at the Strickland residence. Megan had come here to Wells because a post was advertised by the bishop's wife, although without a reference her chances of success were minimal.

The moment Evangeline heard the companion's name, she had abandoned all thought of Christmas with Jane in order to give pursuit. In a few moments now she hoped to come face-to-face with the young woman who had no connection with her whatsoever, but whose welfare was vital to her peace of mind. She reached inside her cloak to finger the beautiful gold locket at her throat.

Maybe it was all going to be in vain, but whatever the outcome, she would have tried her best.

Rollo broke into her thoughts by suddenly clearing his throat. "Wilt thou hear my soliloquy now, mistress?" he asked hopefully.

"Master Witherspoon, your wretched soliloquy will have to wait until we are home in Brighton, for this is neither the appropriate time nor place for *Hamlet*!" Evangeline replied tartly.

His footsteps crossed to the abandoned greenery, which he kicked pettishly. "Yon surly Ramsbotham taketh a plaguey long time," he grumbled.

"I dare say he is being deliberately slow to spite me," she replied.

"A knave, if ever I perceived one." The ghost sighed. "Mistress, art thou *quite* sure of all this? Might it not be that Master Ralph spoke truthfully? What if Mistress Mortimer is a trollop after all?"

"I've already told you, I'm not sure of anything," she replied a little impatiently, for they had argued about this all the way from Bath. Of *course* there was a chance that Ralph had been honest for once, but she rather thought pigs would sew fishing nets on the Steine first!

At that moment there came a timid knock at the door. Evangeline braced herself for her first glimpse of Miss Megan Mortimer. First impressions were so very important. . . . "Enter," she said.

Chapter 2

Megan came in. She was in her early twenties, and of medium height, with a small-waisted figure and heavy nut-brown hair that was pinned up beneath a white muslin day bonnet. Her mustard wool gown was high-waisted and tightly buttoned at the cuffs, and there was a plain white shawl around her shoulders. Her face was striking rather than pretty, for her mouth was a little too wide and her nose perhaps a fraction too straight, but her complexion was without fault. Her eyes, light brown and melting, were respectfully lowered as she came in and closed the door.

Evangeline's heart quickened, for the likeness was quite uncanny, especially those eyes. She drew herself up sharply. Don't let your heart rule your head completely! "Look at me, girl, and come closer, that I may see you properly," she instructed.

Megan obeyed, and then asked. "Why do you wish to see me, Lady Evangeline?"

The question was answered with another. "Does my name mean anything to you, Miss Mortimer?"

"I have heard Lady Jane Strickland speak of you, and know that you are to spend Christmas with her this year, but that is all I know. Lady Jane was my last employer," Megan added.

"Yes, I am aware of that. So my name has never been mentioned in the past? Before you went to Lady Jane?" Evangeline held her breath.

"Before?" Puzzlement shadowed Megan's eyes. "No, Lady Evangeline."

Well, that was only to be expected, Evangeline supposed. "May I inquire why you left Lady Jane's employ?" Let's see how discreet the girl could be.

Megan met her inquisitor's gimlet gaze. "I left because I felt it was time to make a fresh start."

"Pastures new?"

"Yes."

"Hmm. And you have made this momentous decision immediately before Christmas, when you have no new position to go to, and no reference either? With all due respect, I find that hard to believe."

"I came here because I knew of a post with the wife of the Bishop of Bath and Wells, but the place has been filled. There is an element of doubt, however, so I thought it might be prudent to stay for a few days, in case the vacancy should arise again. When Mr. Ramsbotham told me someone wished to see me, my first thought was that it was someone from the Bishop's Palace." Megan avoided Evangeline's eyes, for the truth of it was that her lack of a suitable reference from Lady Jane had raised doubts in the mind of the bishop's wife.

Evangeline smiled. "I commend your reticence, Miss Mortimer, for I know you to have been greatly wronged by Ralph Strickland and his wretched wife." She saw hot, embarrassed color flood into Megan's cheeks, and went on. "Ralph is known to my nephews, who speak of him as an unconscionable womanizer, and as for Sophia, well she is a Garsington, and her family are my near neighbors in Brighton. That is a misfortune for both Brighton and me, I assure you. Now, then, enough of others, for I wish to know more about you, my dear. You told Lady Jane that you were left destitute on the unfortunate early demise of your parents?"

"Yes. My father owned a modest Northamptonshire estate called Berengers, and my mother was from a noble but far from wealthy Scottish family. They died in a boating accident in the Lake District eight years ago, when I was a pupil at a seminary for young ladies in Bath. It transpired that my father had neglected to take full account of my position in such a tragic event, and everything he owned went to a distant male cousin, who saw

no reason to provide for me." Megan glanced away, for
since being forced to become a companion, she had
never once mentioned her one and only relative; indeed,
she had done her utmost to banish him from her
memory.

Evangeline sympathized, although she exulted inside
because she now knew beyond all shadow of doubt that
this was the Megan Mortimer she sought. "I fear that in
this day and age there is a great deal of such heart-
lessness, Miss Mortimer. However, do go on."

"Well, that is all there is to tell, really. Because my
cousin wanted nothing to do with me, I was obliged to
leave the seminary and seek employment. I was only
sixteen at the time, and therefore very fortunate to find
the post with Lady Jane. I am sorry I have had to leave
her, but I understand the awkwardness of her position."

"Which is more than I do, for she had no business
supporting Ralph and Sophia. You have too generous a
nature, Miss Mortimer." Evangeline hesitated. "Were
your parents happy together?" she asked suddenly.

It was such an oddly personal question that Megan
was startled. "I-I beg your pardon, my lady?"

Now it was Evangeline's turn to color. "Oh, no matter.
Well, now, Miss Mortimer, I am seeking a companion,
and everything about you meets with my approval. The
post is yours if you wish." The offer was a compromise,
because Evangeline could not bring herself to tell the
truth. All in good time; there was no need to rush bull-
headed at it. . . .

"You—you wish to employ me?" Megan was caught
off guard.

"Yes, Miss Mortimer."

Megan knew she ought to ask questions. "I, er . . .
What duties will you require?"

"Duties?" Evangeline looked blank. "Well, what did
you do for Lady Jane?"

"I read to her, I went shopping for her, I brought her
shawl when she required it, and walked with her. If she
wished to drive out in her carriage, I accompanied her,
and—"

"Yes, yes, well, those are my requirements too." Evangeline didn't care what tasks Megan carried out, just that she came to reside at Radcliffe House. "The terms of employment will be exactly as those you enjoyed with Lady Jane, commencing now. And you may rest assured that I no longer intend to spend Christmas in Bath, but will be returning to Brighton tomorrow."

"I would very much like to accept your kind offer, indeed I would be truly grateful and deeply honored to do so, it's just . . ."

"Yes?"

Megan was embarrassed. "Lady Evangeline, I-I am very anxious indeed that Mr. Strickland's lies about my conduct should go no further."

Evangeline smiled understandingly. "You surely do not fear I will, er, blab I believe the word is?"

"Not exactly, it is just that . . ." Megan didn't quite know how to put it without causing offense, but there was no denying the fact that those of Lady Evangeline's rank usually thought little of the sensitivities of persons well below them on the social ladder.

"It's just that what, Miss Mortimer?" Evangeline prompted curiously.

"You might not think it as important as I do."

"My dear, I think it very important indeed. A woman's reputation is everything in this day and age, so not a word will pass my lips about the circumstances of your departure from Bath. I trust you are reassured?"

Megan gave her a grateful smile. "Yes. Thank you for your understanding, Lady Evangeline."

"Not at all, my dear. It is settled, then. Now, then, I do not wish you to remain in this ramshackle place a moment longer. I have taken rooms at the Angel opposite, and wish you to join me. I trust you like sea air? Brighton has a great deal of it, I fear."

"I have no experience of sea air, Lady Evangeline, but I am sure I shall like it very much indeed."

"Good. The season is in full swing there at the moment, but company will be a little thin at Radcliffe House until New Year's Eve. However, we will make the best of it. Are you interested in amateur dramatics? And by that I do not mean the hothouse vapors of which Sophia Strickland has made such a study."

Before Megan could answer, the greenery on the floor moved slightly. It was only a small movement, and most people would not have noticed, but it happened to catch Megan's eye. She looked down in horror, fearing it might be one of the rats she had observed in the backyard. But then a sprig of mistletoe somehow broke off, and floated up into the air. Megan was transfixed. "I-I'm afraid I have never had cause to follow an interest in theatricals, Lady Evangeline," she managed to stammer, watching the mistletoe's mysterious progress.

Evangeline had not observed anything. "Radcliffe House boasts a very fine private theater, and every year I present a play for my considerable circle of friends. It has been postponed until the new year on this occasion, but it will still take place, possibly for the last time, as I am about to sell the house to the Prince of Wales, who will pull it down to make room for more of his Pavilion. However, that is in the future, and as things are right now, everyone who spends Christmas beneath my roof is obliged to join in the play. You will escape an actual role because everything has already been cast, but I'm sure you will be excellent at prompting."

"Yes, Lady Evangeline." Megan's bemused gaze was still fixed upon the floating mistletoe."

"Master Witherspoon, put that down this instant!" Evangeline breathed, and the mistletoe fell abruptly to the floor.

The hairs at the nape of Megan's neck prickled uncomfortably. Was her new employer a little moonstruck? One thing was certain, if a message were to summon her to the Bishop's Palace right now, she would definitely change her mind about becoming Lady Evangeline Radcliffe's companion! But such a message wasn't likely to be forthcoming, and beggars could not be choosers; so Brighton it had to be.

Chapter 3

One day later in London, at about the time Evangeline and Megan—and Rollo, of course—were setting out from Wells for Winchester, where they would spend the night at the Crown Inn before continuing to Brighton, Sir Greville Seton and Lord Rupert Radcliffe left Greville's fine town house, and went for a stroll in the railed garden of Berkeley Square. Rain threatened from the leaden sky, and they huddled in their greatcoats and pulled their top hats low as the chill breeze shivered through the bare-branched plane trees, some of which bore the scars of the storm earlier in the week. The vanilla smell of fine confectionery floated from Gunter's in the southeast corner of the square, and a rosy-faced countryman selling holly from a donkey cart was calling at the elegant Mayfair houses, many of which were already closed for the holiday; it was very different from the bustle and noise of the marketplace in Wells.

Greville paused by the equestrian statue of King George III in the middle of the garden. "I don't know about you, Rupert, but I'm almost beginning to regret spending Christmas in town."

"So am I, but it can't be helped." Rupert raised his ivory-handled cane to prod His Majesty's horse, wishing the creature would bolt and provide at least some fleeting diversion. His beautifully tailored fawn greatcoat was worn over a wine-red coat and gray breeches, and there were golden tassels on his highly polished Hessian boots. He had fair hair and green eyes, and an aquiline nose. There was usually an amiable smile on his face, but he had been less than cheerful since declining Chloe Holcroft.

Greville drew a heavy breath. "I really thought there would be more going on here than there is, but the *beau monde* seems to have departed. Except Sybil Garsington and her ferocious brother." He said this last with a grimace.

"And Prinny."

"And Prinny," Greville conceded.

By December the Prince of Wales would usually have been ensconced in his adored Marine Pavilion, but this year ill health obliged him to remain in London. However, that had not prevented most people of consequence from removing to the Sussex resort as usual for the winter months. It might have been royal patronage that had made Brighton the second most fashionable town in the land after the capital, but it was high society in general that kept it in such an exclusive position.

Greville continued. "Well, Prinny is not so bad, in fact he can be most agreeable; but to stumble upon Garsingtons at every turn . . ." He shuddered as much as Evangeline when it came to that particular family. Sybil was the younger of Lord and Lady Garsington's two awful daughters, Sophia Strickland being the elder. Their hotheaded brother Sigismund was plump and as bald as a coot, but of such a dangerously combustible temperament that he was known to generally act first and ask questions afterward, as his record of dueling bore witness. In this and this alone he was formidably talented. Unfortunately, he and his entire family also prided themselves on their musicianship, at which they were universally dreadful. Lord Garsington played the cello, her ladyship the spinet, Sybil the harp, Sophia the violin, and Sigismund the hautbois. Musical evenings at Garsington House on the Steine were dreaded by one and all, but were notoriously difficult to avoid. Once there, only the tone deaf or those with the most insensitive eardrums escaped unscathed.

Rupert's gloom lifted for a moment as he grinned at Greville. "Just because Sybil has decided you will make a fine consolation prize."

"I'm glad you find it amusing, because I'm damned if I do," Greville replied with feeling. Sybil had been brought to London in the care of her brother in order to nurse her apparently broken heart. Some fellow in Brighton had not only resisted her advances but made clear his interest in another, so Lord and Lady Garsington had hastily dispatched her to the capital before she ruined her reputation in her attempts to win him back. It was only the thought of his sister's good name that had prevented Sigismund Garsington from challenging the man concerned to a duel. Greville didn't know who the fellow was, but cursed him soundly. If it hadn't been for him, Sybil wouldn't have come to London, and the life of Sir Greville Seton would have continued in its previous tranquil way!

Rupert nodded. "I agree, it's not funny at all."

"Why should I suffer because Sybil's heart is broken. Have you any idea what it's like to be pursued by such a strapping great amazon? It has reached the point where I expect her to leap from behind every tree, her harp lashed to her back, and her alarming bosom heaving as she lisps at me in that huge voice. Oh, Thir Gweville, Thir Gweville, wender me your arm that we may thtwoll together. Thall I play a Thakethpeare thonnet for you?"

"You shouldn't be so devastatingly handsome. It's the tight breeches, you know. All that manly perfection banishes female inhibition."

"She hasn't got any inhibitions to banish."

"True."

Greville gave a slight chuckle. "Mind you, I don't think I've ever laughed so much as I did last Christmas when she had twanged and warbled her way through 'Where the bee thuckth, there thuck I.'" He leaned back against the statue's plinth, his cane tapping against his gleaming boot. He was an arresting blend of the rugged and romantic, with thick almost black hair, and steel-gray eyes that could be disconcertingly cold if he was displeased. When he chose he was possessed of a singular charm, and his dry wit made him popular among his peers. His taste in clothes was impeccable, as his braided charcoal greatcoat, dark blue coat, and tight-fitting cream breeches bore full witness. Nothing could have been more discreet and perfect than the black pearl pin reposing in his starched muslin neck cloth, and there were few who could carry off the rakish angle at which he wore his top hat. On top of all these desirable attributes, he was also immensely wealthy, which made him the target of every hopeful mama with a daughter to marry off. But Greville had yet to find a young lady who even turned his head, let alone stirred his heart; the awful Sybil Garsington certainly wouldn't. He gave a careworn sigh. "I am ashamed to admit it, Rupert, but there have been times when I've felt tempted to shoot the whole Garsington family."

Rupert grinned again. "Oh, that won't do at all, my friend, for Aunt E won't tolerate mass murder in the family."

"More's the pity."

Rupert shivered as the cold breeze blustered again. "Anyway, Greville, why have you insisted on bringing me out in this damned cold? What is it you wish to speak to me about that couldn't be said inside?"

"I didn't want any servant ears to hear because it's about Chloe."

Rupert stiffened. "That is a closed subject."

"No, it isn't, because it's your continuing boneheadness over her that has occasioned you to foist yourself on me for Christmas."

"Look, if you resent my company, why don't you just say so!"

"For heaven's sake, Rupert, don't be so damned touchy. Did I say I resent your company?"

Rupert looked away. "No, I suppose not," he conceded. "Greville, I just don't want to talk about Chloe."

"Why? Because you know you made a disastrous decision when you spurned her?"

Rupert's green eyes swung resentfully back to him. "Certainly not. I like Chloe very much, but only as a friend, so why does everyone think I should marry her?"

Greville studied him shrewdly, deciding the time was right to make him face up to a few things. "Well, if that's the way you feel, then you won't mind the talk I overheard at White's last night."

"There's *always* talk at White's. Sometimes I think

there's more gossip at that club than there is among Billingsgate fishwives!"

"On this occasion the fishwives have it that Chloe will be betrothed to Oliver March in the new year. The odds are apparently on St. Valentine's Day."

Rupert was visibly shaken. "Tell me you jest."

"I fear not."

"But it cannot be so, Chloe doesn't even know March!"

"Oh, yes, she does. The Holcrofts met him at the beginning of November when they came up to town. They were among Prinny's dinner guests at Carlton House, and March was there too. It seems he was much smitten with Chloe, so much so that he has followed her back to Brighton and taken lodgings for the winter. Duchess Place, I believe. He's there now, from all accounts."

Rupert leaned a hand against the statue, and bowed his head. "Well, now we know who he preferred to Sybil Garsington," he muttered.

Greville's lips parted in astonishment. "*March* was the fellow in Brighton?"

"I presumed you knew." Rupert struggled to overcome his emotion, for Oliver March was one of the men he loathed most in all the world.

"No, the actual name was never mentioned to me."

"He and Sybil richly deserve each other, but I still can't believe Chloe could be taken in by him." Rupert was so incensed he struck the statue with his cane.

"You only have yourself to blame if Chloe has cut her losses and turned elsewhere," Greville pointed out bluntly.

"So it's *my* fault that she has apparently fallen into the clutches of a man like March?"

"Yes, as a matter of fact it is." Greville wasn't about to mince his words.

Rupert glowered at him. "I hardly think that's fair!"

"It's very fair," Greville replied without sympathy.

Rupert looked away. "I think I despise March more than any other man alive."

"You couldn't prove he palmed that ace." Greville recalled the occasion, the tense faces caught in the muted glow of the shaded lamp in the center of the green baize table.

"I still know he did!" Rupert snapped.

"Undoubtedly, but it would be a great fool who challenged him without a shred of real evidence. I think he is second only to Sigismund Garsington when it comes to dangerous hotheadedness. If ever there was a man who lives up to his red hair, it's March!"

"Maybe, but that isn't the only reason I abhor him. Did you hear about that so-called drunken waiter at the Union Club a couple of months ago?"

"I don't know any details."

"Then let me acquaint you. March and his bosom bird of a feather, Ralph Strickland, were in it together. The poor waiter hadn't touched a drop except the glass March so generously handed to him. It was liberally laced with some diabolical eastern tincture Strickland acquired in Constantinople. The effect was one of unbridled enthusiasm, so much so that the waiter had to be physically restrained from leaping off London Bridge. March and Strickland thought it all highly amusing, and had no qualms about allowing the unfortunate man to be dismissed. When I found out what they had done, I saw to it that he was reinstated. March and Strickland are without a doubt the two most irredeemable reptiles in the whole of England, and March is certainly not fit to utter Chloe's name, let alone pursue her." Rupert faced Greville. "Damn it, I can't possibly stand by and let her marry him!"

Greville spread his hands. "How can you prevent it? You have slunk here to London, leaving Brighton to him. Just think of all the Christmas festivities, the kissing boughs of mistletoe, the—"

"Oh, do stop!" Rupert was distraught.

"Why don't you just admit that you are in love with her?" Greville suggested quietly.

"Because I'm not."

"Liar."

A conflict of emotions struggled upon Rupert's face, but then he exhaled slowly and bowed his head. "Yes, you're right, I *do* love her. I wish I had known it before, but what's done is done." Having at last admitted the truth to himself, he fell silent. The thought of an angel like Chloe with a devil like Oliver March was too horrible for words.

Chapter 4

"Rupert, you must tell Chloe how you feel before it's too late," Greville urged.

"If there's to be a St. Valentine's Day betrothal, it's already too late," Rupert murmured resignedly.

"Don't be so damned defeatist. It's a rumor, that's all. She isn't wearing his ring yet."

Rupert swallowed. "Call me defeatist if you wish, but after the way I've behaved, I don't think I'll ever have the nerve to approach her again."

"Is she worth fighting for or not?" Greville inquired.

"Of course!"

"Then, you'll have to *find* the nerve, won't you?"

"I suppose so. Why did it have to be March? First he cheats me at cards, now he steals the woman I love!"

"Forget the damned card game, for it's in the past. Chloe is all that matters."

Rupert gave him an incredulous look. "Stop dwelling on the past? By all the saints, that's rich coming from you!"

Now it was Greville's turn to stiffen. "That has nothing to do with it."

"So it's one rule for you, another for me? I think not, coz. The balance is even: I choose to dwell upon March's sleight of hand, you choose to dwell upon your father's marital misdeeds."

Greville looked away, a hint of bitterness shadowing his handsome face. Yes, he *did* dwell upon the past. He had never forgiven his late father for going off with his mother's companion, and as a consequence he loathed companions as a breed. Only a certain type of woman sought such positions, a scheming, ambitious, conscience-less type of woman who would stop at nothing to get what she wanted. They were all the same; nothing would ever change his mind on *that*!

Rupert wished he hadn't tilted the conversation in this particular direction, and changed the subject. "I believe we are very much in Aunt E's bad books for letting her down this Christmas. It's strange that *everyone* has cried off, for the house is usually full to overflowing."

"Perhaps they all dread the theatricals as much as I do," Greville muttered.

"You're the only one with a gripe."

"With good reason," Greville replied.

Rupert gave a shy grin. "But I thought you made an excellent Bottom last year. It was a shame your ass's head got stuck."

"I'm sure you would have found it equally as amusing if the elite of Brighton, including the Prince of Wales and Mrs. Fitzherbert, convulsed at *your* expense. Damn and blast Bottom! The miserable experience of playing him was the last straw for me. I'm determined to stay away from Brighton until at least the end of January." Memories of Aunt E's production of *A Midsummer Night's Dream* would surely torment Greville for the rest of his life.

"January? You can't do that!" Rupert gasped. "You promised her you'd go down with me on New Year's Eve! She's even sent us our roles for *Twelfth Night*!"

"Yes, and you are to be the hero of the piece, hand-some Duke Orsino, while *I* am marked to be Malvolio, the pompous steward who makes a fool of himself in cross-gartered yellow stockings! Oh, I can just imagine the relish with which our dear aunt penned my name in for *him*!"

"You're jealous because you wish to be Duke Orsino!" Rupert declared.

"Rupert, I neither wish to be nor intend to be anything at all."

"For pity's sake, it's only a bit of fun."

"Really? Well, I don't recall you feeling quite like that

last year. You didn't relish being togged out in Oberon's
pink doublet and bright green hose, because you said
you looked like a monstrous tulip."

"All right, all right, I admit it, but that's the only thing
I disliked. I enjoy Aunt E's plays."

Greville held his gaze. "If that is so, and if you have
also decided to ride to Chloe's rescue on your white
charger, why don't you toddle down to Brighton for
Christmas after all? There's nothing to stop you, is
there?"

"Only the small matter of Aunt E not being there
either. Radcliffe House is closed until New Year's Eve."

Greville was startled. "That's the first I've heard of it!"

"I can't help it if I'm a good correspondent, whereas
you delay your letter-writing as long as you can."

"If she's not in Brighton, where is she?"

"Bath," Rupert replied. "When everyone let her
down, she accepted an invitation from Lady Jane Strickland. She's there now, and won't return to Brighton until
New Year's Eve."

Greville raised an eyebrow. "Strickland, did you say?"

Rupert nodded. "Yes. Ralph Strickland's mother, actually, but I gather that she is quite tolerable. At least, she
was. Aunt E hadn't heard from her in an age."

"I ran into dear Ralph and his Medusa of a wife at
the Theatre Royal last night. They have just returned
from Bath, but they didn't mention seeing Aunt E. Mind
you, I had the impression that Strickland had some embarrassing trouble there with his mother's companion,
who had to be dismissed as a consequence. Sophia was
still incandescent about it."

"Doesn't it occur to you that Strickland was more
probably the culprit than the companion?"

"You know my opinion of companions."

"I know your prejudice, if that's what you mean," Rupert replied in a tart tone that was not all that unlike
his aunt's.

Greville coolly returned to a previous topic. "Radcliffe
House is empty, you say?"

"Yes. Well, except for Master Rollo Witherspoon, I

suppose, unless he's gone to Bath as well." Rupert smiled. "Aunt E is delightful company and I adore her, but I also think she is slightly dotty, increasingly so over the past six months. Rollo Witherspoon is in her imagination, nothing more and nothing less."

Greville pursed his lips. "Except we know he existed because we looked him up in the old records at the Theatre Royal. He was the grandnephew of the Bard of Avon, and a member of King Charles II's Company of Actors."

"Agreed, but have you ever actually seen proof that his spirit is now dwelling at Radcliffe House?" Rupert demanded.

"No," Greville conceded. "I just think that Aunt E has become so obsessed with all things theatrical that she has conjured him out of the ether. It's damned embarrassing at times, especially when she seems to answer him."

Rupert gave a sheepish grin. "I know. Actually, when I went down to breakfast at Radcliffe House one morning this summer, I could have sworn I saw a rose drop on the carpet. It must have been a trick of the light, because the rose was probably lying there all along. Anyway, I picked it up and began to put it back in the vase on the table, but Aunt E asked me to give it to her, because Rollo wished her to have it. I obliged, of course. If it pleases her to believe in a ghost, then it does no harm to humor her."

"That's a matter of opinion," Greville said. "There are times when I feel we should tackle her about it, because she'll do it in the wrong place one day, and find herself in the nearest Bedlam! Anyway, why would a *Restoration* actor haunt a mid-eighteenth century house on the Steine in Brighton? If he belongs anywhere, it's at the Theatre Royal, where he was once such a leading player. Oh, it's too ridiculous to talk about." Greville adjusted his top hat a little crossly. "Anyway, to go back to the business of Radcliffe House not being in use until New Year's Eve. What say you we *both* hie ourselves down there without further ado? It can't be that closed up if everyone is descending upon it until after Christmas, so we can insert ourselves quite nicely. That way I can escape Sybil Garsington's amorous intentions, and you can see what's what between Chloe and March.''

Rupert's face brightened. ''I like the sound of it, coz.''

''But be warned that I intend to be sharply away from there before Aunt E *et al* arrive. Nothing, but *nothing* will induce me to run the risk of Malvolio.''

Rupert glanced at his fob watch. ''If we make all our travel arrangements tonight, we can leave first thing in the morning. It's only fifty miles or so, and I doubt if the storm the day before yesterday will have damaged the best turnpike in England. We should be there some time in the afternoon.''

Greville gave a satisfied sigh. ''And if we feel like it, we can indulge in a shampoo at Mahomed's Baths before dinner!''

''We can indeed,'' Rupert agreed. ''Come on, we must send a messenger ahead. It wouldn't do to arrive there and find the fires unlit.''

Chapter 5

After a delay caused by one of the horses casting a shoe, it was the early evening of Thursday, December 18, before Greville's traveling carriage bowled down toward Brighton from the windmill heights of the Downs. The team's hooves rang on the hard road, and the carriage lamps cut cleanly through the darkness as the final mile was covered to the fashionable spa that had once been the insignificant fishing town of Brighthelmston.

The wide grassy area known as the Steine had originally been on the eastern extremity of the old town, and was where the local fishermen had mended and dried their nets. Then the Prince of Wales chose adjacent Great East Street in which to build his seaside palace, the Palladian villa called the Marine Pavilion. The rear of the Pavilion looked out on the Steine, and in order that the royal view should not be spoiled, the locals and their unsightly nets were banished. Equally unsightly Great East Street, at least that part which had the audacity to pass the Pavilion, had been purchased and was being pulled down apace, and where it stood there would soon be tranquil gardens.

The Steine had become the *beau monde*'s favorite promenade outside London. No longer was it on the edge of the town, but was surrounded on three sides by new streets of smart town houses and exclusive shops; the fourth side opened directly on to the crumbling low-cliffed shore, where fishing boats and wheeled bathing huts cluttered the beach. Carriageways and rails enclosed the beautifully clipped grass, and stone-flagged walks were laid out for the fashionable to stroll without fear of puddles or mud.

Immediately to the south of the Marine Pavilion stood

the Castle Inn and its grand assembly rooms, which would in all probability one day suffer the same royal fate as Great East Street and Radcliffe House. A few buildings further on was Garsington House, then the pretty villa of Mrs. Fitzherbert, who was either the Prince of Wales's wife or his mistress, according to one's political persuasion. Like the Pavilion, her house was in darkness because she was in London with the Price Regent, but Garsington House was ablaze with lights, and from it drifted the sound of indifferently played Vivaldi.

Radcliffe House stood directly against the Pavilion and, like the Castle Inn on the other side, its looming redbrick sturdiness dwarfed the royal residence's pale elegance. It was isolated on the northwest corner of the Steine, its access from Great East Street now lost in the frenzy of royal improvement. Fortunately its main entrance was to the north, and it was here that Greville's town carriage drew up. The illuminated fanlight above the door signified the servants' anticipation of guests, and the horses had barely come to a standstill when two of Evangeline's liveried footmen hastened out to attend to the luggage.

Greville alighted, and took a deep appreciative breath of the sea air. Brighton was renowned for its mild winters, but it seemed to him that this year there was an underlying chill, even a hint of snow, perhaps. Snow on the Steine? That would be a novel thing. He looked across the fine open grass toward the terraces of handsome houses opposite. In the middle of them, on the corner of new St. James's Street, stood Donaldson's Circulating Library, a single-story wooden building, painted white and fronted by a columned verandah. It was here that everyone entered his or her name in a register, so that those already in town knew who had just arrived, and in the past he had always signed it. But not this time, oh, no, not this time. Rupert could sign what he wanted, but Sir Greville Seton wasn't about to broadcast his presence to the Garsingtons.

His glance moved to a house in the northeast corner of the Steine. There was a lighted lantern and a Christmas wreath at the door. It was the home of Admiral Sir Jocelyn Holcroft and his daughter Chloe, and outside it stood a dashing red curricle that Greville recognized as belonging to one Oliver March.

Rupert alighted as well, and scowled as he too saw the curricle. "Damn March!" he breathed, and tugged his top hat low over his forehead.

Greville clapped him reassuringly on the shoulder. "He'll soon be saying the same of you," he declared, and ushered Rupert into the house.

Warm air, chandeliers, and the welcome flicker of firelight greeted them in the cream-and-blue hall, where touches of gilded plasterwork set everything off to perfection. The floor was tiled in black and white, and there was a sky-blue velvet sofa and a table on which there would by now have been an arrangement of Christmas greenery if Evangeline had been in residence; indeed there would have been seasonal decorations everywhere, but yuletide was a barren business for Radcliffe House this year.

The portly butler, Fosdyke, hastened to greet them. His receding hair was concealed beneath a neatly powdered white bagwig, and he wore a gray coat and black breeches, both of which were somewhat strained by his girth. He was reckoned the finest butler in Brighton, and he and his wife, a fine cook who made excellent gingerbread, the local delicacy that was Evangeline's great weakness, oversaw the staff of Radcliffe House. They had charge of an assortment of footmen, maids, scullions, grooms, and coachmen. There were also two local gardeners who came in daily from the town, for there was not a great deal of garden to look after, just a railed semicircle of shrubs and flower beds on the Steine side, and a pocket handkerchief of walled garden on the Great East Street side.

"I trust your journey was expeditious, sirs?" Fosdyke inquired solicitously.

"Just a cast shoe to hamper our progress," Greville replied.

Rupert nodded, then looked at the butler. "I say, Fosdyke, I hope you managed to send word to Mahomed's Baths?"

"A running footman was dispatched as soon as your

message arrived, my lord. Both you and Sir Greville are expected. Sheikh Mahomed himself will attend you."

"Excellent." Rupert raised an eager eyebrow. "And what has Mrs. Fosdyke prepared for our evening repast?"

"Mulligatawny soup, roast pork and apple sauce, and syllabub, sir."

Rupert's mouth watered. "I look forward to it. Convey my compliments to her even before we sit down, for I *know* it will be a feast fit for the Marine Pavilion itself."

The butler inclined his head. "I will tell her, my lord. Dinner will be at eight, sirs, but will you be requiring refreshment in the meantime?" Fosdyke asked.

Rupert turned to Greville. "What do you say?"

"I'd rather go straight to Mahomed's, the exertion will give us an excellent appetite for Mrs. Fosdyke's peerless roast pork."

Rupert nodded agreement, and then thought of something. "Tell me, Fosdyke, are Sir Jocelyn and Miss Holcroft in good health?"

"Oh, yes, my lord, and they will both be in Lady Evangeline's play."

Rupert went on. "And, Fosdyke, have you come across a person by the name of Oliver March?"

The butler cleared his throat. "Yes, I have, my lord. He has taken lodgings in Duchess Place, and is often seen driving Miss Holcroft in his curricle." Seeing the stormy expression this information produced on Rupert's face, Fosdyke hurried on. "Shall I send for fly-by-nights to convey you to the baths, sirs?"

"Certainly not!" declared Greville, appalled at the thought of being found in one of the wheeled sedan chairs that were peculiar to Brighton, and were trundled along by two men, one in front and the other behind. In his opinion such conveyances were best suited to the elderly and infirm, not to healthy young men who were perfectly capable of walking the short distance to and from the shoreside baths.

"As you wish, Sir Greville."

"That will be all for the moment, Fosdyke. Just see

that our things are taken to whichever rooms have been aired for us. The usual ones, I take it?"

"Indeed so, Sir Greville. You have the blue chamber, and my lord the green." The butler bowed, then snapped his fingers at the footmen, who had now brought all the luggage in from the carriage. They immediately carried the first of it toward the staircase that led up from the Great East Street side of the hall.

Before setting off for the baths, Greville and Rupert went to the impressive double doors at the far end of the hall, and opened onto Greville's notion of purgatory. Aunt E's beloved private theater, was sandwiched between the main house and the Marine Pavilion next door. Rupert flung the doors open, and the light from the hall shone into a small auditorium decorated in red and gold. It seated fifty guests on elegant horseshoe-backed chairs, and boasted a fine stage with painted backcloths, a drop curtain, and an orchestra apse. Behind the stage there lay two changing rooms, a scenery store, the wardrobe, and even a small green room where the players could relax between scenes. Lady Evangeline took her passion for theatricals very seriously indeed, and at present regarded herself as Brighton's sole upholder of the acting tradition, the old town theater having closed and the new one not being due to open until the following summer.

Greville pulled a face. "Ye gods, how I loathe this place."

"Hee-haw," Rupert replied unfeelingly.

Greville suddenly noticed a black flat-topped tent in the orchestra pit in front of the stage. He knew that it would contain candles, oil lamps, mirrors, hand-painted transparencies, and projecting lenses for the phantasmagoric images that had become a drawing room novelty in recent years. "Well, well, it looks as if Lady E intends *Twelfth Night* to be a very dramatic production indeed," he said, nodding toward it.

"Yes, she told me there will be lighting experiments this year. She has notions of bringing scenes like the opening storm very much to life—you know, towering waves, a foundering ship, and so on."

"Spare me the awful details," Greville muttered. "Come on, let's go to Mahomed's."

Chapter 6

Two hours later, when Greville and Rupert had enjoyed an herb-scented vapor-bath at the exclusive premises of Sheikh Deen Mahomed, shampooing surgeon to the Prince of Wales, and were strolling back for Mrs. Fosdyke's roast pork dinner, a second traveling carriage drew up outside Radcliffe House. Fosdyke was very startled indeed to admit Evangeline, followed by the gray-haired French maid, Annie, who immediately scuttled upstairs to prepare her mistress's apartment, which thankfully was kept aired at all times.

The butler did not observe Megan, who lingered nervously on the threshold, nor did he seem to see or hear Master Rollo Witherspoon, who marched boldly into the house as if he owned it. The sound of spectral footsteps rang out on the tiles as the ghost followed Evangeline to the fireplace; indeed he was apparently so close behind her that he trod on her train. She turned a little crossly. "Oh, do look where you're going, sirrah!" she complained.

Neither Fosdyke nor the footmen reacted in any way, yet they could not have failed to hear what she said; on top of which Rollo had passed within two feet of the butler! Megan was very aware of it all, however, as indeed she had been from that first moment in Wells. By now she knew that Evangeline was not mad at all, simply well and truly haunted; a fact with which her ladyship might be able to cope, but her new companion found rather difficult.

Having spent the entire distance from Somerset in the knowledge that a spirit was in the carriage as well,

Megan was still a little uneasy about remaining in Lady Evangeline Radcliffe's employ. From the incident of the floating mistletoe at the lodging house, to Evangeline's asides to apparently thin air, and the mark of an invisible posterior on the carriage's velvet upholstery, Megan *knew* Rollo Witherspoon was there. Annie had not seemed to notice anything, and now that Fosdyke and the footmen likewise seemed not to notice anything, Megan was forced to conclude that they were probably ignorant of the ghost's actual existence, and were all making allowances for a mistress they thought to be a little eccentric.

This was the first time Megan herself had encountered anything supernatural, but in spite of her unease she was intensely curious. Who *was* Rollo Witherspoon? How old was he? What did he look like? Why was he haunting Evangeline? She longed to ask, but knew better than to broach such a delicate and potentially embarrassing matter. It remained to be seen whether or not the wraith realized that the new companion was aware of him, for as yet she had been very careful to show no sign.

Evangeline discarded her muff and held her hands out gladly to the fire as she glanced around the hall. "How very unseasonable we are, to be sure. Fosdyke, first thing in the morning I wish you to see that Christmas greenery is acquired. It must be lavish, because this holiday is going to be very special after all—at least, it is from New Year's Eve onward."

"My lady." What was going to be "very special" about it? the butler wondered. He did not know about Evangeline's personal plans, or indeed about the sale and subsequent demolition of the house.

Evangeline continued. "It goes without saying that the mistletoe by the summerhouse is not to be touched."

"Yes, my lady."

"I'm very proud of that mistletoe. I vow it must be the largest example in the realm."

"Undeniably, my lady."

Lady Evangeline eyed him again. "I trust that my rooms have been kept aired and warm since my departure?"

"Oh, yes, my lady."

She looked shrewdly at him. "What's afoot, sir? You have discomfort written all over you. Has something happened of which I should know?"

"Yes, my lady. My lord and Sir Greville arrived earlier this evening, and are at this moment at Mahomed's Baths."

Evangeline paused. "Well, that is an agreeable surprise, and hastens things along."

"My lady?"

"No matter. Have they indicated why they have chosen to grace Radcliffe House with their presence after all?"

"No, my lady, but the message they sent from London informed me that although my lord intends to stay on, Sir Greville will return to the capital again on New Year's Eve."

"To avoid *Twelfth Night,* no doubt," Evangeline observed caustically, recalling the shambles Greville had made of Bottom. "Is he accommodated in the blue chamber as usual?"

"Yes, my lady."

"Which presumably means it is nicely aired?"

"Oh, yes, my lady."

"Well, Sir Greville will have to relinquish it, I fear, for I wish Miss Mortimer to sleep there as it is next to my apartment."

"Miss Mortimer, my lady?" The butler was still unaware of Megan in the doorway behind him.

"My companion. Where is the girl?" Evangeline looked past him at Megan. "Ah, there you are! Come in, come in, don't fidget on the threshold."

Nonplussed, the butler turned as Megan stepped reluctantly into the hall. His critical glance took in the plain maroon hooded cloak she wore over her mustard woolen gown, and the modest black hat beneath her raised hood. He guessed her to be an impoverished gentlewoman, as indeed were most ladies' companions, but why on earth would Lady Evangeline suddenly employ such a person? And not only that, but give her the blue chamber as well? There was surely more to all this than met the eye. . . .

Another footman had emerged from the kitchens in time

to hear about Megan. He was in his mid-twenties, with sandy hair, small eyes, and full lips, and the withering look he gave her was also one of outrage that a companion should be shown such undue favor as to be accommodated in one of the grandest bedrooms. Megan was accustomed to resentment, for companions did not rate highly either above or below stairs, being neither one thing nor the other, but she was herself a little startled to be given a chamber that was clearly more suited to a guest.

Evangeline spied the footman. "Ah, Edward. Remove Sir Greville's things from the blue chamber without delay. The mauve room will do for him, for the color will no doubt suit his temper when he finds himself evicted from his usual cozy place."

Fosdyke nodded at Edward, who gave Megan another dark glance before he went swiftly up the staircase. Megan felt very awkward. "Oh, Lady Evangeline, I do not wish to be the cause of Sir Greville's eviction . . ." she began.

"Nonsense, chit. It will do him good. He and Rupert are most presumptuous, first declining my invitation, and then taking possession of my house behind my back. I intend to have stern words with them. No doubt Greville thinks to avoid my play this year, but his timely presence will enable rehearsals of *Twelfth Night* to get under way a little sooner than expected. That will teach him."

Megan fell silent. One thing was certain, Sir Greville would regard *her* as the presumptuous one, not himself. Edward and the butler clearly already did!

Suddenly Evangeline began to feel familiarly hot and uncomfortable, and she stepped hastily away from the fire. She longed to rush out on to the Steine for some cold air, but to her relief the disagreeable flush passed after a few moments, which was more than could be said for a few exceedingly disagreeable occasions during the journey from Wells. Recovering, she waved Megan toward the drawing room, which lay on the Steine side of the house. "Wait in there until your room is ready, Miss Mortimer. Fosdyke, see that a dish of tea is brought to my apartment *tout de suite*." With that she gathered her skirts and bustled toward the staircase.

"My lady." The butler bowed solemnly after his departing mistress, then took himself off to the kitchens.

Megan went into the gray-and-gold drawing room, where lighted candles in sconces illuminated exquisite furniture. Theatrical prints adorned walls hung with Chinese silk, and a portrait of the famous actress Mrs. Siddons as Cleopatra had pride of place on the chimney breast. A longcase clock ticked slowly in a silence that was broken only by Evangeline's voice in the distance, issuing instructions to Annie.

Megan flung back her hood and went to the deeply bowed window to hold the fringed velvet curtain aside. She saw the lights of the houses across the Steine, and at an upper window of the first one, a young woman looking back at her. Slender, with short blonde hair, she was dressed in a white evening gown with a blue sash, and the room behind her was lit by a dazzling chandelier. She seemed taken aback to see someone looking out of Radcliffe House, and stared so obviously that Megan hastily let the curtain fall into place again.

In the house opposite, Chloe Holcroft continued to gaze at Radcliffe House in astonishment. She had been at the window of the second-floor drawing room to watch Oliver March drive off after dining with her father and her, and she had been startled to see lights at Evangeline's house. Now she was even more startled to see a young woman she did not know.

She turned back into the room. "Papa, I believe one of Lady Evangeline's Christmas guests must have arrived after all."

"Mm?" Admiral Sir Jocelyn Holcroft didn't look up from the new newspaper, the *Brighton Herald,* which had only been in print for a month or so. He was still a handsome man, although his features were now marred by an eye patch over his left eye, and a livid white cutlass scar down his right check to the corner of his mouth, the result of an encounter with pirates in the Mediterranean. Once a distinguished uniformed figure commanding from the quarterdeck of one of the Royal Navy's finest first-raters, he was still impressive in the formal black velvet coat and white silk breeches of a civilian gentleman who had just had a guest to dinner.

Chloe gave him a cross look. "The French fleet has just appeared on the horizon," she remarked in a conversational tone.

"Mm?" The paper rustled as he turned the page.

"And they are putting longboats ashore to raid the town," she went on. "Can't you hear the warning bells of St. Nicholas's?"

He looked up with a start. "Eh? Warning bells?"

"Oh, so you *do* listen eventually," she declared. "I vow the French really could be at the door, and you would still be browsing contentedly through that newspaper. The next time we have someone to dinner, I am going to insist that you take less port afterward, for I vow it makes you far too dull at the edges."

He gave her a charming but rather sheepish smile. "I'm sorry, my dear. Now, what was it you were saying?"

"Lady Evangeline is away for Christmas, but the lights are on at the house, and I have just seen a strange young woman looking out of the drawing room window."

"Strange? In what way? Does she have two heads?"

Chloe became cross again. "You know perfectly well what I mean, Papa!" He raised a teasing eyebrow, and she colored. "I-I was wondering if perhaps one of her guests has arrived after all," she added.

"We know all her usual guests," he pointed out.

"Yes, but—"

"But?"

Chloe bit her lip and looked away. "Well, perhaps I should go across—"

"And see if there is news of Rupert?" he finished for her.

"Certainly not!"

"That is a great pity." He folded the newspaper and put it on the table beside his chair. "From the heated manner of that last response. I must presume that you are still angry with him?"

"Angry? I'm not anything anymore, Papa. Rupert

Radcliffe is of no interest to me, especially now that . . ." She didn't finish.

He got up and went to pour himself a large glass of cognac. "I do hope that you were not about to mention Mr. March's name," he murmured.

"And if I was?"

"I know that he has come to mean much to you, my dear, but I do not care for him."

"Why not?" she asked in dismay. "He has just been all that is charming and courteous."

"I know, but I can't help how I feel," her father replied, resuming his seat.

"Just because you and Lady Evangeline have decided that Rupert and I would be a fine match! That's it, isn't it? Well, I do not need to remind you that it was *Rupert* who broke our friendship, not me."

"No, my dear, you do not need to remind me. Nor, I dare say, would you need to remind Rupert himself, who I am sure now regrets his actions."

"I doubt that very much."

"Chloe—"

"Papa, I do not wish to speak of Lord Rupert Radcliffe, indeed I do not even wish to *think* of him. Oliver is in my heart now, and I intend to continue to see him. Unless, of course, you mean to forbid it?"

"No, my dear, I will not do that, for I know only too well that to forbid you will only make you the more determined."

"So you will not mind if he takes me to St. Nicholas's church in the morning, to help with the Christmas decorations?"

"I will mind very much, but I will not prevent you from going."

"Well, that is that, then," she declared, as she gathered her skirts and hastened from the room.

Her father gazed sadly after her. He didn't want Mr. Oliver March as a son-in-law, but he very much feared he was going to get him. He glanced toward the window. It was very tiresome of Evangeline *et al* to be away this Christmas. If things had gone on in the usual way, there might have been a chance to rectify the sorry situation, but with Evangeline in Bath and Rupert in London . . . well, the way was clear for Mr. March.

With a sigh, the admiral drained the glass of cognac, then grimaced.

Meanwhile at Radcliffe House, Megan had put the young woman in the house opposite from her thoughts, and was studying the portrait of Mrs. Siddons. Suddenly Rollo's footsteps crossed the hall again, and she turned with a gasp, having momentarily forgotten all about the ghost. Her curiosity got the better of her as the steps moved away, and she went out into the hall to follow the sound to the theater. She halted at the entrance, listening to Rollo walk down through the auditorium, past the strange black tent, then up on to the stage, where the curtain shivered slightly as he halted in front of it.

He cleared his throat dramatically, and to her astonishment began to declaim one of Shakespeare's most famous soliloquies as if wishing to be heard out on the Steine. " 'To be or not to be: that is the question . . .' "

A ghost who recited Hamlet at the top of his spectral lungs? It was so unexpected that Megan almost curled up with stifled mirth, although she doubted if he intended to be anything other than serious.

He continued his flamboyant oration. " 'Whether 'tis nobler in the mind to suffer the slings and arrows of outrageous fortune. Or to take arms against a sea of troubles. And by it . . . And by the . . .' " There was a loud sigh as the next line eluded him. "Oh, plague take it! *When* will the words remain in this foolish noddle?" he grumbled in quaint old-fashioned English, then the hem of the curtain was raised briefly by an invisible hand, and the ghostly footsteps retreated to the back of the stage. After that there was the sort of silence that told Megan he had departed for the time being.

Suddenly she felt a great deal better about her new post, for how could one be afraid of—or disconcerted by—a spirit who fancied himself a great actor? No *wonder* Lady Evangeline put up with him! Still smiling, she turned back to the hall, and was immediately confronted by Edward the footman, who had been watching her.

"What are you doing out here? You were supposed to stay in the drawing room!" he said haughtily, thus making clear his inflated opinion of himself, and low opinion of her.

"I-I'm sorry," she replied. "I thought I heard someone making a speech in the theater."

"No one is allowed in there unless her ladyship is present. That applies to you too."

"I'll try to remember."

"Your room's ready. Come on." He paused. "And don't think that because you're in the blue chamber, you can lord it over the rest of us."

"I know my place." Which is more than you do, she added silently.

He eyed her for a moment as if sensing her unspoken thought, but then he conducted her up to a fine second-floor room on the Great East Street side of the house. "This is yours," he announced pushing the door open. "Just don't forget you're still a servant, and while there are guests, you'll be eating with us in the kitchens, so don't think you can treat us to airs and graces."

Megan was provoked as she went inside. "If anyone has airs and graces, it's you," she replied, and closed the door firmly in his face. She guessed that he would now paint a very black picture of her to the other servants, but she was philosophical about it, for she had endured a similar situation at Lady Jane's, but had managed to rise above it and make some good friends. With luck she would do the same here.

She glanced around the room. It warranted its name, for nearly everything was blue, except for a rose marble fireplace and a white ceiling that was richly picked out with gold. A fire crackled in the hearth, and there were lighted candles on the mantel, on either side of a garniture of fine blue-and-white Chinese porcelain vases. The four-poster bed had sapphire-blue hangings, and she lifted her portmanteau on to it to begin unpacking. Her back was to the door, and her hood fell over her hat again as she bent over it.

Suddenly the door was flung open. "You impudent light-fingered scoundrel!" someone cried, and before she knew what was happening, an assailant had launched himself at her. She was knocked sprawling facedown on the bed beneath him.

Chapter 7

Megan screamed and fought for all she was worth to escape, but her attacker—Sir Greville Seton, no less—was infinitely stronger and kept her pinned to the bed. After a struggle that lasted only a minute, but seemed a lot longer to Megan, she stopped fighting and lay still.

Greville thought he had apprehended a male intruder, and knelt roughly astride her. "You damned villain! Let's see your face!" he cried, and snatched back her hood. But he wrenched her hat off as well, and then froze as her long brown hair tumbled down in only too feminine profusion. "A-a woman?" he gasped, and leapt from the bed as if scalded. Then his glance went belatedly to the luggage, which was clearly not his. "What's going on? Who *are* you?" he demanded.

Angry and frightened, Megan scrambled away on the other side of the bed from him. "How *dare* you assault me so!" she cried.

"I dare because at the last time of reckoning this happened to be *my* room, and I caught you apparently rifling my belongings. I see now that I was wrong."

"You are indeed!" she replied angrily. They gazed warily at each other, their eyes bright with instinctive dislike and mistrust. Neither intended to give an inch, because both felt in the right. Megan spoke again. "Am I to understand that you are Sir Greville Seton?"

"You have the advantage of me, madam. Am I to have the honor of your name? Or is that to remain one of life's little mysteries?"

"I am Megan Mortimer, Miss Megan Mortimer, and I am Lady Evangeline's companion."

He stared at her. "Lady Evangeline's *what*?"

The sharp altercation brought Evangeline at the double from her apartment directly opposite. "Miss Mortimer is with me, sirrah, and this is her room!" she declared as she halted in the doorway to survey them both. She had changed into a peach taffeta dinner gown, and Annie had not quite finished her coiffure, so that several long gray ringlets hung down a little untidily. The little Frenchwoman peered over her mistress's shoulder to see what the noise was about.

Greville whirled about in disbelief, for she was supposed to be far away in Bath! Rupert came running as well, and he too stared at his aunt. "Aunt E? What are *you* doing here?" he cried.

"I live here, if you recall," that lady replied waspishly, "and I was under the erroneous impression that I was going to spend a quiet Christmas alone with my new companion. Instead I find that my home has been rather presumptuously invaded in my absence!"

Rupert colored. "I, er . . ." Then he fell silent, for what she said was quite true. Then the import of what she had said about Megan began to sink in, and his glance slid uncomfortably toward Greville, whose opinion of companions was hardly a secret.

Greville was appalled. Not only had he and Rupert walked into the lion's Christmas den after all, but there was a damned companion here as well!

Evangeline's peach taffeta rustled irritably as she came into the room. "Now, then, sirs, since you are here, allow me to formally present Miss Mortimer, who was Lady Jane Strickland's companion, but is now mine."

Greville's face became very still, and Rupert recalled what had been said in the garden at Hanover Square. This was the same companion who had so brazenly attempted to seduce Ralph Strickland? She certainly didn't *look* brazen, he thought, nor would Aunt E have employed her if there was any truth in the story Ralph was putting about.

Evangeline continued. "I trust you will both make her feel welcome, for she is about to become very much part of my household. She will be taking her meals with us, and is to be treated with respect in every way."

Megan's lips parted. Take her meals with them? Oh, that was not at all the thing! Her place was in the kitchens with the other servants.

Evangeline observed Greville's stony expression. "Sir, pray do not forget my wishes in this, for your private attitudes are not to be aired while beneath my roof. It is hardly Miss Mortimer's fault that your fool of a father ran off with your mother's companion when you were only six."

He was nettled that she should express such a derogatory opinion in front of Megan. "Aunt E, I hardly think Miss Mortimer is interested in my childhood," he replied in a tone as blunt as hers.

Evangeline already regretted her sharp tongue. "I shouldn't have said that. Please forgive me. It's just that it grieves me to see you still so bitter about something that happened such a long time ago. On top of which, I hardly think it is fair of you to direct your antagonism toward Miss Mortimer without her knowing *why* you feel as you do."

Greville didn't reply, and his silence conveyed that he didn't consider it to be any of Miss Mortimer's business.

Evangeline looked at him. "Greville, if only you would understand and accept that with your father gone, the last five years of your mother's life were far happier."

"I beg to differ on that point."

"But you were only eleven and away at Eton when she died. She *was* happier, believe me. Anyway, I wish you to let bygones be bygones while you are in this house." Evangeline decided to give him a moment or two to consider this, so she introduced Rupert to Megan first. "Miss Mortimer, this is my nephew and heir, Lord Rupert Radcliffe."

Rupert had been observing Megan, and was now of the firm opinion that she could not possibly be the scheming witch Ralph Strickland claimed, so he stepped gallantly forward to raise her hand to his lips. "I'm delighted to make your acquaintance, Miss Mortimer."

"Lord Rupert," she replied with a grateful smile. At least *he* was a gentleman!

Evangeline braced herself as she turned to Greville again. "And this disagreeable fellow is Sir Greville Seton. I forget what his relationship to me is exactly, but suffice it that he is definitely family."

Greville had no intention of emulating Rupert, but if Aunt E required politeness, politeness she would have. "Miss Mortimer," he murmured, and showed the limit of his chivalry by merely inclining his head.

"Sir."

Evangeline wasn't about to let him off lightly. "Sir, I think you should apologize to Miss Mortimer for your disgraceful physical attack upon her."

Greville was provoked. "Aunt E, this was my room when I departed for Mahomed's Baths, so it was reasonable enough to presume that it was still my room when I returned. When I found someone in a hooded cloak apparently examining *my* luggage, of *course* I thought it was a thief!"

"So you acted first, and asked questions afterward. I'm deeply disappointed in you, Greville, for I thought such lamentable conduct was the preserve of half-witted hotheads like Sigismund Garsington."

Megan felt dreadful, and wished the whole business could be dropped.

"Aunt E," Greville answered in a labored tone, "if I were Sigismund Garsington, I'd have fired a pistol at Miss Mortimer, not simply apprehended her. However, you are right to castigate me for my actions, and so I will indeed apologize." He turned to Megan. "I trust you are able to forgive me, Miss Mortimer, for you may be sure that if I had realized, I would not have dreamed of acting as I did."

"Of course I forgive you, sir." She didn't really, but there was little else she could say.

Evangeline was satisfied. "I have removed you to the mauve chamber, Greville, because I wish Miss Mortimer to be close to me. Fosdyke has aired it and had a fire kindled there, so it will be sufficiently warm by the time you retire tonight."

"As you wish, Aunt E, but it would have been pleasant if I had been informed of this when Rupert and I came back from the baths. Such consideration would have prevented me from making such an error."

"Fosdyke was instructed to do so, but he clearly did not realize you had returned. Besides, who are you to carp about being kept informed? I do not recall being informed that you were going to take liberties with my home in my absence."

He knew he was beaten, and gave her a wry smile. "I concede defeat, Aunt E. The laurels are yours."

"Yes, I rather think they are," she declared archly.

"Do you really mind us being here?" he asked, knowing she didn't.

"Of course not, you silly boy." Evangeline fingered the gold locket at her throat. Mind? On the contrary, for their timely arrival on the scene speeded up her plans considerably. "Now, then, gentlemen, I believe you have both forgotten something." She presented her cheek for a kiss.

Rupert obliged warmly, but as Greville kissed her as well, she tapped his sleeve with her fan. "Why, your shampoo has left you smelling of rosemary. It is quite appetizing. I almost wish Mrs. Fosdyke were preparing some mutton, or better still, some sweet Welsh lamb."

"It was not my intention to smell like a roast dinner," he replied.

"Nor, I'll warrant, was it your intention to spend Christmas with me," she observed shrewdly.

"That isn't so. I'm more than pleased that you have returned," he protested untruthfully, then added. "Er, why *have* you returned?"

"Oh, this and that," she murmured, studying his face. "Acting will never be your strong suit, will it? Be honest, sir, you are absolutely *horrified* to see me, and already you begin to suffer the onset of stage fright! How is your Malvolio coming along?"

"He isn't," Greville replied frankly. "Aunt E, I may as well be honest; I have no intention of being Malvolio or anyone else."

"Nonsense." Her eyes were wickedly knowing. "Greville, I can just *see* you in cross-gartered yellow stockings, and although I concede that it will be out of period, I think it might be amusing to fit you with the *Henry VIII* codpiece as well."

Rupert made a strangulated noise, and Greville was aghast. "Aunt E, I positively, absolutely refuse to even consider that—that *thing*!" The codpiece in question had been hidden away at the very back of the theater wardrobe for two years now, because of its shocking size. It had been intended for a production of Shakespeare's *Henry VIII*, but Evangeline had been so certain that its appearance onstage would result in charges of indecency, that it had languished among the wardrobe cobwebs ever since.

She pursed her lips. "Well, on reflection perhaps it *would* be a little too much, but the stockings stay, for they are essential to the play."

"Essential or not, I will still not be wearing them," Greville replied doggedly.

She shrugged. "Well, no one is forcing you, so if you wish to scuttle back to London, I will quite understand. I am sure that Mr. March will leap at the opportunity to play alongside Chloe, who is to be Olivia. I did write to one of you about Mr. March, did I not?"

Rupert scowled. "I don't want that scoundrel leaping into anything, unless it be a pit of vipers."

"Well, at least we are agreed on something, for he is indeed a scoundrel, but Chloe seems quite taken with him," Evangeline replied. "Still, Greville's craven desertion means a replacement is needed, and I happen to know that Mr. March is very fond of amateur theatricals, so he will have to do."

Greville saw the anguish on Rupert's face, and felt obliged to reverse his decision, even though it meant Malvolio, stockings and all. "I'm not cravenly deserting anyone, Aunt E, I'm staying right here."

"Then, you are going to be Malvolio, and that, sir, is that."

"I know," he answered heavily, and Rupert looked away to hide his unutterable relief. Megan cordially hoped Malvolio would cause Sir Greville Seton endless embarrassment.

Evangeline was triumphant again. "It is settled, then. You are to be Malvolio, Rupert is Duke Orsino, Chloe is to be my Olivia, and Sir Jocelyn will be my Sir Toby Belch. Your cousin Ada is to be Viola, her husband will be Sebastian, and her sister insists upon being the maid, Maria, although with her squeaky little voice I fear it may be a disaster. Your other cousin Archibald, who as you know is very shy and retiring, has very bravely undertaken to be Sir Andrew Aguecheek. He promises faithfully not to hide behind the scenery as he did last year. After that I quite forget who is to be who, but they are all rather minor considerations."

"And who, pray, are you going to play, Aunt E?" Greville asked curiously, noticing the singular omission.

"Feste."

He raised an eyebrow. "Isn't he the clown?"

Evangeline twiddled the locket. "Er, yes, he is."

Greville folded his arms. "And doesn't he wear bells and brightly colored hose?"

"Yes." Evangeline wouldn't look at him.

"And doesn't he *sing*?"

"Yes."

Rupert groaned. "Oh, no . . ."

Evangeline was cross. "I may not have a voice like Catalini, but—"

"No, you have a voice like Caterwauli!" Greville interrupted crushingly. She was tone deaf in his opinion, and the prospect of her off-key trilling was almost worse than that of Sybil Garsington.

Evangeline drew herself up indignantly. "I'll have you know that I have been taking lessons, Greville, and I think you will be agreeably surprised by my Feste."

"I await your performance with bated breath."

"So do I, sirrah, for I have some information that will

surely pay you back for your sharp tongue. I happened upon Lady Garsington at the circulating library recently, and she informed me that Sigismund and Sybil are returning to Brighton for Christmas. So if you imagine that by scuttling here you have eluded her, I'm afraid you are very much mistaken." For Megan's sake, Evangeline omitted to add that Lady Garsington had also said that her other daughter, Sophia might be coming as well, together with her husband, Ralph Strickland.

Greville closed his eyes for a moment. "Please assure me this is a tease," he begged faintly.

"It is the plain, unadulterated truth. She will soon be upon us, harp and all." Evangeline glanced pointedly at her little jeweled fob watch. "It is almost time for dinner, gentlemen, so I suggest you go to your rooms to change," she declared, thus bringing the conversation to an end.

Chapter 8

When Greville and Rupert had withdrawn, Evangeline turned to Megan. "I am sorry about Greville, my dear, but I am sure he will come around. Now, then, I realize you do not have the sort of wardrobe necessary for taking your place among us, but from tomorrow I trust that particular situation will be rectified."

"Rectified? I-I don't understand." Megan was alarmed. Her small income would not stretch to the purchase of a modish wardrobe!

"I have sent a footman to Mrs. Fiske, the dressmaker and milliner in St. James's Street. She has long had premises in Mayfair but has now opened a repository in Brighton as well, specializing in Parisian dresses, trimmings, pelisses, oh, everything that a lady could require. To my certain knowledge, she almost always has uncollected items of which she is anxious to dispose."

Megan's misgivings increased. Clothes of style and fashion for a *companion*? It wasn't right, it wasn't right at all. . . .

"I have informed her that I estimate you to be the same height and size as Miss Holcroft," Evangeline continued, "so if she has anything suitable, she will have it waiting."

"Miss Holcroft?"

"Chloe Holcroft. She is the dear, sweet, kind daughter of my good friend, Admiral Sir Jocelyn Holcroft, and if Rupert had any sense at all, he would be betrothed to her by now. Instead she seems set to slip into the unpleasant grasp of Mr. Oliver March."

Megan was transfixed with shock on hearing Mr.

March's first name. "Have—have you met Mr. March, Lady Evangeline?"

"Why, yes, not that I took to him at all."

"Does he have chestnut hair and a rather pointed nose?"

"Chestnut? I would not dignify it with such a name, for it is more carrot, but his nose definitely seems well suited to poking in where it has no business to be. Why do you ask?"

"Oh, it's nothing really. I just think I may have met him once." Yes, Megan certainly had met him, for Mr. Oliver March was the cousin who had inherited her family's estates and thrown her penniless into the world!

Evangeline looked curiously at her. "What is it, my dear? You have gone quite pale."

"I-I think I am just tired after the journey."

"I fancy we will both sleep like tops tonight," Evangeline replied, still studying her. "May I ask where did you and Mr. March meet?"

"I really don't recall, for it was a long time ago now." Megan wanted to tell her the truth, but did not feel in a position to do so. After all, Oliver seemed on the point of becoming the son-in-law of one of Evangeline's dearest friends, so even though Evangeline herself clearly disliked him, it wouldn't do at all for her companion to presume to reveal distasteful facts about him.

Evangeline smiled. "Well, I will leave you now, or you will not have time to change before dinner."

"Lady Evangeline, I-I really appreciate your kindness in providing me with new clothes, but . . ." Megan didn't quite know how to express her worries without giving offense.

Evangeline smiled. "Do not feel awkward, my dear. I wish you to look your best when you are with me, which you cannot do if you are drably clad."

"Then, of course I gratefully accept your generosity, Lady Evangeline, but for meals surely my proper place is with the other servants?"

"I will not hear of it, Miss Mortimer. What use is a companion who isn't with me? I like conversation at the table to be properly balanced, which it will hardly be with only Rupert and Greville. Another lady is required, and that means you, my dear.''

"But, Sir Greville—''

"Sir Greville has no say in the matter! He is my guest here, and as such will mind his p's and q's. I am afraid it is time he learned that he cannot allow his personal feelings to intrude upon everyone else. I spoke the truth when I said that he and his mother were better off without his philandering father, so if anything, the companion was to be thanked not vilified.''

"I do not think Sir Greville will ever see it that way."

The folded fan touched Megan's cheek kindly. "Don't let him upset you, my dear, for he is just being a stubborn bear. The trouble is that the most vivid memory he retains of that time is of his mother weeping one day when she took him to St. Nicholas's here in Brighton, not long after the scandal had broken. St. Nicholas's was the church where she and Greville's father were married, where she was laid to rest, and where Greville himself was baptized. You will be able to see it from your window in the morning, for it stands on a hill at the western edge of the town.''

"Have Sir Greville's family been in this part of Sussex for long?" Megan asked.

"Oh, yes, there were Setons here in Brighton before Prinny made it à la mode. Their seat was east of the town, but when Greville inherited a fine estate in Oxfordshire, he decided to sell up here. He still spends a great deal of time in Brighton, however, for he visits me a great deal." Evangeline smiled fondly. "Anyway, where was I? Oh, yes, his feckless father. It all happened just before Christmas, which did not help at all, and as it is Christmas again now, I suppose it still doesn't help. At the time it was understandable enough that his mother wept so, for what woman does not feel sad for happiness lost? But Greville does not understand that this particular happiness was lost a long time *before* the companion entered the scene. So let that be the end of your anxiety, my dear, for the problem is his not yours. Now, then, I recall that at the Crown in Winchester you wore a green gown with a little chenille trimming at the throat and cuffs. It will do well enough here tonight."

"Yes, Lady Evangeline."

As the door closed, Megan sighed unhappily. Sir Greville Seton, fine clothes, and dining with the family were bad enough, but the presence of cousin Oliver in Brighton was even worse. He was an unscrupulous, heartless knave who would not wish to be faced with the relation he so cruelly abandoned, especially now he was dancing attendance upon Chloe Holcroft. Chloe sounded far too nice a person for him, maybe even nice enough to send him packing if she found out what he had done.

Megan knew it would be wise to keep out of his way if possible, although it would be too much to hope that she could avoid him entirely. With a heavy sigh, she took off her cloak, and began to look through her luggage for the green gown.

Meanwhile in the mauve chamber at the other end of the house, Greville and Rupert were discussing Megan. Rupert spread his hands. "Look, Greville, I can't believe Strickland. Miss Mortimer just isn't the sort to do what he claims."

"Because she looks as if butter wouldn't melt in her mouth?"

"No, because Ralph Strickland wouldn't know the truth if it jumped up and bit him on the backside!"

Greville gave a cynical laugh. "It is clear you are taken in by Miss Mortimer's air of angelic innocence."

"And it is equally clear that you are guided by your preconceptions about companions. Aunt E isn't a fool, Greville. Do you imagine she would have engaged Miss Mortimer without first making inquiries of Lady Jane? No, of course not; so I dismiss Strickland's lies out of hand."

"I believe that on this occasion he was speaking the truth," Greville replied a little annoyedly.

"Well, with all due respect, that's because it suits you to believe him. You know him for a slippery toad who cannot be relied upon for the correct time of day, yet when he utters the dreaded word 'companion,' suddenly you credit him with absolute veracity!"

Greville didn't reply.

Rupert pressed his point home. "I prefer to place my faith in my own judgment, and in Aunt E's, for she would not employ anyone about whom there was a single doubt. So let's ask her, mm? That should settle the matter."

"It is clear to me that Aunt E knows nothing about this business. Besides, she clearly dotes upon the creature, so I will need more than Ralph Strickland's say-so anyway."

Rupert looked at him in puzzlement. "What do you mean?"

"I intend to make further inquiries. I know someone who happens to reside only a door or two from Lady Jane, so I will send him a note posthaste. His servants will be thick with her servants, and what isn't known to them won't be worth knowing."

"And if you discover Miss Mortimer to be innocent?"

Greville smiled coolly. "She isn't."

Chapter 9

That night, after a truly awful dinner during which Greville had hardly said a word to her, and Rupert did his level best to make up for it by drawing her into the conversation, Megan retired to her bed in the certain knowledge she would never enjoy mulligatawny or roast pork again!

She lay with her arms folded behind her head, and gazed up at the canopy as she thought about Greville. The blue velvet hangings were burnished to rosy lilac by the soft glow from the fire, and the scent of roses filled the warm air from the open potpourri jar in the hearth. At the window the shutters and curtains were firmly closed to keep out the raw chill of the December night, and she wished she could similarly exclude Sir Greville Seton from her mind. Why, oh, why, had his wretched father had to choose a companion to run away with? Why couldn't it have been a governess, or even his son's nurse?

Sleep came gradually, but an hour or so later she awoke with a start to find moonlight flooding into the room. Someone had just flung open the shutters and curtains! There was a vague silvery shape outlined against the window, a tall middle-aged man in the clothes of Charles II's time; at least, she *thought* that was what she saw, for he was ethereal, almost like gossamer, and the moon and stars shone through him. A faint floral scent other than roses seemed to hang in the still air, and for a moment she could not think what it was, but then she realized it was orange blossom.

She sat up slowly, and rubbed her eyes to make sure

she was not dreaming, then she looked at the apparition again. Plumes curled from his wide-brimmed hat, and a periwig fell to his shoulders in row after row of regimented curls. He was clean-shaven except for wisps of mustache flanking the corners of his mouth, and he wore a short, unbuttoned jacket that was fastened with bows at the throat. There were more bows on his shirt, his baggy breeches were finished with deep lace ruffles at the knee, and his buckled shoes had high heels. He carried a cane that was almost as tall as himself, and there was a sword in a decorative baldric over his right shoulder. She knew she was looking at Rollo Witherspoon, but he might so easily have been Old Rowley himself, or the Sun King of Versailles.

He was staring at something in the distance, but then raised his eyes to the heavens, assumed a theatrical pose, and declared. " 'I have a good eye, Uncle: I can see a church by daylight.' "

Shakespeare again, Megan thought with commendable calm, possibly *Much Ado About Nothing*. She didn't quite know how to proceed. Should she speak to him, or just stay silent? But even as she deliberated he suddenly strode from the room, and the scent of orange blossom water wafted over her as he passed. Quickly she got out of bed, put on her cream woolen wrap, then followed him. He went downstairs to the theater, where he again uttered his interpretation of the Bard of Avon: *As You Like It* this time.

" 'All the world's a stage. And all the men and women merely players: They have their exits and their entrances: And one man in his time plays many parts, and . . . And then . . . !' " The words eluded him once more. "Oh, fool, fool, to be able to recall quotations only to forget speeches!" The curtain was wrenched up, and he strode away into the recesses of the stage. Then silence descended.

Megan gazed across the darkened auditorium. Now, when it was too late, she wished she'd spoken to him. She returned to the staircase, but as she began to ascend, candlelight suddenly flickered at the top and Greville barred her way. His hair was tousled from sleep, and his maroon paisley dressing gown was tied loosely at the waist. "What have we here, Miss Mortimer? A little nocturnal perambulation for the good of your health?" he inquired coolly.

"Please let me pass, sir."

He didn't move. "Why are you wandering around the house in the middle of the night?"

"I heard something," she replied truthfully.

"What, exactly?"

"Footsteps. Didn't you hear them too?"

"I heard nothing at all." He really didn't *know* why he'd awoken, but something had then compelled him to leave his room.

She thought it prudent not to mention Rollo, for Sir Greville the Grim was unlikely to believe in such things. All she wanted was to return to her room and close the door upon all things Seton. "Well, I was probably dreaming," she said.

"Undoubtedly." His candle fluttered as he stood aside suddenly. "Well, don't let me keep you from your slumbers a moment longer, madam."

She hurried thankfully past him, wishing hot candle wax would splash on his bare toes.

Megan opened her eyes to bright sunshine the next morning. It was Friday, December 19, and she could see by the ice-fringed ivy leaves around the window that there had been a sharp dawn frost. There was a great deal of noise coming from outside, hammering, shouting, and the occasional rumble of falling masonry. She flung the bedclothes back and went to look out, for everything had been in darkness when she and Evangeline arrived last night.

She found herself gazing out over a small walled garden and the Radcliffe House stables toward what was left of the northern end of Great East Street. Most of it had already been demolished, and gangs of workmen were bringing down what was left. There were clouds of dust, and carts were hauling away the rubble.

Several miles to the north of Radcliffe House were the ice-whitened Downs, where windmills awaited the breeze, but immediately to the south lay the present quite modest grounds of the Marine Pavilion, which would soon be greatly extended when the intrusion of Great East Street was no more. Already a great stable was abuilding, comprising an immense dome that to Megan's eyes looked as large as St. Paul's Cathedral itself. The main entrance to the Pavilion was from the undisturbed section of Great East Street, and beyond it lay the rest of the old town. Then there was the sea, sparkling brightly in the winter sun, and far out on the horizon a squadron of Royal Naval frigates sailing toward Portsmouth.

The walled garden of Radcliffe House was well tended even in the depths of winter, and although the frost precluded any work as yet this morning, it was clear that Evangeline's two gardeners were assiduous about their duties. There was a quite astonishing display of chrysanthemums, goldenrod, and Michaelmas daisies for so late in the year, as well as borders of pansies and violas. A gravel path edged by a low box hedge encircled a small lawn, in the center of which was a raised lily pond that was covered in ice. Beside the pool there was a little white-painted summerhouse. It was open in front, had a little bench inside, and was overhung by a gnarled apple tree, in which flourished the prodigious mistletoe Evangeline had mentioned the evening before.

Remembering how Rollo had appeared to be gazing at something in the distance, Megan looked in what she thought was the same direction. The only thing of note was a hilltop church with a countrified churchyard at the very edge of the town. Was that what the ghost had been looking at? Suddenly she remembered the quotation he'd used. *"I have a good eye, Uncle: I can see a church by daylight."* Yes, that was what he had been looking at.

A little later, dressed in her mustard gown, with her hair pinned up in a neat knot on top of her head, she went reluctantly down to take breakfast with Lady Evangeline, Rupert, and Greville. She was determined not to catch the eye of the latter, or speak to him unless spoken to first.

Chapter 10

The dining room was next to the drawing room on the Steine side of the house, and was decorated in gray and gold. It caught the full flush of the morning sun, and the warm air was scented with coffee, toast, and crisp bacon, as well as the bowl of roses that adorned the center of that same white-clothed table where the previous evening Megan had been so wretched. Edward, as supercilious and sour-faced as ever, was standing to attention by the sideboard, on which an array of silver-domed platters indicated a goodly selection. Outside, ladies and gentlemen of the *ton* paraded on the Steine's fine pathways, and several gleaming town carriages bowled around the perimeter roads. More carriages were drawn up in front of Donaldson's Circulating Library, and the sound of a German band playing Christmas carols could be heard from the front lawn of the Pavilion.

When Megan entered, she found everyone else already at the table. Rupert and Greville rose to their feet. They were both in pine-green coats and beige breeches, signifying an intention to ride after breakfast, and Evangeline was resplendent in a long-sleeved navy blue silk morning gown and lace day bonnet. She bestowed a gracious smile upon Megan.

"Good morning, my dear. I trust you slept well?"

"Good morning, Lady Evangeline. Sirs. Yes, I slept excellently," Megan replied, and was immediately conscious of Greville's raised eyebrow. But he said nothing.

Rupert hastened to draw out a chair for her, and as she sat down the door opened again. A maid came in with more bacon, and did not enter alone, for Rollo's spectral steps followed. The ghost crossed to the table, and halted right beside Megan. He was totally invisible again this morning, but the scent of orange blossom was heady, and she was sure that if she reached out she would be able to touch him. After all, if he could leave his imprint on carriage upholstery, surely he would be substantial enough to touch?

She heard him inhale deeply. " 'But, soft! Methinks I scent the morning air,' " he murmured, and she looked swiftly at the others to see if they heard, but only Evangeline seemed to have done so, for she tutted as she reached for the marmalade.

The maid went out again, and Evangeline smiled at Megan again. "What would you like to eat, my dear? I vow we have every breakfast item in creation."

"Oh, just some bacon and an egg," Megan replied, and as Edward brought them, she wondered if he would contrive to spill everything in her lap out of spite.

Rollo was evidently intent upon Evangeline, for suddenly he spoke to her. "What ho, my lady? Dost thou not think this to be a fine morning?"

"Enough, sir," she hissed, at which Rupert and Greville exchanged glances. Edward paused, a slice of crisp bacon impaled upon his serving fork, but then he went on with what he was doing.

Rollo sighed. " 'Fair is my love, and cruel as she's fair,' " he quoted.

"Sir, I will not have this at the breakfast table!" Evangeline whispered crossly.

" 'O tiger's heart wrapped in a woman's hide!' " But the phantom fell silent, and Evangeline began to talk about the Christmas decorations which Fosdyke and two footmen were at that very moment acquiring in the town.

Megan picked up her knife and fork, but then a slice of toast suddenly rose from the rack in front of her, and floated over to the window seat, where it was eaten with relish. Megan stared. Ghosts could *eat*? She glanced around the table again, but this time not even Evangeline appeared to have noticed.

Silence prevailed for some five minutes, but then Rupert glanced so sharply toward the window that Megan was sure he had suddenly perceived Rollo. But it was something else he had noticed. "Good Lord! That fellow's all in white!"

Everyone turned—even Rollo, Megan felt sure—and saw a gentleman clad from head to toe in white, riding by on a white horse. He was not new to Evangeline. "That is a busybody and tittle-tattler by the name of Mr. Mellish. He is a crony of the Garsingtons, and is *always* to be found at their wretched musical *soirées*, although I am convinced his purpose is solely to discover their latest foolishness. He spreads spiteful chitter-chatter to every drawing room into which he can worm his way, for he is the most unprincipled gossipmonger in Brighton. He thinks he cuts a dash to end all dashes with his penchant for white, but he is actually relatively restrained compared with Mr. Cope, who thankfully is no longer in Brighton," she declared, beckoning Edward to bring her some more bacon.

Rupert was intrigued. "And who might Mr. Cope be?"

"A gentleman as green as Mr. Mellish is white. Mind you, Mr. Cope's eccentricities verged on the alarmingly odd."

Greville raised his eyes to the pelmet, thinking that those last two words might occasionally apply to his aunt herself.

Evangeline glanced at Edward. "You may go now."

"My lady." The footman bowed and withdrew, closing the dining room door behind him.

Evangeline then elaborated upon the green man. "Mr. Cope wore only green, right down to green seals at his fob. His house was furnished in green, he only ate green vegetables, his wigs were powdered in green, and he even attempted to have his horses dyed green, but it all washed out in the first downpour. He was much given to studying ladies with his quizzing glass, and examined complete strangers as if under a microscope. He alarmed more than one gentle soul, I can tell you. As you can imagine, he brought the Steine to a halt when he appeared, not that he will appear again for the time being.

In October he jumped out of his bedroom window because he heard noises and thought he had to escape a riot. Fortunately, he wasn't badly hurt, but his friends deemed it best to take him somewhere quiet to, er, recover."

"An asylum, perchance?" Rupert suggested.

"Most likely." Evangeline looked at him. "By the way, have you and Greville entered your name at Donaldson's?"

Rupert nodded. "Well, not yet. I intend to do so this morning, but I can't speak for Greville."

She turned to Greville. "Sir?"

That gentleman stirred himself to answer. "Aunt E, the circulating library is the very last place you will find me. To go there is tantamount to informing the town crier."

"You surely don't imagine your presence here is going to pass unnoticed? You will be observed the moment you sally forth for your ride."

Greville shrugged. "I intend to turn my collar up and pull my hat low, and since we are going to make for the Downs, I doubt if I will see all that many. Word can get around if it pleases, but I do not have to oblige Brighton by flinging myself into the thick of society. I wish to be quiet, and quiet I will be."

"Well, that makes things a little awkward. You see, now that you, Rupert, and I are here in Brighton after all, I had planned for us to attend tomorrow night's Christmas *bal masqué* at the Old Ship Hotel. I presume you will not be coming?"

"That is correct."

Evangeline sighed. "Oh, well, I suppose it will even things out conveniently if you are not present."

"What do you mean?"

"Sir Jocelyn and Chloe are bound to be there, which means Mr. March will be with them. Rupert and I will join their party, and Miss Mortimer will bring the number up to a perfect six."

There was silence, and the playing of the German band seemed suddenly more intrusive. Megan lost what little appetite she had; indeed she felt quite sick. Wear fine clothes, eat at this awful table, face Cousin Oliver, *and* go to a fashionable ball? It was too much. She couldn't do it, she simply couldn't!

Evangeline beamed at them all. "An excellent balance, don't you think?"

Greville's cool gray eyes swung toward Megan. "Perhaps I'll attend the ball after all, Aunt E," he said, and Megan was sure he had changed his mind simply to be at hand to deny her any hope of enjoying herself. He need not have troubled, for enjoyment was the very last thing she would experience!

Evangeline frowned at him. "Oh, do make up your mind, sir. Am I to take it now that you are definitely going to join us?"

"Yes, so it's an uneven seven after all, I fear."

"It cannot be helped. Now, then, Greville, I have a favor to ask of you."

"A favor?"

Evangeline nodded. "I find myself with so much to do today that I really do not have the time to fit everything in. What with overseeing the Christmas decorations, sorting out the costumes for the play, and summoning my dressmaker to bring the new jester's costume I ordered before leaving for Bath, there really isn't time to go to Mrs. Fiske's in St. James's Street as well. Mrs. Fiske herself is only in attendance between twelve and five, and Miss Mortimer is expected there at twelve, so would you be an angel and take her for me? After your ride, of course."

"If something you've ordered requires collection, surely a footman can do it?" Greville suggested, thinking it odd to send Megan.

"It isn't anything for me, sir. Mrs. Fiske is to provide Miss Mortimer with suitable new togs, including, I trust, a gown that will do for tomorrow night."

Greville stared. His aunt had finally taken leave of her senses! An evening gown for a companion? Oh, feline Miss Mortimer had indeed fallen on her feet!

"Well, Greville?" Evangeline eyed him.

"If you wish me to take Miss Mortimer, I will do so."

Megan's heart sank, for she had been silently praying he had something else to do, but Evangeline beamed with satisfaction. "Excellent. Now, if Miss Mortimer finds the things to her liking, you are to instruct Mrs. Fiske to have them delivered here without delay. The bill is to be sent to me, naturally."

"Naturally."

"By the way, I have invited Sir Jocelyn and Chloe to join us tonight to discuss *Twelfth Night*." Evangeline placed her napkin by her plate. "Rupert, I expect you to conduct yourself with dignity where Chloe's friendship with Mr. March is concerned."

"Yes, Aunt E."

"Miss Mortimer, I shall not require you until this afternoon, when I wish you to read through Feste with me."

"Yes, Lady Evangeline."

Rollo murmured from the window seat. " 'Well, God give them wisdom that have it; and those that are fools, let them use their talents.' "

Evangeline hesitated, then went on speaking to Megan. "In the meantime you may do as you please, just be sure to make arrangements with Greville before he goes off on his ride."

"Yes, Lady Evangeline."

"Oh, dear, it's beginning to get very hot in here. I think I will stroll in the garden a while." Evangeline got up hastily, for her face was beginning to go a familiar red. Greville opened the door for her, but as he began to close it again he almost trapped Rollo, who was following her.

The ghost was most indignant. "Ye gods and small fishes! Thou art plaguey impatient, sirrah! Canst thou not allow a person time to pass through in peace?"

But Greville's ear was unhearing.

Chapter 11

Having reluctantly agreed with Greville that she would be ready in the entrance hall at a quarter to twelve precisely, Megan decided to use the intervening free time to walk the half mile or so to St. Nicholas's. Wearing her maroon cloak, mustard gown, and little hat, she set out directly after breakfast, before Greville and Rupert had left for their ride on the Downs. Her hands were thrust deep into a warm fur muff that Evangeline had kindly insisted she take, and she was glad of her little ankle boots, for there was quite a bite in the sea air.

Her route took her away from the Steine, across another fairly open area and the remnants of the very end of Great East Street into Church Street, which led past an army barracks, then steeply up toward the church on the hill. The sun had melted the frost and a light breeze had picked up, and during a lull in the demolition she heard the German band again. It was playing "The Holly and the Ivy."

There were side streets and courtyards along Church Street, as well as a number of houses and other buildings, but they became fewer the farther up the hill she walked until by the time she reached the churchyard wall, she seemed almost in open country. From here the view was wonderful. Brighton was spread out below, and she could clearly see Radcliffe House and the Marine Pavilion. The sea glittered bright green-blue, with many sails dotted out toward the horizon, and it was so clear that in the western distance, some sixty miles away, she could make out the Isle of Wight. It was a lovely day, and could not have been further removed from the storm of less than a week ago, when parts of southern England had suffered damage and flood.

The main gate into the churchyard from the town lay on the other side, and led directly to the south-facing porch, but from Church Street there was a small gap in the wall. Beside the gap there waited a gleaming scarlet curricle, the two chestnut horses in the care of a small boy who had been paid for his services. Megan did not give the vehicle a second glance as she entered the churchyard. A path led around the surprisingly quaint old church to the porch. Over the centuries medieval St. Nicholas's had acquired several additions of differing heights, and the uneven roof had dormer windows and even a tall chimney. The golden weathercock atop the church tower shone brightly against the vivid blue of the sky, and seagulls wheeled overhead, their cries echoing across the hillside.

She walked slowly, glancing at the many gravestones, almost expecting to see the name Rollo Witherspoon upon one of them, but there was nothing. Then, as she turned the corner to approach the porch, a young lady and gentleman emerged arm in arm and came toward her.

The lady was vivacious and beautiful, in a matching cornflower-blue pelisse and gown braided with gold. She had short blonde hair, and the golden tassels of her white fur shako-styled hat bounced as she walked. There was an elegant shawl over her shoulders, with one end trailing along the ground behind her, as was the latest mode, and she was laughing at something the gentleman said. But it was the gentleman himself who so arrested Megan's horrified attention that she came to a standstill—for it was her abhorred cousin, Oliver March.

She may only have been sixteen when last she saw him, but she remembered him very clearly. He was tall and narrow-shouldered, with wiry ginger hair, a thin face and long pointed nose, and, unusually, his pale complexion was free of freckles. While not handsome, his looks were certainly attractive to many woman, and by the smile of the lady on his arm, she numbered among them.

His attire was elegant. There were large brass buttons on his donkey-colored coat, his fawn breeches were faultlessly tailored, and his boots were the work of a very exclusive boot maker in London's St. James's. He carried a brown beaver top hat under his right arm, and a diamond pin flashed in the very center of his neck cloth. Everything about him smacked of the sort of wealth and privilege that had no need to throw a destitute kinswoman out of her modest home, especially when he only intended to leave Berengers standing forlorn and empty anyway. All that mattered in Oliver March's world was Oliver March—and possibly the beauty he had on his arm. Presumably it must be Chloe Holcroft, for she was the young woman who had looked out of the window across the Steine the evening before.

Megan was so transfixed that she could not move. Thus, he could not help but see her. For a moment he looked at her with a perplexed "Don't I know you?" quizzicality on his face. His steps slowed as he pondered whether or not it might be disadvantageous to acknowledge such a modestly clad person, and Chloe looked up at him in surprise. "Is something wrong, Oliver?" she asked. "Are you acquainted with this lady?"

"Er, I have a feeling I may be," he admitted, and doffed his top hat to Megan. "Pray forgive my poor memory, madam, but have we met before?"

Relief flooded through Megan. He didn't recognize her! Long may it stay that way. "Not that I can recall, sir," she replied, deciding to postpone the truth while she could.

Chloe smiled at her. "Have you been in Brighton long, Miss er . . . ?"

"I only arrived yesterday." Megan affected not to have noticed that her name was sought. She knew that the chances of Oliver remaining in ignorance for long were rather slender, for he was sure to hear Evangeline's new companion referred to by name at the ball. When that happened, Megan did not doubt that his memory would be jogged rather sharply.

Chloe smiled again. "Yesterday?" Ah, that explains

why I have never seen you before. Are you here for Christmas?"

"No, I have taken a new position here."

"A new position?"

"I am companion to Lady Evangeline Radcliffe." That admission at least had to be made.

Chloe's eyes cleared. "I saw you looking out of the window of Radcliffe House last night!"

"Yes."

"I confess I was all nosiness, because as far as I was aware Radcliffe House was closed until New Year's Eve. I also confess I was puzzled when I saw an unknown hooded lady peeping out of the dining room window. I had no idea Lady Evangeline was taking a companion." Chloe's expression became a little self-conscious. "Oh, what a rattlebrain you must think me, for I haven't introduced myself. I am Miss Holcroft, daughter of Lady Evangeline's old friend, Admiral Sir Jocelyn Holcroft. This is Mr. March."

Megan managed a smile. "I am honored to meet you, Miss Holcroft. Mr. March."

"I vow you are most fortunate in your mistress," Chloe went on, "for Lady Evangeline is without a doubt the most delightful lady of my acquaintance."

"I am fortunate indeed," Megan replied, warming to the other by the moment. No wonder Evangeline was so fond of her—and so regretful that Rupert had apparently bungled his chances. Chloe Holcroft did not seem to have an unpleasant side. There had been no change in her attitude on discovering she was addressing a companion; she remained warm and friendly. Oliver's manner, on the other hand, had changed perceptibly.

Chloe spoke to Megan again. "I believe you and I will see each other again later today, for Lady Evangeline sent a footman over last night inviting Father and me to Radcliffe House this evening to discuss the Christmas play."

Oliver took out his fob watch. "We should be leaving now, Chloe," he said pointedly.

"Oh, yes, of course. Decorating the church *did* take longer than expected, didn't it?" Chloe slipped a hand over his arm again, but then paused to address Megan again. "I understand from Lady Evangeline's message that Rupert and Greville—I-I mean Lord Rupert and Sir Greville—have come to Brighton for Christmas after all?"

"Yes, they have."

"Please convey my best wishes, and to Lady Evangeline as well, of course."

"I will be sure to pass on your message, Miss Holcroft."

Chloe smiled again, and Oliver showed grudging politeness to a nobody of a companion by touching the brim of his hat, then they walked past Megan, and around the church toward Church Street.

Megan couldn't help slipping to the corner to watch. She saw Oliver hand Chloe into the waiting curricle, but then suddenly he whipped around to look back, and by the expression on his pale face, Megan knew he had realized to whom he had just been speaking. Her heart sank like a stone, for even at a distance she could see the veil descend over his eyes, and the way his lips set into a thin line of unease and displeasure as he perceived what a very unwanted pigeon had come to roost in Brighton. For a moment he stood stock-still, then he climbed swiftly up beside Chloe, the whip cracked, and the curricle sprang away down the hill.

Megan felt so uneasy she had to dig her fingernails sternly into her palms to try to keep calm. She knew of old that Oliver March was a very unpleasant foe, and that as far as he was concerned, water was thicker than blood. But what could he do to her now? After a moment or so the almost panicky feeling subsided, and she took a long breath. She was about to walk on to the porch, when she noticed some wooden steps leading up to a door on the side of the church, beneath a dormer window. Curiosity got the better of her, and she went up to open the door. Inside, she found galleries that had been installed to accommodate the much larger congregations now that Brighton was so fashionable.

It was cold and quiet, with that odd musty smell of ancient stone, and the sunlight slanting through the windows lay brightly across the altar and aisle. The sound of women's quiet voices made her lean over to look down, and she saw two ladies putting the finishing touches to a garland of holly, ivy, and myrtle they were fixing to one of the pews at the edge of the aisle. No mistletoe, Megan noticed, for it was considered unsuitable for a church. The women finished what they were doing, then left, and silence descended. Megan remained where she was, just savoring the peaceful atmosphere, when suddenly the door of the porch was flung open, and loud masculine steps entered the church.

For a split second Megan thought it was Rollo, but then she saw they belonged to someone only too real: Greville. She drew back out of sight as he walked down the aisle, then over to an ornate tomb against the wall opposite. Carved from white marble, and topped by cupids and angels ascending toward heaven, it was the most splendid resting place in the church. He halted on a brass memorial that was set into the floor in front of it. Dressed in a pine-green coat and pale gray riding breeches, he was bareheaded and had his top hat and riding crop clasped behind him. There was so sign of Rupert, and Megan presumed they must have elected to go their separate ways for the ride on the Downs.

Greville turned toward the altar, paused to glance back toward the porch, then took a little jeweled snuffbox from his pocket. He removed something from it, and slipped whatever it was into a hiding place in the wall behind the altar. Then he left the church.

Megan had to investigate, so she descended the steps from the gallery into the nave, and hurried first to the tomb, being careful to step around the memorial set into the floor. The inscription in the costly white marble read: IN LOVING MEMORY OF ARABELLA, LADY SETON, PATIENT WIFE OF SIR HENRY SETON, ADORED MOTHER OF GREVILLE. BOTH 14th JULY 1753 DIED 29th APRIL 1788.

When she then went to look in the wall behind the altar, she found a loose stone behind which there was a space containing sprigs of mistletoe. Some were clearly years old, but one very fresh indeed.

Chapter 12

After crossing the Steine to Donaldson's Circulating Library, outside which there was a considerable gaggle of carriages, curricles, phaetons, and gigs, to say nothing of the ladies and gentlemen who had walked there, it was only a few doors around the corner into St. James's Street to Mrs. Fiske's premises. The fact that the fashion repository was very select indeed, with clientele from only the superior levels of society, was the second reason Megan felt so daunted; the first was Greville's presence at her side.

The walk from Radcliffe House had been accomplished with the minimum conversation, for which Megan did not really know whether to be relieved or not. His public conduct toward her could not exactly have been faulted, but then neither could it have been praised; the simple fact was that Sir Greville Seton was not an easy man, and she was fast concluding that his unmarried state was no accident. To begin with, she could not help noticing how he kept the brim of his top hat low, and averted his head if he saw anyone who might recognize him. He clearly had the unbelievable vanity to think that every unmarried lady in creation had designs upon his person and his fortune.

It was a shame he was so difficult, for he really was exceedingly handsome, and no fault could be found in his appearance, which was all that a gentleman of style and fashion should be. Today he wore a gray Polish greatcoat with an astrakhan collar, a top hat that was utter perfection, tasseled Hessian boots with gold spurs, and he carried an ivory-handled cane in a tightly gloved hand.

Beside such a paragon, she felt very inferior and insignificant indeed, so much so that she almost felt tempted to walk a respectful six paces behind!

But as they passed through Mrs. Fiske's tasteful chocolate-brown door, which was fixed with a discreet knot of holly and was set between two fine bow windows containing a display of hats and bonnets, Greville ceased to be uppermost in her thoughts. It was agreeably warm inside after the bracing air of the street. A fine coal fire glowed in a hearth that had a polished brass fender and blue-and-white Delft tiles, and there was a sumptuous smell of costly materials: velvets, silk, exquisite Indian muslins, and richly colored winter merino. Beautiful clothes of every description hung haphazardly from a curtain rail that ran around every wall except by the windows, and there were several tall floor-standing mirrors in which one's appearance could be admired or lamented.

Two ladies, one tall and thin, the other short and buxom, were at an oak counter examining a selection of lace trimmings that had been brought for them by a young man wearing a cream coat and blue-spotted neck cloth. Female voices came from behind a maroon velvet curtain that was drawn across one alcove next to the fireplace, while in the other there was a sofa where a lady was turning the pages of a catalog of the latest designs. Her face had the dry look of one who had failed to protect her complexion sufficiently from the rigors of the Madras sun, and lolling beside her was a wheezy pug with a jeweled collar that glittered in the light from the windows. The only other gentleman was a high-ranking cavalry officer who Megan guessed was the pug lady's husband.

The alcove curtain was jerked aside, and Mrs. Fiske emerged with a figured velvet pelisse over her arm. She was a severe woman of about forty-five in a charcoal gown and starched muslin bonnet, and Megan's heart sank still further at the way she snapped her fingers at the young male assistant, who immediately bore the pelisse through another door at the rear of the premises. The lady whose garment it was came out of the alcove with her maid, who was still endeavoring to arrange the long gauze scarf of her mistress's jockey bonnet, and the cavalry officer gallantly opened the front door for them to go out to the carriage waiting at the curb across the street.

Mrs. Fiske came over to Greville with an ingratiating smile. "Why, Sir Greville, what an unexpected honor," she declared, then bestowed a withering glance upon Megan's hat and cloak.

Greville explained his errand. "I am charged by my aunt, Lady Evangeline, to bring her companion to you to be fitted for some new clothes. I believe you know what is required?"

A *companion* was to be fitted for clothes? Shocked eyes turned upon Megan, to whom it seemed that even the pug dog gasped. Mrs. Fiske's gaze was impenetrable as she inclined her head. "Ah, yes, I received her ladyship's message last night, and everything is in readiness. Sir Greville, if you will take a seat, I will attend to Miss, er . . . ?"

"Mortimer," Megan supplied, hoping her face wasn't as aflame with embarrassment as it felt.

"This way, if you please, Miss Mortimer." Mrs. Fiske returned to the alcove, and held the curtain aside for Megan to go inside, then hurried away, leaving Megan alone inside.

Megan was glad of the privacy. This was an ordeal, not a pleasure, and the sooner it was over, the better she would feel. She glanced around. There was an uncomfortable wrought-iron chair with a pink satin cushion, and a cheval glass that looked as if it might once have graced a French chateau. The only garment was a midnight-blue evening gown that had been tossed almost carelessly over the chair. Made of sequined gauze over watered silk, it was one of the most beautiful gowns Megan had ever seen. If only it were there in case it would do for Lady Evangeline Radcliffe's new companion! Megan touched the glittering sequins on the low-cut bodice, and imagined herself dancing in it at tomorrow night's Christmas *bal masqué* at the Old Ship. The gauze and silk were exquisitely matched, the sequins must have taken an age to stitch, and the craftsmanship was of matchless quality. Why, Queen Charlotte herself would not be ashamed of such a gown.

The curtain was jerked aside again, and Mrs. Fiske returned with various clothes over her arm. She hung them one by one on a rail, and then turned to cast a knowledgeable eye over Megan's figure. "Yes, Lady Evangeline was right, you and Miss Holcroft are indeed the same size," she declared, and began to remove Megan's hat and cloak.

Greville had seen the clothes taken into the alcove, and considered them far too good for mousy Miss Mortimer, who did not warrant such plumes. The curtain hadn't been properly drawn across, and he could just see the flick of a ruby dinner gown in part of the mirror. Thus was a companion being raised above her station in life, he thought sourly. Then he saw Megan's profile for a moment. With her smile and soft brown eyes, and her thick brown hair made unexpectedly rich by the ruby of the gown, she was perhaps more handsome than he gave credit for, and there was something very graceful and ingenuous about the way she turned her head to see herself from a different angle. Had she been anything other than a companion, he would have found her tolerable. Annoyed with the route his thoughts were taking, he looked out of the window instead.

Half an hour later, the better by the ruby dinner gown, an apricot-and-white-striped woolen morning gown, a simple white silk evening gown that would serve well for the following night's ball, a gray velvet spencer, and a fine dark-green woolen cloak richly trimmed with honey-colored fur, all of which would soon be on their way to Radcliffe House, Megan and Greville left the repository again.

As they emerged on to the pavement, Megan was dismayed to see Oliver drive past toward the Steine like a fox pursued by hounds. He was dressed as he had been in the churchyard that morning, and he clearly considered his driving to be very much the tippy, for he brought the swaying curricle to a flourishing standstill by the crush of vehicles on the corner by Donaldson's. Vaulting down, he vanished into the library after flinging the reins and a coin into the eager hands of one of the local boys hanging around for just such lucrative tasks.

Greville glowered after him. "March is a fellow I would delight in seeing overturned," he muttered.

"I would too," Megan said without thinking. She knew it was simply postponing the evil moment, but nevertheless she still hoped she and Greville would pass by without encountering her loathed cousin.

"You are acquainted with him?" Greville asked.

"I-I met him once a long time ago, and this morning I encountered him again with Miss Holcroft by the—"

"You are acquainted with Miss Holcroft as well?" Greville interrupted in surprise.

"Well, not exactly. I happened to meet them both when I was out walking this morning."

"And where was this?"

"In St. Nicholas's churchyard."

Greville halted. "Did you indeed? And what were they doing there?" he inquired, beginning to fear things might have progressed as far as the ordering of the banns.

"Miss Holcroft had been helping with the Christmas decorations."

"Ah, yes." He relaxed a little, but still looked at her. "I went to St. Nicholas's myself this morning, after changing my mind about riding with Rupert on the Downs."

"Oh?"

He gave a dry laugh. "Miss Mortimer, I can tell by your face that although I did not see you, you certainly saw me."

She flushed a little. "I happened to be up in the gallery when you came in, but I made certain to keep out of your way."

"Indeed? Well, I dare say that is an honest reply."

"I dare say it is too," she replied.

"Don't presume to employ the edge of your tongue upon me, madam." For a split second he was tempted to tell her he knew all about her disgraceful behavior in Bath, but he didn't. He intended to write to his friend when they returned to the house, and as soon as confirmation had arrived of Miss Megan Mortimer's wrongdoing, he would expose her for what she really was.

Megan had been stung into forgetting herself. "Then, you should not punish me for events in which I had absolutely no hand! I have grievances too, not least that when I was sixteen I was thrown out of house and home by my male cousin. Am I then justified in tarring *all* gentlemen with the same odious brush? Why not? If such an abysmal standard is fit for you, then it is fit for me as well!"

His gray eyes became icy. "You overreach yourself, Miss Mortimer."

Caution now eluded her completely. "Perhaps, but after enduring you for an hour that might as well have been a lifetime, I feel very much better! You may rest assured that in future I will avoid you to the best of my ability, and if I am able to keep out of your way entirely, I will be more than glad of it!" With that she stepped into the road right in front of a fly-by-night.

Chapter 13

Megan might have met with a terrible accident, had not Greville pulled her back in time. "Damn it, woman, look where you're going!" he cried.

She was too shaken to reply. She heard the growled curses of the two chairmen, and caught a glimpse of the fly-by-night's middle-aged male passenger's startled face; then it had gone.

Greville drew her away from the curb. "Are you all right?"

"Yes. Thank you."

"Perhaps in future you will know your place."

She wrenched her arm away from him. "And what exactly *is* my place, Sir Greville? Somewhere below kitchen scullion and above street urchin? Or would even that be too grand?"

"Miss Mortimer—"

"Maybe you would prefer to see me press-ganged? A few winters on the Atlantic would no doubt do me good!"

"*Miss Mortimer!* When I spoke of your place, I meant on my arm, *away* from the curb!"

She gazed at him in dismay. "Oh."

"Oh, indeed. Now then, can we please proceed back to Radcliffe House, and bring this disagreeable expedition to an end as quickly as possible?"

She took his arm without another word, and they walked on in a silence during which they heard the band still playing Christmas carols in the garden in front of the Marine Pavilion. But then they both saw Oliver bow-

ing over Chloe's hand as she stood with her father on
the verandah of the library.

With Rupert's interests very much in mind, Greville
decided that Radcliffe House would have to be temporarily postponed, and his own desire for anonymity abandoned. "Miss Mortimer, I, er, have decided to call in at
Donaldson's before going on to the house. I trust that
will not inconvenience you at all?"

Megan had observed the expressions crossing his face
as he witnessed the scene on the verandah, and knew he
had changed his mind out of consideration for Rupert.
For this she could almost have favorably revised her
opinion of Sir Greville Seton, indeed she probably would
have had it not been that she was filled with trepidation
now that another meeting with her only kinsman was
almost certainly imminent.

She was in a cleft stick. In spite of Oliver's intimacy
with the Holcrofts, should she have revealed to Evangeline that he was her despicable cousin? It was too late now
for she had held her tongue, and if Oliver mentioned their
relationship, her silence on the subject was going to convince Greville still more that she had an ulterior motive
for everything she did—probably even for drawing breath!
She could explain to Evangeline that she had kept silent
because of the Holcrofts, but Greville wouldn't believe
that!

"Miss Mortimer?" Greville prompted curiously, still
awaiting her response.

"Of course it will not be an inconvenience, sir," she
answered, and they continued toward the corner.

The circulating library had been run by Mr. Donaldson
only since June, having previously been in the hands of
a Mr. Gregory. It was open all the year around for the
convenience of persons of rank and fashion, and was
almost always crowded and busy. Within its walls one
could not only borrow the latest novels, plays, or poems,
but also examine portfolios of watercolors and carica-
tures. Materials for painting and sketching could be acquired, new pieces of music tried out, tickets for balls
and lotteries purchased, and cardplaying indulged in; but

above all, people went there to append their names to the all-important register.

Summer and winter, the verandah was the favorite gathering place, because it was visible from both inside and outside the library, and if the Prince of Wales should be at the Marine Pavilion, he could look across and see who was in town. Today he would have observed his Carlton House dinner guest, Miss Chloe Holcroft, blushing and smiling as another of his Carlton House dinner guests, Mr. Oliver March, paid court to her with every display of gallantry.

Megan studied Oliver as she and Greville drew closer. To see him now one might take him for a veritable Robin Hood, not the ruthless mixture of Prince John and the Sheriff of Nottingham he really was. Sir Jocelyn stood at his daughter's side in a frogged olive-green greatcoat and a black beaver hat with the brim turned down against the cold. There was a rather impenetrable expression on his face, and if Megan had to hazard a guess, she would have said he was none too happy to encounter Oliver March. Maybe the admiral was of Evangeline's persuasion, and would much have preferred Rupert for a future son-in-law.

Chloe, on the other hand, was obviously pleased to see Oliver again; at least, if she wasn't, she was hiding the fact very well. She still wore the cornflower-blue clothes of the morning, and her smile was radiant. Suddenly she looked up and saw Greville. "Greville! How good it is to see you again!" Her eyes went to Megan. "And you too, of course, Miss er . . . ?"

"Mortimer," Megan supplied, knowing there was no longer any point in hiding it. She felt Oliver's hard gaze upon her, but did not look at him.

"Miss Mortimer." As Chloe smiled she wasn't entirely able to eliminate the speculation in her eyes. She was wondering why Sir Greville Seton was out walking with his aunt's new companion. Was there something between them? Realizing what was going through the other's mind, Megan hastily removed her hand from Greville's arm, and by so doing unwittingly caused Chloe to wonder even more.

Greville stepped on to the verandah to kiss Chloe on the cheek. "It's good to see you again too, Chloe," he said, and clasped her hands warmly to look at her. "You are blooming, as always."

"Why, thank you, sir." She bobbed a mock curtsy.

The admiral leaned forward with an outstretched hand. "Greville, m'boy, I thought you were shunning us all this Christmas."

"A last-minute change of plan," Greville replied as they shook hands, then he turned to Megan. "Miss Mortimer, allow me to present Admiral Sir Jocelyn Holcroft, Miss Holcroft's father."

The admiral raised Megan's hand to his lips. "So *you* are the strange young lady my daughter espied at the window last night, eh?"

"Yes, Sir Jocelyn."

"I'm relieved to note that you do *not* possess two heads."

"Sir?"

He smiled again. "Oh, nothing, my dear, just an old man's notion of humor." He looked more closely at her with his one good eye. "I trust you will forgive me, for although I realize we have met before, I'm afraid I cannot remember where or when."

"But we haven't met before, Sir Jocelyn" she replied.

"We haven't? Are you sure?"

"Absolutely certain, sir."

"But you seem so familiar. Upon my soul, I truly thought we must have been introduced at some time. Ah, well, clearly my memory is even worse than I feared."

Oliver had very definitely been left in the wings by all these greetings, but now he reached for Megan's hand and made a pretense of bending over it. "How fortunate to encounter you again so soon, Miss Mortimer," he murmured, using the display of civility to squeeze her fingers until they hurt.

By doing that, and by deliberately addressing her as Miss Mortimer instead of Cousin Megan, she knew she was being warned to hold her tongue about being his relative. Such an arrangement suited her admirably. "Mr. March," she replied.

Oliver held her gaze with his pale, cold eyes, and she was the one who lowered her glance. It was the reaction of someone who did not wish to cause trouble, and it satisfied him that—for the time being at least—he had successfully intimidated her. His eyes flickered away to Greville, whom he greeted with every appearance of suspicious dislike. "Seton," he said briefly.

"March," was the equally abrupt reply.

Antagonism crackled between them, and once again Megan was reluctantly moved to credit Greville with some approval; anyone who abhorred Oliver March could not be entirely beyond redemption. She felt Sir Jocelyn still looking at her with that "I'm-sure-I-know-you-from-somewhere" light in his eyes. She must look like someone else, she thought.

Chloe was addressing her again. "Have you been a companion for long, Miss Mortimer?"

"Since I was sixteen. I was with Lady Jane Strickland before being employed by Lady Evangeline." From the corner of her eye, Megan saw Oliver's startled reaction.

"Like Sir Jocelyn, I too thought I knew you. Now I know why," he said.

She looked warily at him. "Sir?"

"I am a close friend of Ralph Strickland's, and met Lady Jane with him once. I must have seen you then."

Her dismay returned. He and Ralph Strickland were friends? Somehow she managed to sound level as she replied. "Oh, yes. How could I have forgotten?"

"I encountered Ralph in London only two days ago, when I paid the capital a fleeting visit."

Megan's spirits plunged. She could tell that he had heard Ralph's version of the dismissal of Lady Jane's companion. No name could have been mentioned at the time, but now she herself had kindly provided him with the information, and by the cold, knowing glitter in his gaze she knew he was prepared to use this as ammunition to make her do as he wished. He wanted his past callousness toward her to remain secret, and if she told tales about it, he would spread lascivious tales about her.

She felt close to tears. All she wanted in life was a suitable position, a roof over her head, and a peaceful, dull existence; instead she seemed unable to avoid trouble. Oliver obviously thought Evangeline did not know the truth about Bath, and of course in that he was wrong, but would Evangeline feel able to continue employing a companion whose notoriety was the talk of Brighton? Probably not. And again there was Greville, who would take the tale as proof that all companions were jezebels. She didn't like the latter, but she did not want him to think his prejudice against her was fully vindicated! If she had glanced at his face at that moment, she would have realized that he had already heard Ralph's account, and believed it.

Greville tapped his cane thoughtfully against his boot. If March had met Strickland within the last few days, then he was bound to have heard some very unflattering facts about Miss Megan Mortimer, yet he gave no hint of it. The sudden acquisition of honor was hardly likely to be the case where he was concerned, nor was Strickland likely to have painted the lady pure white after all, so why was March being so courteous? Consideration for Chloe's sensitivities? Possibly. Perhaps it would be interesting to probe a little. So as the conversation turned to *Twelfth Night,* he drew a rather surprised Oliver aside.

Chapter 14

"How was Ralph when you saw him?" Greville asked Oliver.

"In excellent fettle. Why do you ask?" Suspicion oozed from Oliver, for it was most unlike Greville to make a courteous inquiry about Ralph Strickland's health.

"Oh, just that I too have seen him recently, and both he and Sophia seemed a little, well, overwrought concerning something that had apparently happened in Bath."

A veil descended over Oliver's eyes. "I don't know what you're talking about, Seton. Besides, if there had been anything untoward at Bath, surely Lady Evangeline would know? Ralph told me that she had arrived there before he and Sophia left."

Greville gave a facile smile. "Yes, and she is now here in Brighton for Christmas, when she intended to spend it with Lady Jane. She will not volunteer a reason for the change of arrangements, and I was hoping you could shed some light. Clearly you cannot." He glanced at Megan, who was endeavoring to seem interested in *Twelfth Night,* but was actually more concerned about not being able to hear what he and March were saying. Her inordinate perturbation about the little tête-à-tête convinced him more and more that something was going on. Greville was certain that March knew all about events in Bath, and was equally certain that Megan knew March knew. That she would wish to keep the shameless circumstances of her dismissal a secret he could understand, but what was March's motive? Clearly not discretion in front of Chloe, otherwise the salacious details would be being divulged man-to-man right now!

Oliver was shaking his head. "No, I cannot shed any light at all because I know nothing."

"I see. Well, that's that, then." Greville gave another facile smile, and turned back to the others just as *Twelfth Night* was abandoned in favor of London gossip. Chloe was anxious to hear everything. "You have been in London for some time now, Greville, so I expect you to be bang up to the mark with *on dits*."

As Greville began to recount the news from the capital, Megan wondered greatly what he and Oliver had been talking about. Surely Oliver could not have regaled him with her inappropriate advances? No, somehow she thought not, because that would mean the very real risk of his own past misdeeds being exposed. Her gaze moved to Oliver, who was once again dancing attendance upon Chloe with such doglike devotion that it was impossible not to know he had marriage in mind. No wonder Brighton daily expected an announcement, she thought, marveling anew that Chloe and her father could be so easily duped into thinking him suitable.

From London the conversation moved to Brighton, and the social calendar up to Christmas. Chloe enthused about the next night's masked ball, and expressed immense delight that Megan would be attending as well. When Rupert's name was mentioned, however, she did not seem in the least enthusiastic, indeed she made much of changing the subject. Megan wasn't quite sure whether it was for Oliver's benefit, or she really wasn't interested in Rupert, or if it was a screen to hide her true feelings. It had to be one of the three, and this time Megan did not care to hazard a guess.

Another carriage pulled up alongside the other vehicles by the library, and a middle-aged lady and gentleman alighted. Megan did not know who they were, but she saw the appalled expression on Oliver's face, and could not help but notice how he immediately tried unsuccessfully to persuade Chloe to take a drive with him in his curricle. Greville smiled sleekly at Oliver's discomfort, for the lady and gentleman were Lord and Lady Garsington.

The head of the unmusical family of musicians was a stout, beak-nosed man who still liked to wear the powdered wig and tricorn hat of his youth. Not for him the elegance of a greatcoat; instead he preferred a fur-trimmed cloak, as did his bespectacled wife. Lady Garsington was his equal when it came to stoutness, but had a small upturned nose and buck teeth, putting Megan in mind of a studious, overweight mouse. Her ladyship's shortsighted gaze soon alighted upon Greville, and she nudged her husband.

They bore down upon the small group on the verandah, and immediately made their feelings very plain where each person was concerned. Greville and Sir Jocelyn received warm smiles and kind inquires regarding health, Megan—introduced merely as Miss Mortimer—was granted a brief glance that assessed her as a nonentity who did not warrant the condescension of a greeting, Oliver was frozen out completely because he had committed the unpardonable sin of casting aside their daughter Sybil, and Chloe was given a fixed smile because although she was the reason for Oliver's defection, she was also Sir Jocelyn's daughter.

The purpose of the Garsingtons' foray to the library was soon apparent; they had decided to mark Christmas Eve with another musical extravaganza, and at such short notice they were at a struggle to find guests. Mr. Mellish was always ready to accept, but apart from him their hopes had to rest with those who had just come to town and who had yet to fill their diary, or those they caught unawares, like poor Sir Jocelyn.

"Ah, Admiral," gushed her ladyship. "I *do* trust that you and dear Miss Holcroft will be able to attend our little *soirée musicale* on Sunday evening?"

Chloe's father, that grand seafaring man who had faced many an enemy without flinching, gave a start like a nervous rabbit. "Eh? Oh, I—"

"Good," Lady Garsington interrupted smoothly. "We will expect you at eight. Oh, and you, of course, *dear* Sir Greville."

Megan lowered her eyes, for the omission of Oliver and

herself was so pointed as to be rude. Why Oliver was in the woman's bad books Megan couldn't imagine, but her own exclusion was clearly due to her less than superior appearance. Yet for all Lady Garsington knew, she might be an eccentric princess who liked to travel incognito! Megan hid a smile at this preposterous thought, but nevertheless it was true to say that Lady Garsington's manners and judgment left a great deal to be desired.

But if Megan was considered beneath consideration, Greville certainly was not. Lady Garsington knew he had replaced Oliver in Sybil's affections, and so singled him out for particular indulgence. "Sir Greville, what a very agreeable surprise it is to find you here in Brighton after all. Your dear aunt told me you were staying in London this Christmas."

"I was." He saw the tit-for-tat smirk on Oliver's face.

Lady Garsington continued to gush. "Well, you can only just have arrived here, so *do* tell me how my dearest Sybil was when you left."

"I have no idea how she was," he replied, hoping to convey his complete lack of interest in Sybil Garsington.

Lady Garsington gave a twitter of laughter, and reworded the question. "Well, how was she when last you saw her?"

"Er, in excellent spirits," Greville answered. Excellent spirits? The unmanageable creature had been as frisky as a cart horse in season!

"I'm sure you will be delighted to hear that she and Sigismund are also returning in the next day or so. Oh, how foolish of me, for of course you must already know."

The implication that he was only in Brighton in order to be close to Sybil was almost too much for Greville's sensibilities. Something had to be done that would make absolutely clear his indifference to her frightful offspring. Oliver had done it by besieging Chloe instead; Greville's thoughts raced, and on impulse he took Megan's hand, startling her greatly by drawing it very deliberately over his sleeve and leaving his fingers resting warmly on hers. Then he beamed at Lady Garsington. "No, I'm afraid I didn't know Sybil and Sigismund were returning," he said untruthfully. Nor do I care, he added silently.

The taking of Megan's hand caused Lady Garsington's face to alter most comically, and she drew back as if a vile odor had suddenly assaulted her nostrils. After murmuring something about having much to do, she and his lordship then stalked away into the library, which suddenly sinking ship was immediately subjected to the scrambled exit of fashionable rats. Nothing could be more guaranteed to disperse a gathering than the approach of the Garsingtons.

The sudden departure of people obliged the party on the verandah to divide, and Megan found herself stepping aside with Greville. She took the opportunity to make her displeasure known, for companion or not, she would not be treated like that. "I do not like being used, sir," she said, snatching her hand from his sleeve.

"I concede that it was ill done on my part, Miss Mortimer, but if you knew their daughter . . ."

"I don't care what reason you have, Sir Greville, for the fact that I am only Lady Evangeline's companion does not entitle you to—"

"I know," he interrupted. "I can only ask you to forgive the imposition, Miss Mortimer."

She gave a curt nod. "The matter is at an end, sir." She turned to go, meaning to quit the library and scurry back to Radcliffe House.

"Miss Mortimer . . . ?"

"Sir?"

"Thank you for not saying this in front of Lady Garsington." The acknowledgment was uttered with the enthusiasm of one whose teeth were being drawn.

Megan hesitated. "I thought her to be an unmannered person who did not deserve any more consideration than she showed to me."

"Oh, believe me, you are fortunate to be omitted from her wretched *soirée musicale*. Evenings at Garsington House are to be avoided at all costs. Why else do you imagine the library has emptied so sharply?" He nodded toward the evacuation just coming to an end. So many vehicles had already pulled away that Oliver's curricle was one of the few still remaining. Oliver, Chloe, and Sir Jocelyn were now at the far end of the verandah, warning newly arriving acquaintances of the hazard within. Chloe glanced back, and her manner intimated that she was now more convinced than ever of something going on between Sir Greville Seton and his aunt's companion.

Greville looked at Megan. "So my bacon was only saved because Lady Garsington is beneath contempt?"

"Yes."

"Your capacity for blunt speaking is—"

"Almost a match for yours? Yes, Sir Greville, I suppose it is."

Chapter 15

When Megan and Greville returned to Radcliffe House, they found the hallway piled high with the Christmas greenery Fosdyke and the two footmen had purchased in the town. Rupert was still out on his ride, having decided to make a virtual day of it, but he was expected back soon, and from the kitchens there wafted the delicious smell of gingerbread.

Evangeline usually supervised the decorations, but her fitting for her jester's costume was running late, so no start had been made. She was in her apartment with the dressmaker, whose store of patience was rapidly diminishing because the little folly bells on the bright red and yellow outfit's shoulders had been rearranged five times over the past hour, and *still* Evangeline was not entirely satisfied. On hearing from Annie that Megan and Greville had returned, she immediately sent the maid to bring them to her, so that she could call upon their advice as to the bells' most becoming position.

Her apartment was on the east of the house, with a splendid view over the Steine. A fire crackled brightly in the hearth of the blue silk dressing room, where she was standing upon a stool the better to assist the dressmaker. The room contained wardrobes, a chest of drawers, and a washstand behind an elegant black-lacquered screen. There was also a dressing table upon which lay a three-horned jester's hat, and a lute with long ribbons that floated in the fierce heat from the fire.

The sight of Lady Evangeline Radcliffe in a tight-fitting fool's suit was not conducive to solemnity; indeed it en-

couraged the sort of mirth that was not on any account
to be revealed, on pain of her considerable wrath. Her
figure was a challenge for any needlework, and the unfortunate costume strained alarmingly along every seam.
She was red and yellow lozenges from head to toe, her
face was crimson from another flush, and she tinkled with
so many bells that Greville could not help recalling a
herd of goats he once encountered in the Swiss Alps.

She confronted Greville in all seriousness. "Well? How
do I look? Am I not the very personification of Feste?"

He swallowed. "I, er, think you look quite exceptional,
Aunt E," he replied.

Then she turned to Megan. "What do you say, Miss
Mortimer?"

"I have never seen anything quite so singular, Lady
Evangeline."

Evangeline beamed. "There, I *knew* it looked excellent," she declared with some satisfaction.

Megan could not help glancing at Greville, and she saw
his lips were pressed together in an effort to maintain a
straight face.

Evangeline surveyed herself in the dressing table mirror, and saw nothing comic at all. "My cap! Bring my
cap!" she cried, pointing to the item on the dressing
table. Megan took it to her, and watched in fascination
as Evangeline tugged it over her hair. Now my lute!"
she commanded next, and Megan brought that as well.
Evangeline posed in the mirror, and then struck a few
exceedingly discordant notes. "Oh, I *am* looking forward
to all this," she declared.

Greville caught Megan's eyes. The dressmaker gazed
at the floor, and Annie, who stood by the door, was so
still that she might have been a statue. No one dared to
speak. Except Rollo, who suddenly revealed his presence
by murmuring. "Mistress, thou lookest fit to explode."

Megan felt as if *she* would too, but Evangeline's expression did not alter. "I am considering hiring a proper
manager for my theater," she said in a matter-of-fact
tone that hinted at a task virtually accomplished. Rollo

gasped, then hurried from the room. Evangeline's lips twitched with satisfaction. That would teach *him* a lesson!

Greville had heard nothing, of course, and so expressed surprise. "A manager? Aunt E, you don't require such a person."

"I know. It was just a passing thought, and best forgotten," Evangeline replied, holding out a hand to be assisted down from the stool, and her bells jingled as she went to the window. "I am informed by Mrs. Fosdyke's bunion that against all the usual odds, Brighton is about to have a great deal of snow," she said.

Greville smiled. "And this bunion is infallible, is it?"

"Oh, yes, and I'm truly delighted to know there is snow on the way."

"Why?" Greville asked curiously, for snow wasn't exactly to be recommended.

"Because I have Prinny's permission to use the royal sleigh. It was brought to the Pavilion from Windsor in the snow of '98, and has never been returned. I enjoyed driving in it so much on that occasion, that he graciously told me I was at liberty to use it again should the opportunity arise. I am greatly looking forward to it."

Megan trusted that the bunion was indeed to be relied upon, otherwise Evangeline was going to be deeply disappointed.

Evangeline turned from the window again. "Now, then, *mes enfants,* I trust you took note of the Christmas greenery downstairs?"

"It would be hard to miss it," Greville replied.

"All the wires, silver and gold paper, red ribbon, fruit, flowers, and so on are in the drawing room. I wish you and Miss Mortimer to commence making some arrangements."

"*Me?* Aunt E, I don't know the first thing about decorations!"

"No? Well, I'm sure Miss Mortimer does, so off you go."

Greville dug his heels in a little. "Aunt E, why can't we just dispense with decorations this year?"

"Oh, shame on you, sirrah! The ingredients have already been purchased, so I am hardly *not* going to use them. Besides, where is your Christmas spirit? Each Yuletide is precious, Greenville, and should be treated as if it may be your last. Who knows what may have happened by this time next year?" She was thinking about the sale of Radcliffe House to the Prince of Wales, but they did not know that.

Greville looked at her in puzzlement. "What do you mean, Aunt E?"

"Oh, nothing. Now, you and Miss Mortimer are to get on with the adornments. I will join you presently." She shooed them both out of the door, her bells jingling nineteen to the dozen.

Megan had no option but to oversee the decorations, because there was no sign at all of Evangeline. It was Greville's fault that she found herself in such a position, for he expressed complete incompetence where such things were concerned, and informed her that he was at her bidding. Fosdyke, Edward, and several maids therefore had to do as she said, and because Greville was present, they did not dare to quibble. He was put to cut silver and gold stars, that seeming to be the extent of his artistic ability, while she helped the others to incorporate fruit, red ribbons, and artificial flowers into the various ropes, garlands, wreaths, and arrangements of laurel, bay, rosemary, box, pine, holly, ivy, and mistletoe.

Only once did Megan find her attention drawn to Greville, and that was when he briefly left his star-cutting to snip a tiny sprig of mistletoe—two leaves and three berries—which he proceeded to place in the little jeweled snuffbox from which he had removed the previous sprig in the church. Megan could not help wondering what lay behind it all.

Rupert returned at last from his long ride on the Downs, and he lent a helping hand to the decorations. Soon the entire downstairs was a festive bower. Every chandelier was twined with leaves, every mantelshelf and cornice was festooned, arrangements burgeoned in every vacant corner, tables boasted elegant vases and bowls, and the staircase was decked with greenery that seemed to sprout from the very banisters and newel posts.

Candles had been lit when Evangeline at last put in an appearance, looking much more comfortable in blue-gray taffeta. She declared that she had been so tired that she had dozed for a while, but now felt as fresh as a daisy; which was more than could be said for the gallant workers who had labored so hard on beautifying her residence for Christmas. The only major item now remaining was the kissing bough, and even that had almost been completed. When the last length of red satin ribbon had been tied into place, the bough was conveyed ceremonially into the hall, where a hook in the middle of the ceiling had served this particular purpose ever since the house had been built.

The footmen hauled the bough up on a rope, but when everyone stood below admiring it and thinking their tasks were over, Evangeline frowned and shook her head. "It is far too high," she declared.

Rupert was puzzled. "But it's *always* that height, Aunt E."

"Nevertheless, I don't like it now. Lower it if you please," she instructed, and the footmen slowly let out the rope. "More," she said, and the bough descended gradually until it was barely six feet above the floor.

Rupert disapproved. "That's far too low, Aunt E!"

"Do you think so?"

"Of course I do. Greville is the tallest of us, and if he walks beneath it, he'll surely tangle in the ribbons! So will Sir Jocelyn."

"Will they? Show me, Greville. Walk beneath it. Well, go on." She waggled her closed fan impatiently at him.

Greville did as he was told, and sure enough the ribbons brushed his dark hair.

"Ha!" declared Rupert triumphantly. "See? It will have to go up again."

"Yes, but how high?" Evangeline inquired lightly.

"At least two feet to be sensible."

"Oh, I disagree," she said. "It must be just right if it is to serve its purpose to the full. I have it! Miss Mortimer, will you please stand with Greville?"

"Stand with him?"

"The instruction is perfectly simple, miss. Which word do you not understand? Stand, with, or him?"

Megan lowered her eyes quickly, and went to join Greville beneath the bough.

Evangeline tapped the fan thoughtfully to her lips. "Oh, I don't know. Something isn't quite right. Stand closer to each other."

They did as they were told.

"No, closer than that!"

They brushed together.

"Not side by side, face-to-face! For heaven's sake, don't either of you *know* what a kissing bough is for? Greville, please be so good as to put your hands to Miss Mortimer's waist." As Greville obeyed, she fingered her gold locket. "Look at each other. That's better. Now, make as if to kiss."

Greville's eyes were a mirror of his inner feelings as he bent his head closer to Megan, whose face was now almost the same color as the ribbons fluttering overhead. Her heart was beating swiftly, and she could feel the warmth of his hands through her gown; and the softness of his breath on her face. His lips were so close that she feared he was going to actually kiss her, but then Evangeline pronounced her approval.

"That's it! Perfect! Tie the ropes if you please, Edward. Now, then, everyone, I think we have all worked so hard that a glass of champagne is in order."

Greville moved away from Megan, and raised an eyebrow at his aunt. "We? I'm *so* glad you feel able to include yourself among our hard-working number," he observed wryly.

Evangeline took no notice. "Fosdyke, bring a bottle to the drawing room, if you please. You and the other servants may enjoy some of the usual wine in the kitchens."

"Thank you, my lady." The butler bowed, then ushered the footmen and maids away.

Evangeline gazed approvingly around the hall. "At last it begins to seem like Christmas," she murmured.

Chapter 16

Megan wore the ruby silk from Mrs. Fiske's to dinner that evening, but would have felt far more comfortable in her old gown. Sir Jocelyn and Chloe, who looked quite bewitching in lavender satin that became her golden coloring to perfection, arrived just as everyone was adjourning to the drawing room after the meal. To everyone's dismay, the Holcrofts brought Oliver with them, he having expressed a huge interest in all things theatrical.

Rupert's face assumed a stormy aspect the moment he spied his enemy again, and as they all gathered in the hall to admire the Christmas decorations, he seized the first possible opportunity to get Chloe alone. But when he presumed to warn her against Oliver, she haughtily reminded him that he had chosen not to be part of her life, and would he kindly mind his own business from now on. She could not have made herself more plain; indeed she was more than avenged for the hurt he had caused her. He was quite stricken as he realized how low he had apparently sunk in her estimation; but as she walked away from him, Chloe's expression was one of barely concealed triumph. There was a new light in her big blue eyes, and a knowing little smile curved her lips. It was a look that would have discomforted Oliver, but would have imparted a modicum of encouragement to Rupert. His battle might not be entirely lost—at least, not yet.

The decorations having been profusely admired, and Sir Jocelyn having ventured to fondly peck Evangeline's cheek beneath the kissing bough, everyone adjourned to the candlelit drawing room to enjoy cherry liqueurs before any thought of going into the theater. They discussed which scenes should be rehearsed first, and Evangeline obliged Greville to cross his heart and promise that Malvolio's first appearance would be word perfect by the following afternoon. It was Act I, Scene 5, in which Evangeline's fool also appeared, as did the characters played by Chloe and Sir Jocelyn. In the absence of Cousin Ada and her sister, who were to play Viola and the maid, Maria, who figured prominently in the scene as well, Megan was informed she would have to read for them.

Left to her own quiet devices, Megan would have played the mouse all evening. It was a part she had learned well, and which often proved very rewarding, for it enabled her to observe from the wings. She sat in a corner, hoping to do just that; instead she found herself used again, this time by Rupert, whose response to Chloe's rebuff was to pay undue attention to his aunt's long-suffering companion. Megan understood his actions, even if she did not appreciate them. Her problem was made worse by the dark glances Greville directed toward her, for they suggested he thought she was *encouraging* Rupert. She bore it all heroically, but really would have liked to tell them *both* what she thought. Rupert she could forgive because she sympathized with his wretchedness over Chloe and Oliver, but she had no time at all for Sir Greville Seton. In vain did she tell herself he did not matter, because he mattered too much. She was constantly sensitive to him, even starting nervously when he cleared his throat. It was almost as if he twitched her upon a string!

Megan was able to observe a little, however, and had noticed that Lady Evangeline was set all of a secret quiver by Sir Jocelyn. Oh, it was well concealed, but Megan had been aware of it from the moment of the brief kiss beneath the mistletoe. Whether or not Sir Jocelyn felt the same way was not so easy to perceive, for he was one of those men who gave nothing away of their innermost thoughts. Megan could quite understand why her mistress felt the way she did about him, for he was a very attractive man: warm, amusing, thoughtful, and endearingly proud of his lovely daughter. He was also amusingly perplexed about Megan, whom he was still convinced he had met before. He went so far as to say so, but fell silent on the matter when Evangeline informed him he had definitely not encountered Megan until now.

Megan was relieved when Evangeline rose from the sofa, her gown of green-and-blue shot-silk shining in the candlelight. "Right, my company of actors and actresses, let us proceed to our stage," she said. "I plan a phantasmagoria of awe-inspiring lighting effects that will bring the Adriatic of the seventeenth century to modern Brighton. I intend to give you a demonstration of the opening of Act I, Scene 2—you know, the storm scene."

There was a sudden whiff of orange blossom water, and Megan realized that Rollo had crept up softly beside her, for he spoke to Evangeline. "Lighting effects? 'Angels and ministers of grace defend us!' What sacrilege! Is not ye Bard perfection as he is?"

Evangeline's nostrils flared. "Oh, do be quiet, Rollo!" she said.

Everyone exchanged glances, but no one said anything. Except Oliver, who was mystified by her strange remark. "Er, who is Rollo?" he inquired.

"Who is Rollo? Who is Rollo?" The ghost was dismayed by such ignorance. "What manner of ginger-headed pippin asks this?" he demanded.

Megan lowered her eyes quickly, and bit her lip to prevent herself from laughing. Ginger-headed pippin? Oh, if only Oliver could hear!

Evangeline ignored the specter. "Come, *mesdames et messieurs,* for if we delay any longer, we will not have time to see anything tonight, and I am so looking forward to showing off my grand *Laterna Magica.*"

"Your what, Aunt E?" inquired Rupert.

"My *Laterna Magica,* magic lantern, or sorcerer's lamp, call it what you wish. This one is larger than any you may have seen before, and can project the most astonishingly lifelike images."

Greville spoke up quickly. "I will see your wonders in due course, Aunt E, but first I have to write an important letter for tomorrow's mail. I meant to write it earlier, but it slipped my mind. It is little more than a note, and so will not take long."

Evangeline was rather miffed with him. "Oh, very well, but I vow I will be very displeased indeed if you linger."

"You have my word," Greville replied, and as everyone else—including Rollo—followed her from the room, he went to the writing desk and reached for a sheet of his aunt's fine monogrammed paper.

Evangeline hovered by the entrance to the theater as everyone else went in, and when the ghost tried to pass as well, she hissed angrily at him. "Sir, you vex me with your carping!"

"Sweet lady, I do not seek to vex," he protested, his steps halting as he apparently turned to face her.

Megan waited dutifully just inside the theater, placing herself just so to eavesdrop. Evangeline was still irritated with the specter. "I wish I knew what you *do* seek, sirrah! You hound me everywhere, yet will not say why! How am I supposed to help you end your haunting if I do not know what it is all about?"

"It is for thee to discover my purpose, not for me to tell thee. 'But for now, cudgel thy brains no more about it,' " he replied infuriatingly.

"I'll give you *Hamlet*! Oh, you are a most tiresome spirit, and no mistake. I am fast becoming a laughing-stock because you prick me into responding to your sly remarks!" Evangeline's wrath was palpable.

"I suffer ye earth's very end of ennui, mistress. Pray envisage an eternity of waiting, and thou hast my predic-ament."

"Waiting for what?"

"For thou to do what must be done."

"Which rather brings us back to where we were before. How can I do what has to be done, if I don't know what it is? And anyway, to return to your carping, why exactly do you find fault with my plans for lighting the play? I am sure Master Shakespeare would be flattered by my wish to do him full justice."

"I think not, mistress, I think not."

"How can you presume to be so sure?" Evangeline demanded smartly.

"Because I am grandnephew to ye sainted Bard, as well as a member of King Charles II's Company of Comedians, and keeper of this theatrical house. I know my business through and through again, and can vouch that the Poet of Avon would abhor thy fancy lighting effects. His words stand upon their own merit, and were the actors, feeble as they are, to be upon a naked stage, his star would not shine less."

His pompous tone provoked Evangeline still more. "Fie, sir, I believe you have no connection whatsoever with Master Shakespeare, and that your knowledge of acting is confined to being prompter at farthing shows in country barns."

"O, villain, villain! I will have thee know that I was king of Drury Lane. My Mithridates could not be surpassed! Nor my Falstaff!"

"Aye, sir, but in what way could they not be surpassed? In excellence, or mayhap in execrableness?"

"Such heinous lies! Such disrespect! Oh, may thou be forgiven!" cried the spirit, then stomped irately past Megan into the theater, where everyone else had now gathered around the black tent containing the prized lighting equipment.

Evangeline followed him in, on her face an expression of some satisfaction. She had had a little of her own back a little on the vain, sharp-tongued specter, and the feeling was clearly good. But then she remembered something. "Oh, my notes!" She noticed Megan. "Ah, Miss Mortimer, would you be so kind as to bring my notebook? I left it on the writing desk."

"Yes, Lady Evangeline." Megan returned very reluctantly to the drawing room, where Sir Greville the Grim was at the writing desk.

Greville was so intent upon his letter to Bath that he did not hear her enter, nor was he aware as she came up behind him. She saw her name and that of Lady Jane Strickland, then he straightened with a start and hastily drew another sheet of paper over what he had written. "Are you *much* given to creeping up behind people, Miss Mortimer?" he inquired acidly.

"I-I didn't creep, sir," she replied. "Lady Evangeline sent me back for her notes." She reached quickly past him for the little book, then fled the room with it.

But Oliver was waiting for her in the hall. She hesitated in alarm, then tried to pass him, but he caught her arm. "Stay now, coz, for we have things to clear between us," he breathed, keeping a wary eye on the open door of the drawing room.

To her relief there came the sound of Greville's chair scraping as he got up. Oliver released her, and she hastened into the theater with the notebook.

Chapter 17

Everyone was now assembled for the phantasmagoric illusions. The theater was in shadow, and the only light permitted to escape the tent's thick material was through a small hole, from which a bright beam struck the stage curtain as if wishing to burn a hole in it.

Evangeline was secreted in the tent with so many lighted candles and lamps that her face was quite hot and red as she fussed with painted transparencies and complicated equipment. Suddenly she waved a frantic hand outside. "A glass of water, if you please, Jocelyn! Fosdyke will have left a jug and glass by the stage steps."

The admiral hurried to attend to it. "It must be a positive oven in there, Evangeline. Are you sure you are all right?" he asked in concern as he pressed the glass into her fingers.

"All is well, Jocelyn. Besides, it will not take much longer. Please tell everyone to be seated." The hand withdrew into the tent's fastness, and there came the sound of turning pages as she looked through the notebook Megan had retrieved.

The small party went to sit down, but as Megan tried to place herself well behind the others, Evangeline remonstrated with her from the tent. "Don't seek splendid isolation, my dear. Sit in that empty chair next to Greville."

Megan looked at the tent in puzzlement, wondering how on earth Evangeline could see anything from where she was.

"Well, do as I say, my dear."

"Yes, Lady Evangeline."

Megan had no choice but to obey, for Greville had already risen politely to his feet. She refused to look at him as she sat down, but his closeness affected her. From beneath lowered lashes she noticed how he toyed with the shirt frill protruding from his cuff, how his heavy gold signet ring found light even in the shadows, how strong and graceful he was; how heartstoppingly attractive he would be if only she liked him a little . . .

From the tent there came more page rustling, accompanied by impatient muttering, but then Evangeline's hand emerged again, this time with a lighted candlestick. "Rupert? Please be so good as to raise the curtain! You will require a candle to see what you're doing."

"Certes, Aunt E," he replied, and got up. As he did so he caught Chloe's glance, and she smiled hesitantly at him. He smiled back, and then hurried up the steps on to the stage with the candle, then vanished behind the curtain.

"I'll give you a hand," Oliver said, and went after him.

A moment later the drop curtain was hauled up to reveal a shadowy set of rather unrealistic rocks, with a badly painted background of a wrecked ship and a headland topped by a Greek temple, presumably to convey a sense of the Adriatic, for *Twelfth Night* was set in the ancient land of Illyria. The beam of light from the front of the tent fell so brilliantly upon the vessel's rigging that it showed up the inferior brush strokes.

Rupert's candle fluttered brightly as he and Oliver returned and began to descend from the stage. But then Oliver stumbled, and Rupert was pitched right to the bottom of the steps. The candle went out as it fell from his hand, and Chloe leapt to her feet with a cry of dismay.

As Greville and Sir Jocelyn ran to help the fallen man, Oliver lingered wretchedly on the steps. "Oh, I say! I say! I do hope you're all right, sir!" he cried, apparently much put out that his clumsiness should have caused such a mishap.

Light flooded dazzlingly as Evangeline thrust back the

flap of her tent. "What has happened?" she demanded anxiously.

Rupert sat up awkwardly to rub his elbow, which he'd struck during the fall. "It's all right, there's no harm done, Aunt E."

Chloe rushed to him in a flurry of lavender satin. "Are you sure, Rupert?" she cried. "Have you broken any bones?"

"Of course not. It was only a little fall," he replied nobly, and accepted Greville and Sir Jocelyn's assistance to haul him to his feet.

Chloe was not reassured, so the moment he could, Rupert caught her hand and drew it gallantly to his lips. "I am perfectly all right," he said gently, and gazed into her anxious blue eyes.

As she responded with another little smile, Oliver hastened solicitously down the rest of the steps. "Can you ever excuse my clumsiness, Radcliffe?" he said. "I completely misjudged the steps, and—"

"It was an accident, March," Rupert replied.

But Oliver's apology was not good enough for Chloe. "He might have been badly hurt, sir!"

"What more can I say except that I am truly contrite?" he protested.

Rupert wished the matter at an end. "Think no more of it, March," he said magnanimously.

"That's good of you, Radcliffe," Oliver said with a grateful smile.

Behind Megan, Rollo suddenly whispered another quotation. " 'O villain, villain, smiling, damned villain!' " Her glance flew to Oliver. Did the ghost suspect him of stumbling deliberately?

Evangeline was still anxious. "Rupert, are you *absolutely* certain you have not suffered an injury?" she asked.

"Will you all please stop fussing?" he said, but then had second thoughts and turned quickly to Chloe. "Perhaps I do feel a little unsteady. If you could assist me . . . ?" he asked, a weak note creeping into his voice.

"Oh, yes, of course." She took his arm solicitously,

and he glanced smugly at Oliver, whose immediate scowl was ample reward.

Everyone resumed their places, and Evangeline closed the tent flap again. As the shadows returned, Megan mulled over what Rollo had said. She glanced toward her cousin, whose profile she could just make out in the dim light. Oliver was quite capable of foul play, as she knew to her cost, so it was well within the realm of possibility that he would attempt to incapacitate a rival. He probably regarded the smiles exchanged between Rupert and Chloe as more than enough cause to act. A few timely broken bones would keep Rupert out of the way . . .

The thoughts broke off as Evangeline addressed them all from the depths of the tent. "Very well, ladies and gentlemen, I trust you are prepared. Envisage if you please a storm-swept beach in Illyria, with Viola, a captain, and several sailors struggling ashore, the only survivors of a shipwreck. Viola is distraught because she believes her adored brother Sebastian has been lost overboard, presumed drowned." Light flickered and lurched, then suddenly the stage was drenched with lurid color. A jagged streak of permanent lightning was caught against skies where ominous clouds jerked to and fro as Evangeline tried unsuccessfully to pull the painted transparency smoothly past the source of light. Seagulls wheeled dramatically, and Evangeline mewed unconvincingly in an endeavor to imitate their cries. Then everyone jumped as she picked up a thin sheet of metal and rattled it to make thunder.

Megan watched with fascination as everything jolted, flashed, and resonated, but then her eyes widened as Rollo suddenly strode on to the stage, clearly visible in the shaft of intense light from the tent. He came to a swaggering halt in front of the shipwreck, and raised his voice above Evangeline's racket. " 'O my prophetic soul! This is all unworthy flimflam!' " he cried.

Megan saw and heard him so well that she was sure everyone else could not help but do the same. However, although Evangeline immediately dropped the sheet of metal and poked her head out of the tent to glare at the spirit, the four men did not seem to notice anything. Chloe was a different matter. She had been quite enraptured with the lighting illusions, but then Rollo's translucent figure appeared. That was all, just his vague outline; she didn't hear anything. She rose to her feet with a little cry of fright, then fainted gracefully to the floor in a cloud of lavender satin.

Rollo made himself guiltily scarce as consternation broke out. Megan rushed forward, in the process managing to unwittingly block Oliver's way so that Rupert was the man to reach Chloe first. Excluded, Oliver could only stand with Greville as Sir Jocelyn flapped anxiously over his unconscious daughter. Rupert, his bruises entirely forgotten, gathered Chloe into his strong arms and bore her off toward the drawing room. Everyone crowded after him, including Evangeline, who was now more incensed with the ghost than ever.

"Oh, just *wait* until you and I meet next, Master Witherspoon!" Megan heard her mutter under her breath.

Rupert laid Chloe gently on a drawing room sofa, and Evangeline produced some sal volatile from the writing desk drawer as Sir Jocelyn knelt beside his daughter, chafing her limp little hand between his large manly paws. "Chloe? My dearest? Please open your eyes!"

The smelling salts pricked Chloe's nostrils, and she stirred a little. Her lashes fluttered prettily against her pale cheeks, then she looked up. "Papa?"

"Are you all right, my darling?" he cried.

"Yes . . . What happened?"

Evangeline leaned over her. "You fainted, my dear," she explained.

Much to Rupert's chagrin, Oliver was the one who thought of hurrying back to the theater for Evangeline's glass of water, which he now made much of putting to Chloe's lips.

She smiled wanly up at him. "Thank you, Oliver," she whispered, but then remembrance flooded back and her breath caught. "I-I thought I saw . . ."

Oliver gazed at her. "Yes, dearest? What did you think you saw?"

She glanced around at everyone. "There was a man on the stage."

Megan and Evangeline met her gaze as if they did not know what she was talking about, and the four men were genuinely puzzled. Rupert shook his head. "There wasn't anyone there. It must have been Aunt E's wonderful illusions."

Chloe bit her lip. "Now I feel foolish. I was so carried away that I let my imagination go too far." She sat up and smiled sheepishly at Evangeline. "I think your illusions are quite amazing. The thunder was, well, thunderous, and I even liked your seagulls."

Evangeline shifted a little uncomfortably. "They need a little attention, but will come along nicely, I'm sure."

"I cannot wait to see what else you have planned."

"Nothing more for tonight, that is certain. If you are feeling well again now, my dear, perhaps Sir Jocelyn should take you home. A good sleep, and all will be well come the morning."

"All is well now, truly," Chloe replied.

"Tomorrow we will rehearse a scene."

Oliver spoke up swiftly. "I do trust you have a task for me, Lady Evangeline? I gladly proffer my services, even if it is only to move the scenery."

"Why, yes, Mr. March, that will be most helpful. Please come along as well."

Rupert glared at his aunt.

Chloe was still embarrassed about fainting. "I really did think I saw a man," she said again, shaking her head at such a silly notion.

"Light can play tricks, especially *phantasmagoric* light," Sir Jocelyn said kindly, then he looked at Evangeline. "Do you recall what happened at the Marine Pavilion? It was just such an eerie display—ghostly monks amid the ruins of a monastery, I believe—and Mr. Sheridan the playwright sat suddenly and very deliberately upon the lap of a very gullible, fainthearted Russian dowager?"

"Madame Gerobtzoff. Yes, I recall it very well," Evangeline replied with a chuckle.

Sir Jocelyn rose to his feet. "However, that is an aside, for I think you are right; I should take Chloe home now."

Chloe looked quickly at Evangeline. "I have a great favor to ask, Lady Evangeline?"

"What is it?"

"May I borrow Miss Mortimer tomorrow morning? I wish to go into the town to do some shopping in readiness for the ball, and I would like some *female* company," she said pointedly, as both Rupert and Oliver began to offer their services.

Evangeline was only too pleased to surrender her companion to Chloe. "Of course, my dear, in fact it would please me immensely because there are a few errands I wish her to do for me."

Megan smiled at Chloe. "I look forward to it, Miss Holcroft," she said, studiously avoiding Oliver's steady gaze. She knew he wanted her to find a reason to decline, but there was little she could say when Evangeline wished her to go.

"I will call at ten," Chloe promised, and raised a hand for assistance from the sofa.

Rupert and Oliver reached out in unison, jostling against each other in the process, so she tactfully accepted her father's hand instead. Evangeline rang a hand bell to summon Fosdyke, and everyone went out into the hall to say farewell to the guests.

As the butler assisted Chloe and Oliver with their outdoor things, Sir Jocelyn noticed Evangeline fingering her locket as she glanced up at the kissing bough. "Memories are sweet, are they not?" he said softly.

"Mayhap I now have a little more than just memories."

"What do you mean?"

"What's in a name, sir, what's in a name," Evangeline replied enigmatically.

Sir Jocelyn stared at her, and then gave a slight gasp and glanced fleetingly at Megan. "So *that's* it! Why didn't

I make the connection before? I knew there was something familiar—"

Evangeline tapped him with her fan. "Not a word to anyone just yet. Promise?"

"Of course."

As the front door was opened and Oliver stepped out with Chloe, Sir Jocelyn paused to look back at Megan, as if something had suddenly become blindingly clear to him.

When they had gone and Fosdyke closed the door, Rupert turned heavily to Greville. "I need a large cognac to wash Oliver March from my mind," he said, and returned to the drawing room. Greville followed.

Evangeline nodded at Megan. "You are excused until tomorrow now, Miss Mortimer. I wish you to read to me while I take my morning tea in bed. I keep a volume of *Gil Blas* at my bedside. Do you know it?"

"Oh, yes, for it was my father's favorite too."

"Ah, yes."

"Lady Evangeline. I noticed the bookcase in the drawing room, and wondered if—?"

"If you could borrow a volume?"

"Yes."

"Of course you may, my dear. If you have a liking for gothic novels, you will find a copy of Mr. Walpole's *The Castle of Otranto*." Evangeline smiled, then walked away toward the theater. Megan heard her summon Rollo in a tone that augured ill for him. "Right, Master Witherspoon, I require words with you!" Then the door closed.

Chapter 18

It was gone midnight, and Megan had heard everyone retire to their rooms. Comfortably tired but not yet quite ready to sleep, she sat up in the bed to read *The Castle of Otranto*. Radcliffe House was very quiet, the flame of bedside candle fluttered and grew tall, and the fire in the hearth shifted slightly. Mr. Walpole's chapters were quite long, and gradually her eyes began to close. She fell asleep with the book still open.

Suddenly there was a stealthy tap at the door, and her eyes flew open again. "Who—who is it?"

Edward the footman spoke very softly in order not to awaken Evangeline in the apartment opposite. "I have a message for you, Miss Mortimer. You're to burn it when you've read it." Candlelight flickered beneath the door as he pushed a folded piece of paper into her room.

Feeling uneasy, she got out of bed. The note was short and to the point. *Meet me now if you value your post. Edward will bring you.* It wasn't signed, and she didn't recognize the writing, but she still knew it was from Oliver.

"You're to be quick about it," Edward whispered.

She threw the paper on to the fire, and watched flames reach from the dimly glowing coals to lick eagerly around it. The blackened remains curled and shivered, and sparks fled up the chimney toward the night sky; then the flames died back once more.

"Are you coming or not, miss?" Edward hissed, growing impatient.

She didn't want to see her cousin, but knew it was in her best interest to do as he wished. If she could convince him that she wished to keep silent and out of his way, maybe that would be the end of it. Her decision made, she hurried to speak to Edward through the door. "All right, I'll come. Where is he waiting?" she asked.

"The summerhouse. Look, get a move on. I'll be downstairs in the hall." Edward was uneasy, for he knew Evangeline to be a relatively light sleeper.

Megan quickly put on her shoes and mustard gown, and after dragging a brush through her hair, swung her new cloak around her shoulders. She paused to look out of the window at the summerhouse, and at first 'thought it was deserted, but then she saw Oliver. He wore his greatcoat, and his top hat was pulled very low over his face as he still kept well back to avoid immediate detection by any casual glance from an upper room of the house. He had gained access to the garden by means of ladders on either side of the garden wall bordering the remains of Great East Street.

Edward was waiting for her in the hall, his face annoyed in the light from the candle he held. He wore his livery coat over his nightshirt. "About time!" he snapped, still being careful to keep his voice down.

"Are you Mr. March's creature now, Edward?" she asked quietly as she followed him toward the kitchens.

"If I am, it's no business of yours. And if you're thinking of speaking out of turn to her ladyship, you'd best think again, because Mr. March looks after his own."

"If you believe that, you'll believe anything," she replied scathingly. Look after his own? Her dear cousin only looked after himself! She was living proof of *that*!

The sound of their voices had come to Rollo's attention. The ghost, who never slept, was in the theater amusing himself by practicing the levitation of things on the stage. He had never been terribly good at levitation, and sometimes thought he would never get it right. He had managed to make some pieces of shipwreck and Illyrian rocks hover in midair, and some of the ropes from the flies wriggle like snakes, but they didn't do exactly what he wanted or go when he wanted. Frowning, he tried to concentrate his supernatural energy, but then he heard the low voices coming from the hall, and he let everything return to its proper place.

" 'O mistress mine! Where are you roaming?' " he murmured as he went to investigate.

Megan heard his steps and glanced back. She saw his faint outline again as he passed a thin sliver of moonlight that found its way between some poorly drawn curtains, and she wondered why she could see him sometimes but not always. Edward sensed nothing as he conducted her through the kitchens, where he extinguished the candle, then out into the walled garden. The night was bitterly cold, and the clear sky was filled with stars, except to the north, where a bank of cloud lay low in the heavens.

The ghost's steady tread followed, and Megan heard him mutter another quotation. " 'Ill met by moonlight, proud Titania.' "

She halted in front of the summerhouse, where Oliver still waited in the shadows. "You wished to see me?" she said.

"Come inside, and keep your voice down. Sound travels on a night like this."

Reluctantly she did as he asked, and he reached out to pull her right back behind the bench. Then he glanced out at Edward. "Stand away now, for this is not for your ears. And be sure to keep out of sight from the house."

"Yes, Mr. March." Edward hurried toward the black shadow cast by the garden wall.

Oliver then looked at Megan. "Now, coz, we have things to clear between us," he said softly.

"You have already made your wishes very plain, sir."

"I need to be certain that not a word of our past dealings will come to light."

"*Our* past dealings? Sirrah, you were the only one who dealt anything!"

He smiled. "I was within my rights."

"Legally, maybe, but certainly not morally! You didn't even *want* my father's estate, for it brought you little in the way of income, and you certainly did not desire to live in it. Berengers has been left vacant and crumbling ever since you evicted me, and I despise you for that more than you will ever realize!"

"Oh, I realize, my dear, I realize." Still he smiled.

"In spite of that, you may rest assured that I have no intention of saying anything to anyone."

His pale eyes flickered. "I'm not foolish enough to trust your word alone, so let me remind you that I know the full lurid details of your shocking little escapades in Bath."

"Ralph Strickland hasn't told the truth."

"Oh, I do not doubt it, but as far as everyone here is concerned, his account will be the truthful one."

"You are too late, sir. Lady Evangeline already knows what happened, and she heard it from Lady Jane Strickland herself."

It wasn't the response he had been expecting, and he turned slightly away. For a long moment he was silent, then he faced her again. "I am prepared to pay you handsomely to quit Lady Evangeline's service and disappear."

She stared at him. "You cannot be serious!"

"Never more so. I will advance you your wages for a year—half now, half when you have done as I wish."

Rollo heard. "'I like not fair terms and a villain's mind,'" the specter breathed.

Suddenly Oliver caught hold of Megan's arms, his face only inches from hers. "Be warned not to decline my offer, for if you do it will be the worst for you. Cross me at your peril, coz," he breathed.

This was too much for Rollo. It was bad enough that a man should lay hands upon another and utter such threats, but that he should do it to a woman was intolerable. "Vile knave! Insect of insects!" he cried, and fixed his attention upon the path that ran around the lawn as he willed some of the gravel to fly through the air and strike Oliver. But although the tiny stones rustled and jumped about a little, they certainly didn't obey his will. Uttering a curse, the spirit bent to seize a handful and hurl it at Oliver, who suddenly found himself being rained with tiny sharp missiles.

"Great God above!" he gasped, instinctively backing away. More gravel struck him, and he ducked, clutching his top hat on his head for protection.

Megan whirled about to look where she knew Rollo to be. She could see a vague shape bending to gather more ammunition. More gravel hurtled through the air like grapeshot, and Oliver whipped around to look ferociously at Edward, who immediately threw up his hands in alarm.

"It's not me, Mr. March! I swear it!"

"Then, who—?" Oliver yelped as more gravel found a target. By the direction from which it came, he now realized Edward could not be throwing it, so he cast around for the culprit. "Who's there?" he cried. More gravel struck him. "Help me, damn you!" he begged Edward, but the terrified footman couldn't move.

Rollo, well into his ghostly stride now, decided that Edward needed a little punishment too, so he tossed some ammunition at the young man's bare shins, yelling. " 'Out, damned spot! Out I say! One; two; why, then, 'tis time to do't!' "

Edward gaped foolishly down at his stinging legs, and choked back a frightened sob. Then at last he found the wit to take to his heels and make a dash for the house as if someone had set fire to his nightshirt. But as he sprinted for the kitchen door, another barrage of gravel scored a bull on his posterior.

Rollo gave a triumphant snort of laughter, then returned his attention to Oliver, who had begun to back toward the ladder against the wall. The wraith wasn't having any of that, so he ran to cut off Oliver's escape, then hurled gravel again. Oliver made a sound that resembled a squawk, and hastily backed the other way, but whichever way he went he was assailed by the flying gravel. At last he fled headlong toward the ladder, but in his haste he dislodged it, and it toppled over, striking him on the head and knocking him out.

Rollo wasn't in the least concerned. "Ha!" he declared, and as he strode over to examine Oliver, he rubbed his spectral hands together for a job well-done.

Then he prodded the unconscious man with his foot. " 'O Mighty Caesar! Dost thou lie so low? Are all thy conquests, glories, triumphs, spoils, Shrunk to this little measure?' "

Oliver didn't move, in fact he was so still that Megan was apprehensive. "He—he isn't dead, is he, Master Witherspoon?" she asked, going closer.

"Nay, mistress, he is just—" Rollo broke off in astonishment as he realized she had addressed him. "Thou canst see me, sweet lady?"

"Sometimes, but I *always* hear you."

"The saints be praised, now I have two angels to save me! Oh, blessed, blessed fortune. They say miracles are past, but it is not so! he cried, and snatched off his plumed hat to sweep her an eloquent bow. Then he came to seize her hand and shower it with kisses. His touch was strangely warm and firm, like that of a living man.

Oliver groaned a little, and Rollo returned to him. "We will speak again, mistress, but I pray thee do not tell anyone of me. Certainly do not speak of me to the Lady Evangeline."

"But why, if she already knows about you?"

"She hath a special task to perform, and it must be done without her knowing why. Consultation might lead to full understanding, and that she must not have."

"Can you tell me about this special task?"

"No, mistress."

"Why?"

"It is ye unwritten rule, dear lady. A spirit must not explain reasons to the living, except sometimes when the living are unconscious."

"That's silly." She glanced at Oliver, who stirred a little more.

"I will not argue, but nevertheless it is so. I cannot and durst not transgress, for to do so is to be certain of a lonely eternity, and no spirit wishes that. Our existence is made bearable only by the constant hope of redemption."

Megan thought for a moment. "Master Witherspoon,

is this special task something to do with St. Nicholas's church?"

He gasped. "Ah, lady, lady, the quickness of thy intelligence is sweet music to me, and if thou shouldst guess how thou may save me, I will adore thee for all time. But I say again that I cannot explain anything to thee. Now, go inside, mistress. I will wait until this scurvy rogue hath left. And if he should endeavor to plague thee more, thou hast only to tell thy friend Rollo Witherspoon." The specter sketched her another grand bow, then turned to direct his attention to the ladder, which obediently rose against the wall again.

Megan hesitated. "Thank you for coming to my rescue, Master Witherspoon."

"I did but brush aside two flies that were besetting thee, sweet lady."

She smiled at him, then hurried back to the house.

Chapter 19

Megan did not expect to sleep again after that, but to her surprise her head could barely have touched the pillow before she was deep in dreams. She was awoken the next morning, Saturday, December 20, by the sound of Evangeline's gardeners complaining to each other about the gravel on the lawn. She lay warmly in bed, thinking about the eventful night. She would have to face Oliver again soon, and she knew he was not the sort of man to be deterred by just one setback. He would seek her out again, and it would not be a pleasant experience. At least she was prepared for him next time, and had Rollo's promise of assistance, but there ought to be something more. It was something she had to dwell upon very carefully.

When it was time to get up and go to Evangeline, the last thing Megan wished to do was read *Gil Blas*. She was bursting to talk about Rollo, but because the ghost had been adamant about her silence, she knew she could not say anything. It was most frustrating, for she and Evangeline together might be able to discover what it was the spirit required to be done. At least if it was connected with the church she knew where to begin, and she could only hope it wouldn't be too long before she had time to go there again. After dressing in her new apricot-and-white-striped muslin morning gown, and pinning her hair up in a tidy knot, Megan went along to Evangeline's rooms to read to her. The bank of low cloud she had noticed in the night now covered the sky from horizon to horizon, a breeze was blowing, and there was a dusting of snow on the Downs. She thought about Mrs. Fosdyke's bunion, and wondered if it was accurate enough to ensure Evangeline the kudos of driving out in the royal sleigh.

That was what Evangeline was wondering too; indeed all thought of Le Sage's masterly novel was abandoned because she could think only about the sleigh, concerning which she had already dispatched Fosdyke to the Marine Pavilion, Prinny's written consent firmly in his hand. Well, perhaps it wasn't quite true that the sleigh was *all* she could think about, for the costumes for *Twelfth Night* were also very much on her mind. Apart from her jester suit, the contents of her theater wardrobe no longer pleased her. Everything was too gaudy, too drab, too flimsy, too heavy, too anything one cared to mention, except acceptable.

Megan was glad when the time came to go down to breakfast, but first she sought Rollo in the theater. There was no sign of the ghost, however, nor had he gone to breakfast as he had the previous day. A very wan and nervous Edward was in charge of the sideboard, and whenever he brought something to the table, he hobbled because his shins were so sore. He also appeared to be in some discomfort from his rear end, which was hardly surprising, Megan thought with some satisfaction. She wondered how Oliver was this morning. Virtually laid up, she hoped.

Edward avoided catching her eye, indeed he seemed so intent on keeping well away from her that he could barely stretch to place her plate before her. She realized that she thought she had a mysterious ally, with whom he had no desire to risk another encounter. Let him go on thinking it, for it was true!

At first she was alone at the table with Rupert, who had a guilty conscience about the undue attention he had paid her the night before. "Miss Mortimer, about my conduct last night . . ."

"Please think nothing of it, Lord Rupert, for I quite understand," she replied with a smile.

"You do?"

"Of course, and when I go shopping with Miss Holcroft this morning, I promise to do all I can to promote you."

"You are an angel, Miss Mortimer."

"No, sir, I am just someone who hopes Miss Holcroft will soon see the light where Mr. March is concerned, and that she then grants you your heart's desire." Megan glanced at Edward, who must have heard everything, and who would, she trusted, relay it all to Oliver. She had decided upon a way to keep her cousin at arm's length, and she was so pleased with her idea that she did not care if Oliver knew what she said. It was seeing Greville at the writing desk that had provided the inspiration; all she had to do was write a little letter of her own, to be opened in the event of anything unpleasant happening to her, and then let Oliver know of its existence. With that *and* Rollo, she was surely safe.

Rupert sat back. "Do you think I made Chloe just a little jealous last night?"

Megan smiled again, ruefully this time. "I do not think she will ever be jealous of me, Lord Rupert, for she is beautiful and sought after, and I am neither. Besides, what lady is ever going to be jealous of a companion?"

"Greville's mother was," Rupert murmured, then sat forward again. "Miss Mortimer, although you may not aspire to out-and-out beauty, you are nevertheless very attractive, and I think you most charming."

"You are too kind, I fancy," she replied, and reached for a slice of toast from the silver rack.

"Good morning, children," said Greville's voice suddenly, and they both turned with a start to see him standing in the doorway, from where he had heard all they'd said. He raised an eyebrow at their openmouthed silence. "Where are your manners? You are supposed to say good morning in return."

"Good morning, Greville," Rupert replied guiltily, wishing he hadn't made the observation about the late Lady Seton.

"Good morning, Sir Greville," Megan said, and quickly returned her gaze to her toast, but she watched as he went to examine the contents of the domed dishes on the sideboard. He wore a dark blue coat and cream breeches, both of which colors were repeated in the stripes of his waistcoat. His top boots were impeccably polished, a sapphire pin was fixed to the knot of his neck cloth, and some seals hung from his fob. From the thickness of his lashes and ideal proportion of his nose, to the steadiness of his gray eyes and the way his hair curled softly at the nape of his neck . . . She drew herself up in horror, for an unexpected warm sensation had begun to stir treacherously through her veins. This wouldn't do at all! He was too unpleasant to be admired! She buttered the toast so vigorously that it disintegrated, leaving her with little more than a plate of crumbs.

Greville shook his head at Edward and helped himself from the sideboard dishes, then came to sit directly opposite Megan. "Well, Rupert," he declared, "I think you have damned poor Miss Mortimer with faint praise; indeed you were less than gallant. Charm she certainly has, but beauty also."

Megan was astounded to hear a compliment from him.

Rupert was dismayed. "I say, Miss Mortimer, I didn't mean any insult, indeed quite the opposite."

"I saw no insult, Lord Rupert."

Greville looked at her. "You seem taken aback that I should praise you, Miss Mortimer."

"I confess I am, Sir Greville," she replied, deciding that honesty was the best policy.

"Would you like me to revoke my words?" He smiled a little. It wasn't exactly a warm smile, but neither was it cold. Just somewhere in between. "Perhaps I will be able to convince you of my sincerity when I escort you to the ball tonight. I vow I will show you every attention."

The ball! After the excitement of the night, she had quite forgotten it!

"Now I appear to have put you at sixes and sevens again," Greville murmured.

She blushed, and reached for another slice of toast, which she buttered with more care this time.

*   *   *

Chloe was so impatient to commence the shopping expedition that she called for Megan at half past nine, which was rather earlier than agreed. Megan had been just about to write her secret letter, but had to abandon it to hurry upstairs for her new dark green cloak.

A bright buttercup-yellow pelisse trimmed with white fur was Chloe's choice today, and it was very cheerful and sunny when the skies were so cloudy. Megan felt quite dull beside her as they walked down the Steine past the Marine Pavilion, outside which the German band was once again playing carols. A small crowd had gathered to listen, and a woman roasting chestnuts on a brazier was not short of business. With only five days to go till Christmas, the spirit of the season was almost tangible. Children's faces shone with excitement, and among the adults there was a liberal sprinkling of footmen carrying an assortment of presents from various fashionable emporiums.

Megan and Chloe passed the Castle Inn on the corner into Castle Square, where Oliver's lodgings stood next to a silk warehouse. Megan saw the name Duchess Place above the fanlight of the door, and commented upon it.

"Isn't that where Mr. March has rooms?"

Chloe nodded. "Yes, and very tolerable they are too." She blushed then. "I-I only know what they are like because Papa visited Lord Palmerston there about five years ago. They are most comfortable and well appointed for two and a half guineas a week."

"Mr. March is a very fortunate gentleman to have found favor with you," Megan said.

"It is most kind of you to say so, Miss Mortimer."

Megan wondered how far she could go. "It is the truth, Miss Holcroft. It is also the truth that Lord Rupert is heartbroken."

Chloe halted. "Lord Rupert has only himself to blame."

"Yes, he says that too."

Chloe eyed her suspiciously. "Has he primed you to sing his praises?"

"No, I primed myself," Megan replied honestly.

Chloe's lips parted, then she went off into peals of laughter. "You are incorrigible, Miss Mortimer!"

Megan smiled too, and pressed on now that she had started. "I know it is not my place to say so, Miss Holcroft, but I do not like Mr. March at all."

Chloe searched her face. "Papa does not like him either, nor does Lady Evangeline; indeed, I think I am his only admirer, but then to me he has been all that is attentive and chivalrous."

"Maybe, but Lord Rupert is in love with you, Miss Holcroft."

"Is he?" Chloe recalled how Rupert had fussed around his aunt's companion the evening before.

Megan read her thoughts. "Miss Holcroft, if his lordship paid attention to me last night, it was only to make you jealous."

Chloe smiled sheepishly. "Yes, I suppose I know it really." She played with the strings of her reticule. "I'm afraid I find it very hard to forgive him for turning me down as he did. I sobbed for weeks on account of it, and I have no intention of letting him hurt me again."

"He would *never* hurt you again," Megan replied.

"Maybe. Anyway, it will not arise, because I intend to accept Mr. March."

Megan gazed at her in dismay. "He has asked for your hand?"

Chloe gave her a slightly wicked look. "Not yet, but he is on the point of it."

"Miss Holcroft, do you feel the same way toward Mr. March that you did toward Lord Rupert?"

Chloe lowered her eyes, and didn't reply.

Megan feared she had gone too far. "I-I should not say any of this, Miss Holcroft, for it isn't right that a companion should presume."

"Oh, but I *like* talking to you, Miss Mortimer," Chloe said, putting a reassuring hand over hers. "Besides, it gives me the excuse to quiz you."

"Me? What about?" Megan was startled.

"Why, Sir Greville of course."

Megan drew back. "But he and I are barely acquainted."

"That is not how it seemed to me at Donaldson's yesterday," Chloe replied. "I saw how tenderly he took your hand and drew it over his arm. I could scarce believe my eyes, for you are a companion, and I *know* how he has always felt about—" She broke off in embarrassment. "Forgive me, I-I didn't mean to offend you . . ."

"I am not offended, Miss Holcroft, for he has left me in no doubt as to his opinion on that score. Please believe me when I say that at the library yesterday, his sole purpose was to deter Lady Garsington," Megan pointed out.

"On account of Sybil?"

"Yes."

"And that is all?"

"Of course." But Megan flushed as she remembered her reaction to him at breakfast.

"How becomingly pink you have gone, to be sure," Chloe observed dryly.

"Only because I am dismayed at what you think."

Chloe raised an eyebrow. "Hmm. Well, I stand firm, for I *know* there is something going on, and that it is very much to do with you. To begin with, you appear to be the reason why Lady Evangeline curtailed her stay in Bath to return here, and for a companion you are really clothed rather well, don't you agree? Please do not misunderstand, for I do not mean to be rude in any way, I am just making the observation. And now Sir Greville and Lord Rupert have arrived as well, and the former not only singled you out most particularly yesterday, but is to partner you tonight at the ball. If they attend such an occasion at all, companions usually sit meekly on the sidelines, they are certainly not escorted by one of England's most eligible gentlemen. I smell a mystery of some kind, Miss Mortimer, and I am not easily put off a scent."

"There is no mystery," Megan said, but she couldn't help recalling the odd interview in the Wells lodging house, when Evangeline had asked her some very strange questions. And since then there was no denying that this particular new employee had been treated very generously and considerately indeed. First the blue chamber, then joining the family for meals, then the clothes from Mrs. Fiske's, and now tonight's Christmas *bal masqué* at the Old Ship. Chloe was right, there had to be a mystery of some kind. But what could it be? What possible reason could Lady Evangeline Radcliffe have for seeking her out?

Chapter 20

Chloe smiled at the various expressions crossing Megan's face. "I would give a penny for your thoughts right now, Miss Mortimer."

"They are not worth a penny," Megan replied. "Miss Holcroft, I am only Lady Evangeline's companion, I swear it."

"If you say so, if you say so," Chloe murmured dryly. "Anyway, enough of this, for we have shops to visit."

To Megan's relief the subject was dropped, and they embarked upon a very agreeable hour of browsing through the narrow alleys of shops in the old quarter. After that they spent another hour at a rather exclusive haberdashery in Ship Street, where they chose masks and hair ornaments for the ball. Chloe's purchases were lavish, of course: a silver-sequined mask, and for her hair a French star ornament adorned with bright blue rhinestones to match her evening gown. Megan settled for a small black velvet mask and a plain mother-of-pearl comb.

It was almost midday as they walked down Ship Street, near the end of which stood the Old Ship. The hotel was one of the two most important establishments in the town, the other being the Castle Inn, and it boasted sixty-eight bedrooms, although only eight looked toward the sea because a southern frontage had just been acquired in the past few years. It was to the splendid assembly rooms at the northern end of the building that Megan and Chloe repaired, intending to see what preparations were in hand for the ball.

Two liveried footmen guarded the main door, but opened them immediately when one of them recognized

Chloe. Inside everything was wonderfully decorated with greenery, ribbons, and flowers, and the many chandeliers looked as if they had been freshly cleaned for the occasion. As well as the chandeliers, there were wall sconces containing slender scarlet candles and floor-standing candelabra, which together with the chandeliers would make the rooms dazzling come nightfall. Crystal droplets chinked daintily in the draft from the street as the door was closed again, and then there was the seasonal scent of cinnamon and other spices from potpourri bowls in hearths where coal fires glowed.

The crimson-and-gold ballroom was ninety feet long, with a coved ceiling, a balcony for spectators, and a musicians' gallery with a delicate iron railing. Footmen were sanding the floor, upon which lay paper templates of holly, mistletoe, and ivy, and some maids were making a mistletoe bough that was three times the size of the one at Radcliffe House. A consignment of hothouse ferns, considered *de rigueur* for all balls, Christmas or not, had just been delivered from a market garden outside the town. By the evening they would have been arranged around the blocks of ice on stands, which would be necessary to cool the hot air due to all the people, candles, and fires. In the musicians' gallery the orchestra was rehearsing a Mozart minuet, which died away as the first violinist rattled his bow crossly against his music stand and complained about the cellists.

As Megan and Chloe watched from the ballroom entrance, Chloe noticed someone she knew in the adjacent supper room, and excused herself from Megan for a few moments. No sooner had she gone than a cold draft signified the opening of the door from Ship Street. Megan turned and saw Oliver coming toward her.

His clothes were as much the tippy as ever, but there was a large graze on his forehead caused by the falling ladder. After glancing into the supper room, where Chloe was chattering with her acquaintance, he confronted Megan.

"I thought you and Miss Holcroft would never part, coz," he said softly.

"You have been following us?"

"A shabby trick, but one which has now paid dividends," he replied coolly, his eyes sliding once more toward Chloe. However, she was deeply engrossed in conversation and had no idea he was there.

"A shabby trick by a shabby person," Megan responded with mettle, for she was prepared for him.

"We have some unfinished business, my dear."

"No, we do not, sir," she replied.

Oliver held her eyes. "On the contrary, coz, for we were engaged upon negotiations last night when we were rudely interrupted. By the way, who was your rescuer?" This last was added lightly, but was clearly of intense concern to him.

"No one you know," she answered.

"I'm not to be trifled with, madam! Who was it?"

"All I will say is that if you threaten me again, he will come to my assistance, and next time he will not be so gentle with you. As to your financial offer, I have to decline because I wish to stay with Lady Evangeline. And please do not suspect me of attempting to extract more money from you, because that is not the case."

Cold fury darkened his visage. "I'll make you very sorry for this," he breathed.

"I think not. You see, I have written a letter and lodged it in a safe place, to be opened if anything should befall me." That wasn't quite true, of course, but it was as near as made no difference.

"You have more pluck than I expected, coz," he murmured thoughtfully, his voice almost drowned as the orchestra resumed the minuet.

"I fear that you have lived down to my expectations," she replied.

"Does this mean that you intend to regale Miss Holcroft with my past actions? Perhaps you already have?" He saw in her eyes that as yet she hadn't, and he smiled. "Your letter will not protect you from my revenge, my dear, for there will be nothing to connect me with anything that might happen to you. Hold your tongue to Miss Holcroft, or take the consequences."

Megan had no opportunity to respond because Chloe suddenly saw them talking and hurried out of the supper room. "Why, Oliver, what a pleasure this is!" she cried, her lovely face alight with a smile, but then she saw the dressing on his forehead. "Oh, goodness, how dreadful! Whatever happened?"

"I, er, walked into a cupboard," he replied, taking her hand and raising it palm uppermost to his lips.

Her fingers closed solicitously over his. "I do hope it isn't too painful?"

"I am assured it will soon be well again." He gazed into her magnificent blue eyes. "It is most fortunate that I have happened upon you like this, for I have just acquired that new team of roans I mentioned yesterday, and am about to go for a drive along the East Cliff. Would you care to join me?"

"Oh, yes!" Chloe replied eagerly. "Miss Mortimer and I would *love* to!"

Oliver's smile froze for a fleeting moment, but then he was all smooth apologies. "I, er, fear that cannot be so, Chloe, for the curricle will only seat two in comfort. Three might be a little dangerous."

"Oh, yes, I wasn't thinking." Chloe's face fell, and she looked imploringly at Megan, who knew what was expected of her.

"Please go for the drive, Miss Holcroft. I am more than happy to return to Radcliffe House on my own."

Chloe hesitated, well aware that she was in the wrong, but unable to resist the curricle. "If you're sure you will not mind, Miss Mortimer?"

Megan smiled. "Of course I don't," she fibbed, for she minded very much, not on her own account, but on Rupert's. If she could have thought of a way to tweak Chloe's conscience right then, she wouldn't have hesitated to do it.

"I am in your debt, Miss Mortimer," Chloe declared, then linked Oliver's arm to walk out to Ship Street.

Megan watched the stylish curricle leap swiftly away toward the corner, beyond which the sea was gray and choppy beneath the cloudy sky. She heard Chloe's laughter, half exhilarated, half frightened by the recklessness with which Oliver urged the new horses, then they turned the corner and were gone. With a sigh Megan followed them to the bottom of the street, then crossed the uneven track that ran atop the low cliffs of this part of the town. To the west the track ran between the town and the shore, and at first it did the same to the east, but then one of the town's defensive batteries blocked its way, forcing it to swing inland toward the Steine. Now a road, it passed between the Star and Garter Inn and Mahomed's Baths, which actually jutted above the beach.

It was low tide, and wheeled bathing machines stood where the mounds of pebbles by the cliffs gave way to gleaming sand. Fishing boats had been hauled above the high water line by capstans beside Mahomed's Baths, and nets and lobster pots were strewn all around. The air was sharp with the smell of salt water, seaweed, and fresh-caught fish, and a flock of seagulls screamed and dove around a solitary boat that was coming ashore.

Megan walked down some rough stone steps to the pebbles. There was no one using the bathing machines, which was hardly surprising in December, nor did there seem to be anyone around the beached fishing boats, which had cheerful paintwork and lighthearted names. She smiled as she read them. *Martha Mary, Letitia Anne, Salty Sylvia, Philippa's Fancy, Belle Bevington* . . . She looked again at the last one. *Belle Bevington?* Now, where had she recently seen that name before?

A burly fisherman suddenly straightened from the depths of the boat, where he had been applying some tar, and on seeing Megan, he touched his hat respectfully. "Good day to you, miss."

"Good day." Megan stepped a little closer. "Why have you called your boat the *Belle Bevington?* Is it a family name?"

"Oh, no. It was a notion of my late brother's, God rest his soul. He saw the name on a brass memorial up at St. Nicholas's and decided it would be just dandy for the boat he was abuilding."

Of course! The memorial was set into the floor directly in front of Lady Seton's fine marble tomb.

"She was a London actress, I believe," the fisherman added.

"Actress?" Megan's interest quickened.

"That's right. From the time of Nell Gwynne." He clambered down from the boat. "Well, that's me finished for now. I'll bid you good-bye, miss." Touching his hat again, he walked up the pebbles to the steps.

Megan gazed up at the painted name on the vessel's prow. An actress from the time of Nell Gwynne? Surely that was Rollo's time too? Could Belle Bevington have anything to do with Evangeline's actor ghost?

The puzzle was abruptly forgotten because a large ill-tempered black dog suddenly advanced toward her from behind the vessel. It bared its teeth and growled, as if longing for an excuse to attack. As she gave a frightened scream, the dog was struck by a pebble aimed carefully from the steps. With a yelp of pain it ran off, and Megan whirled gratefully about, expecting to see the fisherman; instead she saw Greville.

"Are you all right?" he asked, coming quickly over to her.

"I-I, er, yes . . . Thank you."

He could see that she was shaken, so he made her sit down on an upturned rowing boat to recover. "Sit quietly for a moment, and you will feel better," he said gently.

She managed a little humor. "The dog must share your opinion of ladies' companions, Sir Greville."

"Which rather puts me on a level with savage, ugly hounds," he murmured, and placed a foot upon the rowing boat next to her. Then he removed his top hat and swung it idly in his gloved hands. He wore a wine-red coat and cream breeches, the warmer temperature not disposing him to the extra warmth of a greatcoat, and there was a diamond pin in his neck cloth that caught the pale winter light. "I thought you were accompanying Miss Holcroft this morning?" he said after a moment.

"I did."

"Past tense? I am amazed that Miss Holcroft should

have finished shopping already, for it is her delight to do such things until she has worn out her shoes."

"Well, I'm sure she would have done that, but . . ." Megan fiddled with the package containing her mask and comb.

"But?" he prompted.

"But we met Mr. March, and she has gone for a drive with him."

"I see." He gazed seaward.

"Sir Greville, I fear she has told me that she expects Mr. March to propose to her soon, and that when he does she will accept."

"So as yet there are no plans for St. Valentine's Day?"

"I do not see how there can be if he has yet to ask for her hand. Maybe he will not do so," Megan added without conviction, for Oliver's interest in Chloe was too marked to be anything other than serious.

"I trust you honored your promise at breakfast and did your utmost to dissuade her from all thought of the fellow?"

"I said that I would, and I did." He didn't reply to this, which she immediately took to be a lack of belief in her word. "I suppose you think I am not to be trusted?" she said, unable to keep a confrontational note out of her voice.

He straightened. "I did not say that, Miss Mortimer."

"No, but you thought it."

"Don't speculate upon what I am thinking."

"Why not?" *You* are presuming to accuse me of not honoring my promise to Lord Rupert," she answered illogically, for the whole point was that he hadn't actually *said* anything at all!

Annoyance entered his eyes. "How typical of a woman! I am silent, yet find myself charged with casting aspersions!"

"What else am I to think after you remained so resoundingly silent a moment ago?" Common sense and discretion were winging away into the cloud-laden heavens, but she did not care. Something about this man stung her into behaving in a way she would not normally have dreamed of.

"Madam, I did not say anything because your statement did not seem to require it!" he replied, employing a labored, patronizing tone that goaded her beyond all bounds.

She leapt to her feet, snatched his top hat, and tossed it as far as she could. It landed on its brim on the hard sand, and rolled away like a wheel. Then she stalked off to the steps with as much dignity as she could. She was livid with anger at him, and appalled with herself. There was no doubt in her mind that she had just thrown her new position away with the hat, but it was too late now. She might as well pack to leave! But even as she hurried up to the cliff top, she knew in her heart that her reaction had been due as much to hurt as anything. She wanted to be indifferent to him, but she couldn't; she wanted not to find him attractive, but she couldn't; she wanted . . . Oh, she didn't *know* what she wanted? Choking back a sob, she fled back toward Radcliffe House.

Greville gazed after her in astonishment. Then he glanced toward his top hat, in time to see the black dog tearing it to pieces with its teeth. Then a canine hind leg was raised to deliver a final ignominious insult.

Chapter 21

On reaching Radcliffe House, Megan decided it would be more dignified to hand in her notice than wait to be dismissed, but Evangeline was so flustered and busy with costumes that the moment did not seem right. The deed had still to be done when Greville returned, but to Megan's astonishment he didn't say a word about the scene on the beach. She did not know what to think, except that she didn't really want to leave Evangeline's employ. She knew she would be face-to-face with Greville during the rehearsals planned for that afternoon, so she decided to wait and see what happened then.

In the meantime she had the task of telling Rupert what Chloe had said. He was so crestfallen that Megan could have wept for him, but he had to face the fact that Chloe's regard for Oliver had yet to be shaken, and marriage was very probable. This unhappy interview took place in the drawing room, making it impossible for her to write her letter, so she went to the theater to seek Rollo. Once again there was no sign of the ghost. Having nothing else to do, and there not being sufficient time to walk to the church and look at Belle Bevington's memorial, she went up to her bedroom and read a little more of *The Castle of Otranto*.

All too soon it was time for the rehearsal that had been agreed on the night before, and once again, as if determined to make Rupert's misery even worse, Oliver made his claim upon Chloe very evident indeed. He carried her shawl, hovered constantly at her elbow, found everything she said very witty, and gazed at her with such abject adoration that Rupert declared himself utterly nauseated, which did not go down at all well with Chloe.

Sir Jocelyn attended as well, and Megan soon realized that since the previous night his manner toward her had undergone a subtle change. It wasn't that he was less friendly, just that he seemed conscious of her in a different way. Several times she felt his one good eye upon her, but in a way that made her curious rather than uncomfortable.

Rollo honored the rehearsal with his presence, but Megan had no opportunity to speak to him. He was completely invisible again, and kept his pithy comments to a minimum, from which restraint Megan concluded that the ticking off he had received from Evangeline the night before had been severe enough to curb the sharper edge of his tongue, at least temporarily.

When Oliver first arrived, Evangeline was shocked by the graze on his forehead. "Good heavens, Mr. March, whatever has happened to you?" she gasped as he was shown into the theater, where everyone else had already gathered.

"I rather foolishly walked into a cupboard," he replied.

Rupert did not bother to hide a smile. "Good for the cupboard," he muttered.

His aunt was cross. "Rupert!"

"Sorry, Aunt E," he said, but in far too facile a manner to be sincere.

The poor tone of the rehearsal was therefore set. Rupert did not miss an opportunity to have a sly snipe at Oliver, Oliver fawned upon Chloe, Chloe enjoyed being at the center of both men's attention, and Megan's concentration was so bad that she constantly missed her cue for the parts she was required to read. Sir Jocelyn kept reading Sir Toby Belch instead of Sir Andrew Aguecheek, and Greville was in deep water with Evangeline for not having learned Malvolio's lines as promised. And that was not the worst of it, because before long Greville and Oliver were at daggers drawn by the latter sniggering at the mention of cross-gartered yellow stockings.

Greville rounded upon him. "One more smirk, March,

and so help me I'll throttle you with those damned garters!"

"Oh, come on, Seton, have you no sense of humor?" Oliver replied with a drawl that was almost the very smirk he had been warned about.

"I have an excellent sense of humor, sir, indeed I'd think it hilarious to get a certain *Henry VIII* codpiece and shove it up—"

"Greville!" cried Evangeline, shocked.

"I'm sorry, Aunt E, but it would be no more than he deserves!"

"Hear, hear," added Rupert.

Evangeline put her hands on her hips and glared at them all. "I am *appalled* by the standard of this rehearsal. I do not think any of you, except perhaps Chloe, are making any real attempt to do it properly. Now, then, we will begin again, and this time I expect you to work at it. Do I make myself clear?"

They all shuffled a little and murmured their agreement, and the rehearsal resumed. As the rehearsal droned on, Rollo grew bored. Inspired perhaps by memories of failing to levitate gravel, he passed the time by seeing how adept he could be with berries from the holly and mistletoe that now festooned the front of the stage. Several times he got things wrong, and the berries pattered to the floor, then rolled in all directions. A few people commented about these mysterious occurrences, but put them down to the greenery becoming dry indoors—although how a mere drying would catapult them for yards at a time was not explained. Megan knew what was happening, however, and was thinking about Rollo and the mystery of the church when she missed her cue.

Oliver cleared his throat. "Er, Miss Mortimer?"

She was miles away; well, perhaps not miles, just at St. Nicholas's.

Rollo whispered in her ear. "Thou art dreaming, sweetness?"

"Mm?"

"Thy beastly foe addresses thee. He is in error, but nevertheless he plunges in."

Oliver was irritated by her daydreaming. "Pray keep your mind on the matter in hand. Maria speaks to Malvolio now."

Megan's cheeks flamed. "Oh, yes, er, . . ." She looked hastily at the text.

Evangeline's nostrils flared. "No, Mr. March, it is not Maria who speaks now, but Feste! The lines are mine!"

Oliver colored. "I . . . Oh, forgive me, Lady Evangeline."

Evangeline glared at them all, defying anyone to point out that she had been the one who missed her cue. Not a word was uttered out of place, and after a moment she returned her attention to her pages. " 'God send you, sir, a speedy infirmity, for the better increasing your folly! Sir Toby will be sworn that I am no fox; but he will not pass his word for twopence that you are no fool.' "

Chloe had the next line as Olivia. " 'How say you to that, Malvolio?' "

Greville spoke up in the flat tone he had employed throughout. " 'I marvel your ladyship takes delight in such a barren rascal: I saw him put down the other day with an ordinary fool that has no more brain than a stone . . .' " His voice died away as he felt all eyes upon him, their owners in varying states of suppressed mirth.

His dull, measured delivery left Megan hard put to keep a straight face, and she had to bite her lip when she heard Rollo's disparaging snort. Chloe looked as if she would burst, and Rupert and Sir Jocelyn strove manfully to show no reaction, but Oliver grinned openly.

Evangeline threw her pages down in despair. "Great heavens above, Greville, *you* are the one who seems to have no more brain than a stone! Doesn't the Bard's genius impart anything to you at all?"

Chloe began to giggle, and in a moment Rupert had joined her. Sir Jocelyn bent double with laughter, and then Oliver joined in, albeit in a rather forced way because Chloe and Rupert began to share their laughter. Sir Jocelyn continued to laugh, but his quick glance moved from Chloe and Rupert to Oliver, and then back again.

Greville tossed his script furiously into the air. "Oh, this is insufferable!" he cried.

"This old shade is in harmony with *that*," Rollo put in slyly from the direction of the tent.

The vestiges of Evangeline's patience disappeared. "I warned you about this sort of thing last night, Master Witherspoon!"

"But, sweet lady—"

"Enough! One more word and I will have nothing more to do with you!"

As always when she made such asides, everyone else fell into embarrassed silence. Oliver looked uncertainly at her. Was she deranged? Surely she must be, for she was addressing the tent!

Greville strode furiously out of the theater, and slammed the door behind him. Evangeline sighed. "Well, if he is *that* out of countenance with us, I suppose he must have been doing his best." She turned to Megan. "Miss Mortimer, please go after Greville and persuade him to return."

"Me? Oh, but—"

"Before Christmas, if you please!"

"Yes, Lady Evangeline." Putting her text unwillingly aside, Megan left the theater. She thought that any endeavors from her would make him dig his insulted toes in still further, but a command was a command. At last she found him in the summerhouse, sitting on a bench and gazing at the lily pond. In the apple tree the mistletoe swayed golden against a sky where the clouds were now almost leaden. The breeze was playful, and the noise of demolition not too intrusive.

He suddenly realized she was there, and began to get up, but she hastily prevented him. "Please don't, Sir Greville," she said, and took the liberty of joining him.

"I suppose my aunt has dispatched you to haul me back into the fold?"

"Yes."

"An unfortunate choice of messenger."

She smiled ruefully. "I fear so."

"At least you contained your mirth to some extent."

"Only just."

"I'm delighted to have been of such comic service to you all." He paused, then went on. "I'm also delighted to have provided that damned dog with such a diversion."

She looked quickly at him. "Diversion?"

"It tore my top hat to shreds, and then did something disgusting on the remains."

Megan stared. "I-I did not know."

"Perhaps because you were too busy quitting the scene of the crime."

"I only threw the hat, Sir Greville, I didn't intend it to meet such a horrible end."

He smiled then. "I'm glad to hear it, for if you'd thrown the unfortunate item *and* performed as the dog did, I would be very uneasy about sitting with you now."

She laughed a little, then looked away. "Why didn't you tell Lady Evangeline what I did? I thought you would seize upon it to have me dismissed."

"Perhaps because it was one instance when I *could* see the funny side." He looked away as well. He knew he could have caused a great deal of trouble for her by telling his aunt; he also knew that the letter he'd written to his friend in Bath was still in his pocket. He got up and went to the front of the summerhouse. "You think I have been most unfair to you, don't you?" he said without looking back at her.

"Yes, I do," she replied honestly.

He turned. "What of your unfairness to Sophia Strickland when you attempted to seduce her husband?"

Megan's lips parted. "Did—did Lady Evangeline tell you?"

"So my aunt knows, does she? I did not think she could. No, she didn't tell me, Miss Mortimer, I heard the sordid tale from Strickland himself."

Megan felt dreadful. The entire world appeared to know what Ralph claimed had happened; and those like Sir Greville Seton were only too eager to believe him! She composed herself, determined to be as dignified as possible. "Mr. Strickland did not tell the truth, Sir Greville, whatever you may wish to think to the contrary, and before you call me a liar, perhaps you should know that Lady Jane told Lady Evangeline about it. She did not attempt to defend her son; indeed, she admitted that he was at fault, not me."

"And still dismissed you? Oh, come now . . ."

"She preferred that to another long estrangement from her only family."

Greville studied her. "You sound very plausible, Miss Mortimer."

"Which means that either I am telling the truth, or my acting abilities far outstrip yours."

He gave an unwilling laugh. "Well, *that* would not be so hard to achieve."

"I will not argue, for you are undoubtedly the very worst actor I have ever encountered."

"I perceive that you are not one to spare a man's blushes."

"Whatsoever a man soweth, that shall he also reap," she replied. Why *should* she spare his blushes? He certainly didn't spare hers!

He gave her a wry look. "So the Bible is on your side, is it?"

"That I do not presume to claim, sir, but Lady Evangeline certainly is. Speak to her if you cannot bring yourself to believe me. She will tell you that I was Mr. Strickland's victim, not his pursuer." Megan felt a sudden inexplicable urge to tell him about Oliver, and before she knew it, the words were tripping from her tongue. "There is something I think you should know, Sir Greville, but it must not go any further. Not even Lady Evangeline is party to this."

"A dark secret, Miss Mortimer?"

"Not dark, redheaded. Oliver March is my cousin."

He was startled. "He's what?"

"He is the kinsman who threw me out of my home and obliged me to seek my living. It is a relationship we are both at pains to keep quiet. He naturally wishes to keep his past actions from Miss Holcroft, and I value my position here too much to risk exposing someone who may be about to become Sir Jocelyn's son-in-law. Being dismissed unfairly once is bad enough, to court it a second time would be madness." Megan lowered her gaze, and wondered if it would have been better to have held her tongue.

Greville folded his arms. "Well, I suppose that explains your dislike for him." He looked intently at her. "May I ask why you've decided to tell me?"

"I don't really know. I suddenly wanted you to know." She lowered her eyes. "Perhaps it is just that I needed to confide in someone."

"I would have thought I was the last person on God's own earth you would choose to confide in."

"So would I," she answered with heartfelt candor.

"Well, you have my word that your secret about March is safe with me." The ghost of a smile played around his lips. "You intrigue me, Miss Mortimer, and your company is certainly never boring."

"Is that a compliment, or would I be wise to regard it as another barb?"

"It was definitely a compliment." For the first time his smile was sincere and warm.

Chapter 22

It was almost time to leave for the ball, and Megan was waiting nervously in her room for a footman to inform her she should go down to the hall. The white evening gown fitted her quite perfectly, and Evangeline had sent Annie to dress her hair into an elaborate knot from which there fell several heavy ringlets. The new comb, adorned with a posy of pansies from the garden, was fixed to the knot, and the little black mask was in place. Her attire was completed by a gold-spangled reticule, a gold-embroidered cashmere shawl, and a fan, all of which were borrowed from Evangeline because Megan had no such things of her own.

She stood by the window in a veritable lather of apprehension. How would she be received tonight? Lady Jane would never have dreamed of taking her to such an occasion, but it was clear that Evangeline did not intend her to keep discreetly out of the way. How would Brighton society react to discovering a presumptuous companion in its midst? More than that, a presumptuous companion who had the face to appear on Sir Greville Seton's arm! Would she be seen as a servant who had no business among the *ton?* Or as a gentlewoman who through no fault of her own had suffered a terrible reversal of fortune? Probably the former, it being a regrettable fact that the *beau monde* was not generally disposed to be tolerant; besides, it was what she herself thought, but at least the school for young ladies in Bath had provided excellent dancing tuition, so the overbold employee would not make a spectacle of herself. Except perhaps at the new waltz, of which Evangeline had spoken at dinner earlier in the evening.

"You mark my words, the waltz will soon become *the* dance. I dare say it will take time to become acceptable at Almack's, but then *everything* takes time at Almack's," she had declared to the table in general, as Edward, still hobbling slightly, served the lemon sole.

"And when did you encounter this astonishing new measure, Aunt E?" Greville inquired.

"About two months ago at the Marine Pavilion. Prinny himself instructed me in its intricacies, and at first it made me so giddy that I had to sit down again; but it was not long before I was whirling away like a dervish." Evangeline smiled. "It is a most *immodest* dance, you know, for the gentleman holds his lady around the waist. Did you ever hear of such a thing? Mrs. Fitzherbert was heard to remark that in her opinion it amounted to the first step in seduction!"

Rupert laughed. "And was that Prinny's intention where you were concerned, Aunt E?"

"Certainly not!"

Greville smiled. "Well, I have encountered the waltz as well, and believe that something so shocking can only become exceedingly popular. In fact, I predict it will become all the rage."

Evangeline nodded. "I could not agree more, sir, although it certainly will not be danced publicly in Brighton with our present master of ceremonies. Captain Wade is too old and set in his ways to countenance such a radical new thing. I am relieved he will not be in charge tonight, for he has become such a stick-in-the-mud that he can clear a room almost as swiftly as anything Garsington!"

Megan smiled as she remembered the conversation, but then the sound of singing attracted her attention outside, and she opened the window to listen properly. An occasional snowflake was borne through the darkness as two rather inebriated workmen staggered past the remains of Great East Street, singing *Good King Wenceslaus* at the top of their lungs.

"Thou art beautiful tonight, lady," Rollo said suddenly behind her.

She turned quickly. "Master Witherspoon?"

"Thou knowest another spirit in this house?"

She smiled. "No, of course not. Where are you?"

"By fire, candle, and moon shalt thou see me, mistress." The wraith stepped across the fireplace, and she saw his faint outline against the flames.

"Have you come to tell me how badly I read this afternoon?"

"No, lady, for thy reading was well enough. I have come to see thy fripperies for the ball. I vow thou hast chosen well, and will shine among thy peers."

"It's kind of you to say so, sir, but I doubt there will be many there tonight who will wish to hear themselves termed my peers."

"Then, sweetness, shall I simply say that thou art peerless?" the ghost said gallantly.

Megan smiled. "You are incorrigible, sir. Will we have the pleasure of your company tonight?"

"A ball is not a ball if one is alone."

"If one is without Belle Bevington, you mean?" she ventured.

Someone knocked at the door. "Are you all right, Miss Mortimer?" It was Greville.

"Er, yes. Yes, of course," she replied.

"Pray open the door."

She did as he asked, and found him standing there holding his mask and fiddling with the lace that spilled from his cuff. He wore white silk breeches, a tight black coat—unbuttoned, the better to show off his brocade waistcoat and lace-trimmed shirt—and there was a very singular emerald pin in his neck cloth. "I, er, heard your voice and wondered if all was well?" His glance moved past her, but he saw only an empty room.

"I was rehearsing." It was the first thing that came into her head.

"For what? I wasn't aware that you had a part," he replied.

She floundered in a little deeper. "Oh, it wasn't for the play."

"Then, what for?"

Her mind went blank. "I-I was learning a poem," she said then.

"Indeed? Which one?"

"A Shakespeare sonnet." Oh, how true it was that one lie led to another!

Greville raised an eyebrow. "I'm all interest, Miss Mortimer. Allow me to hear you."

She swallowed. "Hear me?"

"Yes."

Rollo cleared his throat. "Repeat after me, mistress. 'Shall I compare thee to a summer's day?'"

"'Shall I compare thee to a summer's day?'"

"'Thou art more lovely and more temperate.'"

"'Thou art more lovely and more temperate.'" She felt very foolish saying such words. No doubt Rollo had once sighed them to Belle Bevington, but Megan Mortimer felt an utter idiot saying them to Sir Greville Seton!

"'Rough winds do shake the darling buds of May, And summer's lease hath all too short a date.'"

"'Rough winds do shake the darling—'"

Greville continued for her. "'—do shake the darling buds of May. And summer's lease hath all too short a date. Sometimes too hot the eve of heaven shines, And often is his gold complexion dimmed; And every fair from fair sometimes declines.'"

Rollo clapped approvingly. "Oh, finely said, sir, finely said."

Megan looked shrewdly at Greville. "Why, sir, I believe you have been less than honest with Lady Evangeline. You recite quite exquisitely, and could clearly be a wonderful Malvolio if you so chose."

Greville smiled, then looked past her again as he realized the window was open. "Do you suffer from the heat, Miss Mortimer?"

She colored slightly. "I-I was just looking outside at the snow when you knocked."

"While at the same time reciting a Shakespeare sonnet about summer?"

"Er, yes."

"How very strange." He turned to go, but then paused. "You look very well tonight, Miss Mortimer, very well indeed."

"Why, thank you, Sir Greville."

"Not at all." He inclined his head, then walked away.

Megan closed the door, and then the window as well, for the room was now very cold indeed. Then she spoke to Rollo. "Thank you for coming to my aid, Master Witherspoon."

There was no reply, and she realized that the specter had gone.

Chapter 23

Much to Evangeline's open delight, it was beginning to snow quite heavily as the Radcliffe House party set off in the town carriage, and by the time the ball got under way, a thin carpet of white had already begun to settle over the town. As far as Evangeline was concerned, the royal sleigh would be hers the following day.

The Christmas *bal masqué* at the Old Ship was always an important social occasion, attended by everyone who was anyone in Brighton and the surrounding area. It was always a great crush, with so many carriages thronging Ship Street that it took quite a time to reach the doors of the assembly rooms. On arriving, every lady was presented with a wrist favor of ivy leaves, lace, and dainty gold satin ribbons, and every gentleman with a sprig of holly for his lapel.

Megan had been dreading running the gauntlet of Evangeline's many friends and acquaintances, but to her relief she was just introduced as Miss Mortimer. There was no mention of the awkward fact of her being a companion, and people were left to imagine what connection she might have with Evangeline. She was later to discover that the general consensus was that she was another of Evangeline's numerous nieces come to stay with her for Christmas, a green girl from an inferior branch of the family who was bound to waste the éclat of having Greville at her side. Megan had to admit to a sneaking vanity in having such a handsome, eligible gentleman as her official escort. His narrow black mask hardly concealed his features at all, and he seemed to be recognized by many of the masked, veiled, or dominoed ladies present. They were nearly all guilty of much wishful thinking where he was concerned, and so took much catty pleasure in criticizing Megan's simple use of pansies in her hair as verging on the rustic.

Evangeline's party soon met up with the Holcrofts and Oliver, and they all adjourned to the ballroom, where a cotillion was in progress. One of the red velvet sofas around the edge of the crowded floor was providently still free, so they promptly laid claim to it. The three ladies took their seats, and the four gentlemen stood behind. The sofa was flanked on either side with arrangements of ferns, and nearby more ferns concealed a stand on which rested one of the large blocks of ice. It imparted a breath of refreshing coolness to the already overheated air. Fans fluttered everywhere, chandeliers and candles shimmered, and flames licked around Yule logs that had been placed on every coal fire. At the end of the ball there would be carol singing by firelight, and no one would be allowed to depart without a warming stirrup cup of mulled wine. But to begin with, champagne and fruit cup were the order of the evening.

From the moment of joining up with the Holcroft party, Rupert and Greville had politely ignored Oliver, but he drew their attention as a footman hurried over with a tray of drinks. Perhaps it was the glitter of his pale eyes behind his mask as he took a glass of champagne, or the faint smile on his lips; whatever it was, they both suddenly found themselves remembering what he and Ralph Strickland had done to the waiter at the Union Club. They glanced at each other, and knew they were thinking the same thing.

Evangeline sipped a glass of apple cup, then turned to Megan. "My dear, you are to do as you wish tonight. No one knows you are my companion, so there is no need to be a shrinking violet. You may dance every single measure if you feel so inclined."

"That is very kind of you, Lady Evangeline, but don't you wish me to be close by at all times in case you require me?"

"Require you? At a ball? Whatever for? There, a po-

lonaise has been announced, so off with you now. Greville? Step out with Miss Mortimer immediately!"

Megan hardly dared think what he might feel about
being ordered to dance with her, but when she ventured
to glance at him, he did not seem to display any resentment; indeed, when their eyes met behind their masks,
he smiled. To receive a second such smile in one day
made things a great deal easier for her, and suddenly she
realized she could enjoy the night ahead.

The polonaise commenced, and she moved easily into
the steps remembered from her school days. She ignored
the jealous glances of other ladies, for with the benefit
of a mask, she felt equal to them all. After that she
danced every dance; first a polonaise and minuet with
Greville, then an allemande with Rupert, a contredanse
with Sir Jocelyn, and after that a ländler with a plump
bishop who refused to accept that she was not the Duchess of Yeovil, a lady apparently known for an eccentric
abhorrence of jewelry.

Greville's evening was by no means the disagreeable
occasion he had expected, for against all the odds, he
realized he was more than just intrigued by Megan, he
actually enjoyed being with her. Companion or not, it
was no hardship at all to step out with her for another
allemande. But soon his smile was extinguished as he
espied a voluptuous young woman clad in diamonds and
magenta. She was wearing a domino that all but hid her
face, and her dark hair was tucked beneath a gray silk
turban adorned with silver tassels. Greville knew it was
Sybil Garsington, for he would have recognized that stat-
uesque figure and alarming bosom anywhere. She was
dancing with her rotund, bald-headed brother, Sigismund, who shuffled rather than danced. But although
the future Lord Garsington was far from light-footed on
the dance floor, when it came to fighting a duel with
swords, he was very nimble and sure indeed.

"Oh, good Lord above!" Greville breathed, praying
neither of them would glance in his direction.

"Is something wrong?" Megan asked quickly.

"Do you see the vision in magenta!"

"What of her?"

"It's Sybil Garsington, and that is her brother Sigismund with her."

Recalling what had been said at Donaldson's, Megan's head turned immediately. "I fear she has observed you, sir."

He groaned. "Well, at least she cannot descend upon me while the dance is in progress."

"Maybe, but she has the look of an excellent bloodhound," Megan said a little wickedly.

"You point out nothing I do not already know."

"And she is no doubt anticipating your attendance at the *soirée musicale* tomorrow night."

"You have no heart, Miss Mortimer," he replied dryly. The polonaise was drawing to a close, and he looked urgently at her. "I don't care what you do, Miss Mortimer, but I will be eternally grateful if you keep that woman away from me!"

The final chord was played, but as Megan rose from an elegant curtsy, she found herself without a partner, for Sir Greville Seton had made a very hasty and undignified exit from the floor. His parting entreaty was still in her ears as she turned toward the Garsington brother and sister; to her horror they were almost upon her! Fearing to be trampled, she began to move out of their way, but they stepped aside as well and there was a collision. Sybil lost her balance and went down with a furious piglet squeal that brought the ball to a startled halt.

What ensued was a noisy fracas such as only the Garsingtons could create. Sybil continued to squeal, and her lisping outrage was directed at Megan. "Oh, you beathtly cweature! You twipped me!"

"I-I didn't mean to do it, truly I didn't," Megan protested.

Sigismund Garsington hopped up and down and called for assistance as if he feared his sister had been mortally injured.

Megan tried to assist Sybil to her feet, but then the crowded floor parted like the Red Sea as Lord and Lady Garsington surged anxiously to their stricken offspring.

For a second time Megan was obliged to step hastily aside, and this time she was successful, which was as well; otherwise she would have been elbowed out of the way.

At last Sybil was persuaded to get up, but even this she did with considerable volume. Lord Garsington patted her hand and kept asking her if she felt faint, which was exceedingly unlikely given the noise she was making, and Lady Garsington fussed with her crumpled gown and dislodged turban. Sigismund had retrieved her fan from the sanded floor; however, instead of trying to cool his sister, he employed it on himself! As Sybil was led to a sofa, they all four cast such accusing looks at Megan that she was left in no doubt they believed her to have acted with malice aforethought. When she glanced at the rest of the ball, she saw more such looks, mostly from those ladies whose jealousy had been apparent from the outset. She felt quite dreadful, and wished Sir Greville Seton in perdition for being the cause of her scrape.

To her relief the orchestra struck up *Sir Roger de Coverley,* and the ball got under way again. Sir Jocelyn had already come to her side, and now would not take a refusal for the reel. "Ignore the Garsingtons, m'dear, for they are a very silly family," he said, patting her hand as he led her toward a set where Rupert and Chloe had already taken their places.

The reel began, and as the sets whirled to the sound of much laughter, Oliver watched sourly from behind the sofa. He was consumed with jealousy to see Rupert and Chloe getting on well again. Rupert's unexpected return to Brighton had annoyed him greatly, for it did not take great intelligence to see that he was very much in love with Chloe and deeply regretted fumbling his chance with her; it was equally as obvious that Chloe was weakening toward him. That wouldn't do, it wouldn't do at all! Rupert had to be rendered *hors de combat.* It was annoying that the shove down the stage steps had not resulted in a broken leg or worse, but there was more than one way to skin the proverbial cat. Oliver smiled a little, for a fashionable ball was the perfect place to play a little trick upon Lord Rupert Radcliffe.

No sooner had he decided what to do than Evangeline unwittingly aided and abetted him. Seated on the sofa, she was already feeling the heat when suddenly she suffered from one of her flushes as well. "Oh, dear, oh, dear," she gasped. "Mr. March, will you be so good as to procure me another fruit cup? I vow I am hot enough to ignite."

"Certainly, Lady Evangeline," he replied smoothly, and embarked upon the errand almost eagerly, for it was the very excuse he needed. He relieved a startled footman of an almost full tray of apple cup, and spirited it away behind a particularly lavish arrangement of ferns. There he placed it on a small table, disposed of most of the glasses, then took a vial of clear liquid from his pocket. It contained some of the eastern tincture with which he and Ralph had enjoyed such fun with the waiter in London. He emptied it all into one of the remaining glasses, then gave another of his thin unpleasant smiles. "Your health, Radcliffe," he murmured.

Chapter 24

Oliver picked up the tray to return to the sofa, making sure that the doctored glass was right next to his hand, so that if anyone other than Rupert tried to take it he could say it was his own. But then he saw Sybil Garsington and her mother seated alone on another sofa nearby. Lord Garsington and Sigismund had gone off somewhere, probably to the card room, he thought. The two women's heads were together and their fans were in front of their whispering lips, but by the daggered looks they were darting toward Megan on the dance floor, he knew exactly what they were saying.

The little incident with Sybil had amused him greatly because he thought it served his cousin right for daring to stand up to him. But he would have liked Megan to be punished more. He paused as a new idea slid slyly into his head. How entertaining it would be to spread a little selective gossip about dear Cousin Megan, and who better to choose as his town criers than the two Garsington furies!

Oliver almost changed his mind as Mr. Mellish suddenly went over to the sofa ahead of him. The man in white had been very much in evidence since the ball commenced, prancing around the floor to every single measure, his stylish feet twinkling and his coattails swinging. He was most peculiar to watch because he lifted his legs high, kept his arms rigidly at his sides whenever possible, and didn't smile once, so it was impossible to say whether he was enjoying himself or not. But then Oliver remembered that if there was one thing Mr. Mellish *did* enjoy, it was spiteful gossip, which meant that he and the two Garsington women were ideal to employ at Megan Mortimer's expense! Smiling once more, Oliver went over to them.

At first he was not received warmly. Sybil's breath caught, and her face went oddly pale; Lady Garsington's eyes flickered icily, and Mr. Mellish raised his quizzing glass to peruse him. But no one could have been more concerned and solicitous than Oliver March, more intent upon inquiring after dear Sybil's mishap, or more desirous to let unfortunate bygones be bygones. Lady Garsington softened before such earnestness, and Mr. Mellish followed her lead, but Sybil continued to stare at him, her expression still rather peculiar. Oliver's glance moved uncertainly toward her, then he concentrated upon Lady Garsington.

"Dear lady, how very dreadful that such an unworthy creature as Lady Evangeline's companion should have dared to deliberately—"

Lady Garsington's fan snapped closed. "Lady Evangeline's *what?*" she demanded.

"Why, her companion. Didn't you know?"

"Of course I did not know!" replied Lady Garsington, her outraged gaze following Megan, who danced on unknowingly.

Oliver cleared his throat. "Lady Garsington, I realize that what I am about to say is rather, er, delicate, but I think it only right that you should be acquainted with the full facts where Miss Mortimer is concerned. You see, until very recently she was Lady Jane Strickland's companion."

Lady Garsington froze. "Lady Jane Strickland, you say?"

"I fear so."

Her ladyship's nostrils flared, and her lips pursed as if her mouth were full of vinegar. "That— that *creature* is the harpy who endeavored to wreck my dear Sophia's marriage?"

"Indeed so," Oliver said.

Mr. Mellish's eyes brightened, and he hoped some suitably salacious details would be forthcoming. He raised his quizzing glass and made much of studying Megan as she whirled to the invigorating reel.

Sybil gave a horrified gasp. "And Thir Gweville knowth of thith?" she demanded.

"I believe he must, as indeed must Lord Rupert," Oliver replied ambiguously, hoping to cause a little trouble for those two gentlemen while he was about it, but then added quickly. "However, I cannot imagine that Lady Evangeline is aware." Evangeline was held in such too high regard by the Holcrofts to risk implicating her as well.

Sybil pouted disappointedly, but then her speculative glance returned to Oliver, who happened to be looking at her mother and so missed it. If he had seen, he would have been greatly alarmed, for it heralded the full resumption of her interest in him.

Lady Garsington's fan snapped open again, and she wafted it busily before her face. "I will not suffer a servant to ape the lady and get away with it! How *dare* she intrude upon Polite Society!"

Mr. Mellish was all shocked concern as he probed for more information. "But my dear Lady Garsington, how can such a dull mouse possibly have caused any alarm to one as beautiful and vivacious as your daughter Sophia?"

Lady Garsington, ever susceptible to flattery of any description, was unwisely tempted into revelations. "That dull mouse endeavored quite shamelessly to seduce my son-in-law, but failed because he was too noble and faithful. He told my poor darling Sophia, of course, and demanded that his mother dismiss the wench forthwith. Miss Mortimer was sent packing, but it would seem she was not sent far enough because she is now nicely inserted at Radcliffe House. Well, I will not put up with it. Indeed I will not! I shall see to it that the little slyboots is frozen out of Brighton. Sir Greville and Lord Rupert will not escape my revenge either. Come, Sybil, we have whispers to spread."

Mr. Mellish bowed to them both. "I am your fervent ally in this, Lady Garsington, and will labor most strenuously on your behalf." With that he set off eagerly to commence his tittle-tattling.

It was then that Oliver's little plan with the eastern tincture went gravely wrong. He had been standing with the tray throughout, and as Sybil got up from the sofa, she suddenly reached out for a glass. Before he realized what was happening, she'd taken the one intended for Rupert, and had drunk it in one rather unladylike gulp.

Oliver was rooted to the spot. There was nothing he could do, for the deed had been accomplished. Now, instead of Lord Rupert Radcliffe making a very public spectacle of himself, it would be Sybil Garsington! He returned to Evangeline's sofa in dismay, watching as Sybil, her mother, and Mr. Mellish flitted from one person to the next, whispering eagerly to each one. More and more people turned to watch Megan, but Oliver's attention remained upon Sybil. It wouldn't be long now before the tincture started to work.

Sir Roger de Coverley came to a breathless end, and Rupert and Sir Jocelyn led their respective partners back to Evangeline's sofa. Almost immediately another reel was announced, *Chichester Bells* this time, and as soon as Sir Jocelyn and Evangeline had refreshed themselves from Oliver's tray, they hurried back on to the crowded floor to break into one of the sets. Oliver's smile was very forced as Chloe, Rupert, and Megan gratefully partook of the apple cup as well. His only consolation now was that his verbal troublemaking was going on handsomely; Megan might not yet know it, but the ball was positively buzzing about her.

Chichester Bells was a very hectic dance, with much whooping, stamping, and general merriment. Silk skirts fluttered, jewels glittered, plumes jiggled, coattails flapped, and beaming faces grew ever more red as the orchestra increased the tempo. Megan sipped the apple cup and watched the happy glances Evangeline was bestowing upon Sir Jocelyn. She was in love with him, Megan thought. She hoped the feeling was mutual, for she had swiftly become very fond indeed of her new mistress.

But then something happened to banish all pleasant thoughts from her mind. Drawling female voices carried loudly from the sofa on the other side of the ferns, where two very superior ladies were seated. One was in a cloth-of-gold gown and matching turban, the other in blue-and-cream stripes with enormous plumes springing from her hair, and they were passing some very cutting comments about Megan's appearance and situation. They did not mention her by name, but then they did not need to, for it was only too obvious of whom they spoke.

The lady in gold could not have been more condemnatory. "Well, I suppose her gown is well made enough, but so unutterably *dull!* Not a jewel to behold, and those pansies in her hair are so provincial, if not to say bucolic! Did you ever *see* anything so gauche?"

"In my nursery days, mayhap."

"My dear, did you hear she is only a companion?"

"So I understand. *C'est incroyable, n'est ce pas?*" The lady in blue-and-silver tinkled with spiteful laughter.

The lady in gold laughed too. "What *can* Sir Greville be feeling? The poor lamb is having to lower himself to such a degree that he is all but underground. One could not help but notice how he positively fled from the floor at the end of that last minuet. I dare say he could not bear her a moment longer. And then she had the gall to deliberately trip poor Sybil Garsington in order to keep her from him!"

"Did you also hear that the creature made a play for Ralph Strickland, and under his mother's roof as well? Not only that, but his Sophia was staying there too! The trollop has no shame, no shame at all! I am sure that if Evangeline were aware of it all, she would send the little baggage packing!"

Megan's eyes stung with tears, and she wished she had chosen to wear a domino that would have hidden the mortified color that now stained her cheeks. Rupert and Chloe exchanged shocked glances, but Oliver smiled. Society's grapevine was bearing fruit more swiftly than he had dared to hope.

Chloe put a reassuring hand out to Megan. "Ignore them, for they are nasty tabbies."

"I can't ignore them, Miss Holcroft."

"Yes, you can."

Megan looked at her through her tears. "But there is a grain of truth in what they say! I *was* at the center of an embarrassing stir at Lady Jane's house, and I *did* cause Miss Garsington to fall tonight!"

Chloe's fingers rested kindly over her arm. "I am acquainted with Mr. Strickland, and know him for the lecher he is, so I do not for a single moment believe that you pounced upon him. As for what happened tonight, it was hardly your fault. It was an accident, pure and simple. So *please* don't let those dreadful old biddies upset you!" She then raised her own voice in the full intention of being heard on the other sofa. "They are only annoyed because unlike you, their lumps of daughters do not merit a second glance from Greville!" The ladies gave outraged gasps and got up to stalk haughtily away. "Serves them right!" Chloe breathed, so angry on Megan's behalf that she was trembling.

Megan was already distressed, but became more so as she ventured to glance around the ballroom. Misery struck through her as she realized she was the subject of a great many conversations. Faces were turned toward her, quizzing glasses flashed, fans hid whispering lips. This was what she had dreaded.

Chapter 25

Chichester Bells finished, and Evangeline and Sir Jocelyn began to return to the sofa, but before reaching it they were accosted by Mr. Mellish. Megan was to learn later that under the guise of righteous concern he was informing Evangeline what "some persons" were stooping to spread about her companion.

He was still engaged upon this little exercise when a ländler was announced. Chloe turned quickly to Oliver. "May I crave a favor of you?" she asked.

"Your wish is my command," he replied eagerly.

She smiled sweetly. "I want you to lead Miss Mortimer out for this measure."

His smile vanished, and Megan wished the floor would open up and swallow her, but Chloe pressed on. "She is the victim of a campaign of whispers, sir, and it is up to us to show we do not give a fig for such lies."

"Please, Miss Holcroft—" Megan began, but Chloe put up a hand to silence her protest.

"I am set upon it, Miss Mortimer."

Megan became agitated. "Please, Miss Holcroft, it really doesn't matter—"

"It most certainly does!" Chloe fixed her large blue eyes upon Oliver, whose reluctance to comply with her request was only too evident. "I'm sure you do not wish to disappoint me tonight, sir."

"Er, no, of course not." He did not want to be seen dancing with the cousin he had gone to such lengths to make the talk of the ball, but nor did he wish to offend Chloe, so with ill grace he extended a white-gloved hand. "Miss Mortimer?"

Megan did not feel able to refuse, even though that was very much what she wished to do, so she reluctantly slipped her fingers into his. His grip tightened harshly as he led her on to the floor. The ländler was an intimate measure for couples, not sets, and as the orchestra struck the opening chord, he linked her arms to hold her at the elbows. The dance commenced, and all she could see was the cold glitter of his eyes behind his mask, all she could hear were the two piercing voices of the women. Everything whirled almost dizzily past, and she glimpsed the sofa, where Evangeline and Sir Jocelyn were now in urgent conversation with Chloe and Rupert. Then Greville joined them, his face pale and angry as he gestured toward the room in general.

Megan's heart began to pound, and she felt so close to sobbing out loud that suddenly she couldn't bear it any longer. She came to an abrupt halt, and pulled away from Oliver. "I-I cannot go on, sir," she said.

Many nearby couples hesitated perceptibly, for attention was upon the two people now standing stock-still in the middle of the floor. Oliver was dismayed to find himself the center of this particular stage. *She* was the one who was meant to be humiliated, not him! His thin veneer of manners cracked, and he lost his temper. "By all means let us abandon this dance, madam! Believe me, I have no desire to be seen with you anyway!" he declared in a tone that was only too audible to the many listening ears. There were gasps and more whispers as he turned on his heel to walk away.

It was too much for Megan. Catching up her skirts, she fled. She didn't know where she was going, just that she needed to escape from the horrors of the ballroom. The main door of the assembly rooms stood open to the snowy night, and she halted on the threshold. Ship Street was white now, and a passing carriage made hardly a sound, except for the jingle of harness and the crunch of the wheels on the ever deepening carpet. The cold did not seem to touch her at all as she turned her face up to the flakes, striving not to cry. Red tearstained eyes would be the very last straw.

"Miss Mortimer?" Greville said, and she turned in dismay.

"Oh. Sir Greville . . ."

"What happened during that ländler? Why did March walk away like that?" he asked, searching her face in the light that streamed out from behind him.

"Is it not obvious, sir? Please do not tell me that you do not know I am the scandal of the moment. My cousin did not wish to dance with such a shocking creature."

"Then, why did he ask you?"

"Miss Holcroft insisted." Megan searched in her reticule for her handkerchief. "Anyway, it is all too much, and I've come out here for a little fresh air."

"*Fresh?* Miss Mortimer, it is virtually arctic!" He smiled.

"I feel the heat," she replied, managing a very small smile in return.

"Ah, yes, so you do." He leaned against the doorjamb, his arms folded as he continued to look at her. "I have heard what is being said of you here tonight, and think you should know that Ralph Strickland's name is being circulated as well."

She looked quickly away. "At least there is nothing more that can possibly come out." Who had started it? Why, Oliver, of course, for who else would stoop so very low?

"I trust you do not think I had anything to do with it?" Greville said then.

"No, of course not. It would be impossible to prove, but I would guess my cousin to be the instigator."

Greville's lips parted. When he had been keeping out of Sybil's way, he had seen Oliver speaking with her, Lady Garsington, and Mellish. Yes, Megan's blackguardly kinsman *was* the source!

Megan watched the expressions crossing his face. "Please do not say anything to him, Sir Greville, for I am already infamous enough without him choosing to make things even worse for me."

"The fellow needs to be taught a lesson."

"I know, but I would prefer to let things die down."

He hesitated, but then nodded. "If that is your wish."

"It is."

Their eyes met, and he smiled a little. "I do hope you are able to forgive me for the way I behaved when first we met."

"It is forgotten, Sir Greville. Besides, you have redeemed yourself tonight."

"Have I? If I hadn't scuttled off and left after begging you to . . ."

"Keep Miss Sybil Garsington away from you? Sir Greville, I do believe you think I tripped her on purpose!"

He straightened uncomfortably from the doorjamb. "Did you?"

"Certainly not! It was an accident."

He grinned a little sheepishly. "And here I was thinking you'd gone to such noble lengths on my behalf."

"What overweening male vanity," she replied, but smiled back at him.

"That is what comes from being constantly pursued by hopeful brides."

"One day you will meet someone you will not wish to avoid, sir."

He laughed. "Possibly. Although to be truthful I find the prospect of marriage a little daunting. So few unions are an unqualified success that I may take a leaf out of Aunt E's book and remain single."

"But Lady Evangeline does not wish to remain single, sir," Megan replied.

"What do you mean?"

"It may not be my place to say, but I have watched her when she is with Sir Jocelyn, and—"

"Sir *Jocelyn?*" Greville was taken aback.

"Haven't you noticed? She smiles like a young girl whenever he is near, and at such times her pink cheeks are not on account of her flushes."

"But they have known each other almost all their lives."

"So have Lord Rupert and Miss Holcroft," she reminded him.

"True, but I am sure Aunt E only regards Sir Jocelyn as a dear, dear friend. There was someone once, but he broke her heart."

"Who was he?"

"I don't know, but she carries his likeness in her locket."

"So that's what is in it." Megan thought of the many times she had seen Evangeline's fingers creep to touch the locket. She glanced at Greville again. "I still believe she is in love with Sir Jocelyn now, and if I were of a wagering disposition, I would put my money upon it."

"A lady's companion with a gambling streak? What *is* the world coming to?"

Megan laughed. "Rack and ruin, sir, rack and ruin."

He became suddenly more serious. "Those sharp-beaked old broiler hens were wrong to describe you as gauche, for that is one thing you are certainly not, nor is your gown dull or your hair ornament provincial. As to *bucolic . . . !* Miss Mortimer—Megan—I have already complimented you upon your appearance tonight, and now I will say it again. You look very well indeed; in fact, you look quite lovely."

She went a little pink, and hardly noticed the use of her first name. "Oh, come, Sir Greville, we both know that I cannot hold a candle to the other ladies here tonight."

"No?"

"No." She held his gaze. "Be honest, admit that having me as your partner tonight is beneath you."

"I will not admit any such thing, especially as I am about to show this ball that not only do I think you are its most charming belle, but also that I am certainly not demeaning myself by being with you."

She lowered her eyes. "You do not have to do anything on my behalf, Sir Greville."

He put his gloved hand to her chin, and raised her face to make her look at him. "You do both of us less than justice, Megan Mortimer. I have much to thank you

for, not least that you have made me take a close look
at myself. What I saw did not please me, and I am resolved to improve. Tell me, do you think you can be an
accomplished actress for an hour or so?"

"What do you mean?" His thumb moved softly against
her skin, and she suppressed the pleasure that tingled
through her.

"All will soon be revealed. We are going to return to
the ball, and once there I want you to follow my lead.
We're going to give Brighton society something to *really*
gossip about. Come!"

In the ballroom at that moment, Oliver was standing
in glum isolation behind the Radcliffe House sofa. Chloe
had rebuked him very sternly indeed for his disgraceful
conduct during the ländler. Now she refused to speak to
him, and had even made a point of inviting Rupert to
join her on the sofa. Evangeline and Sir Jocelyn, who
were also highly displeased with him for the ländler, took
up the only other places. He would have been ostracized
far more if they had all known the true extent of his
odiousness that night.

He blamed Megan for his predicament, reasoning that
if she hadn't halted as she did during the dance, he
wouldn't have been goaded into losing his temper, so
Chloe would still be smiling at him and Lord Rupert
Radcliffe would not be making headway! That he had
brought it all upon himself, and indeed warranted society's equivalent of excommunication, simply did not occur
to him.

He was so preoccupied with his self-pity that Sybil
Garsington and the tincture had slipped his mind, but
at that moment she was sprawled on her parents' sofa.
Her knees were apart in a most unladylike fashion, her
turban was at a very peculiar angle, her face was scarlet,
and she was staring ardently at him. Abandoned was the
word to describe her, and her parents were thoroughly
alarmed.

Sigismund was more furious than alarmed, for it was
plain to him that this was more than mere inebriation.
His sister had imbibed a drink that had been tampered

with, and if he discovered who that person was . . . ! His
eyes were alight with violent intent, and he was already
mentally deciding whether to gut the villain with a sword
or puncture him between the eyes with a pistol.

Sybil suddenly gave a loud giggle, and got up unstead-
ily to wave across at Oliver. "Cooee!" she screeched,
employing a new word from Australia that she had decided she liked very much. Still waving, she jumped up
and down so that her generous bosom wobbled like jelly.
"Cooee, Mr. March! Pleathe come and danth with me!"

Lady Garsington burst into floods of tears, and her
husband stood there as if possessed of two left legs. Oliver was aghast. Dear God, his brew was working with a
vengeance! Then her overheated gaze met his, and his
heart plummeted as he realized he was once again the
object of Sybil Garsington's desire.

Sigismund caught his sister by the arm. "It's time to
take you back to the house," he said, but that wasn't
what Sybil wanted at all. With another piglet squeal she
broke free of him, then scampered across the dance floor,
scattering couples in all directions. Sigismund set off in
pursuit, but lost her near the supper room. He glanced
around for a long time, then gave up and returned to his
parents. Behind him, the tablecloth on one of the supper
tables was raised, and Sybil peeped out. Then she ex-
ploded into hysterical giggles and drew back out of
sight again.

A cotillion was announced, and it was at this point
that Greville led Megan back to Evangeline's sofa. Evangeline and Sir Jocelyn immediately got up to make sure
Megan had not been too distressed by what had happened, but there was no time to talk because Greville
bent quickly to Rupert.

"I want you and Chloe to make up a foursome for
this cotillion with Megan and me," he said quickly.

Rupert was startled. "So it's *Megan* now, eh?"

"Just do it, there's a good fellow."

Rupert got up, and seized Chloe's hand. "Come on,
we're under orders," he said, and without a murmur she
rose as well.

Greville held Megan by the hand to lead her on to the floor. "Remember, now," he said, "you are just to follow my lead, and I am not simply referring to dance steps." She looked inquiringly at him, but he said nothing more.

Chapter 26

There were renewed whispers as Sir Greville Seton and Lord Rupert Radcliffe escorted their partners onto the quickly filling floor, where numerous sets were seeking a space. But just as the dancers had sorted themselves out, there was a delay because the orchestra discovered a problem. A string had broken on one of the violins, and the violinist had to scurry away to get another.

As the ball waited, Greville caught Megan's eyes and smiled. Evangeline and Sir Jocelyn had resumed their places on the sofa, and when they saw that smile, Evangeline's eyes brightened. "I do believe one of my plans is on the point of success, Jocelyn."

"Only one? My dear, there are *two* plans in that set."

"So there are." She glanced behind to bestow an unsympathetic glance upon Oliver, who was glowering at Rupert as if hoping he would vanish, then she turned back to Jocelyn and lowered her voice. "And plan three stands to the rear of this sofa! I have resolved to see our Mr. March sent packing, which I do believe is what will happen after his shabby behavior tonight. When I think of how he conducted himself in that ländler, I vow I could box his obnoxious ears!"

"Chloe will soon box them for you, I fancy. By the way, she is asking questions about Miss Mortimer."

"Questions?"

He nodded. "It has not escaped her notice that you are showing your new companion a great deal of favor. I happen to know she has asked Rupert, but he says he and Greville know nothing. They are all very curious about your marked interest in Miss Mortimer.''

"I'm sure they are, but until I tell Miss Mortimer herself, I have no intention of confiding in them. You are the only one I have trusted with the truth.''

"I'm flattered.''

She looked toward the dancers, who were still awaiting the violinist. "I was desperately afraid that Greville's detestation of companions would prove too great a stumbling block, but to know her is to be charmed by her. She has spirit too, which he has always liked in a woman. Oh, Jocelyn, I have all my fingers and toes crossed for this, because it would be the match of my dreams. She is the daughter I could have had, *should* have had . . .''

He smiled fondly. "My dear, she is very fortunate to have such a fine mother-by-proxy.''

"What a very cumbersome title, to be sure.'' Evangeline drew a long breath. "To be truthful, Jocelyn, I am unsure what to say to her. I will have to tell her soon, but it will not be easy; after all she is really nothing to do with me. With hindsight, I wish I had been open from the outset, but I dithered, decided to tread carefully by pretending I was in need of a companion, and now I am in a quandary. What if she regards me as a meddling busybody?''

"I think your motives are laudable, Evangeline, and when Miss Mortimer learns them, I am sure she will think so too. She has every reason in the world to be grateful to you, and if your hopes for her future are successful, as they do indeed seem likely to be, then she will have benefited quite considerably from your meddling.''

Oliver's attention had now been drawn to the two on the sofa. What were they talking about so secretively? he wondered. It was obviously something very confidential, and if he stepped just a little closer, perhaps he would be able to hear . . . But as he began to edge forward, a shrill voice made him freeze.

"Cooee! Cooee, Mithter March!''

Sybil Garsington! Oliver glanced right and left like a hunted animal, then took to his elegant heels toward the entrance hall.

Laughter rippled around the ballroom as Sybil gave hot pursuit. "Mithter March, Mithter March, I mutht have wordth with you! There ith thomething vewy important I have to tell you! It'th tewwibly pwivate! Oh, pleathe wait! Cooee! *Cooee!*"

Lady Garsington was so dismayed by the public exhibition her daughter was making of herself that she fell into her husband's arms in a swoon. Sigismund stood in stunned disbelief, a glass of champagne poised halfway to his lips as he watched his sister charge out of the ballroom like a magenta Valkyrie, still cooeeing at the top of her lungs.

The ballroom was abuzz with speculation as to what Sybil Garsington could have to say to Oliver March that was so terribly private. Then it became Chloe's turn to be subjected to undisguised scrutiny, for everyone knew that Oliver had been laying siege to her in recent weeks. Not by so much as a flicker did she display any interest, but instead leaned closer to Rupert to say something at which they both smiled.

Sir Jocelyn nodded approvingly. That's my girl, he thought, and then returned his attention to Evangeline. But he hesitated before speaking, as if unsure whether or not to say something. He put his hand over hers and squeezed it lovingly. "We have mentioned plans one, two, and three, my dear, but I think we both know there is a plan four as well, don't we?"

She looked at him. "Plan four?"

"Yes, and it is very much along the lines of one and two, but definitely *not* along the lines of three."

"Whatever do you mean?"

"Oh, come, now, Evangeline Radcliffe, you are too much the woman to play the coy girl."

She stared at him, then went bright pink. "I-I still don't know what you mean."

He gave her an arch look, and released her hand. "Then, perhaps I should not say any more."

"Oh, please do, Jocelyn!" she said hastily. "Maybe if I change the wording a little and say that I hardly dare *hope* what you mean?"

He smiled then. "That is infinitely more pleasing to my ears, my dear. Still, truth to tell I am not in any position to criticize, for I too have been hovering around this very thing. By Gad, it is easier to face Boney's navy than to pluck up the courage to tell you I love you!"

Tears of joy sprang to her eyes. "Oh, Jocelyn, if you only knew how I have been yearning for you as well, but I was afraid you only saw me as an old friend . . ."

"Ditto, my dearest." He chuckled, and raised her fingertips to his lips. "There are no fools like old fools, mm?"

Her fingers curled elatedly in his, but then the cotillion began and her gaze darted to the sea of dancers. "Now, let us pray for plans one and two," she murmured.

"Ditto again," he murmured.

"Jocelyn, there is something I want you to know, something I haven't yet told anyone. It concerns Radcliffe House."

"Yes?"

"I have decided to sell it to Prinny."

Sir Jocelyn stared at her. "But, Evangeline, you love that house!"

"I know; nevertheless I have decided upon a new start. Now more than ever."

"A new start?"

She smiled. "Yes. As you know, HRH has been pestering me to sell for some time, and suddenly it seems right to give in to him. I fear this will be my last Christmas in Brighton."

He was startled. "You mean to leave *Brighton* as well?"

"Yes. When I said a new start, I meant it."

"And do I figure in this new start, Evangeline?"

She gazed at him. "Do you want to?"

"Of course. In fact, I'll take a damned dim view if you toddle off without me! However, we cannot toddle off together and remain within the bounds of propriety, so it seems to me you will just have to marry me," he declared.

She smiled through tears of happiness. "And I will just have to accept," she replied.

He squeezed her hand again. "I cannot wait to tell them all."

But her fingers tightened urgently over his. "Not just yet, Jocelyn. I want everyone else to be settled first, *then* we will tell them."

"Whatever you wish, my darling, whatever you wish."

The orchestra played the opening chords, and they both settled back to watch as the dance began at last. The cotillion was a vivacious measure involving the giving and taking of forfeits, and as the sequences brought Megan to Greville for the first time, he caught her hand to kiss it on the palm. There was nothing fleeting about the gesture; it was calculated to rivet surrounding attention. She felt herself become rather hot, but then glanced up and became more hot than ever, for the kissing bough was directly overhead. The dance proceeded, and gradually the steps brought her together with Greville for the second forfeit. This time he put his lips to her cheek, before the dance took them apart again.

Other sets nearby were no longer concentrating upon their own steps, for they were too intent upon what Greville might do next. Soon it seemed to Megan that their set was the only one still dancing, and then only just, for Chloe and Rupert were so astonished by Greville's behavior that several times they almost missed their turn.

Megan's trepidation increased as the cotillion moved inexorably toward the third and final forfeit. What would the forfeit be? First he had kissed her palm, then her cheek; next . . . her lips? Would he go that far to prove his point? Perhaps the real question was, did she *want* him to go that far? The thundering of her heart overwhelmed the playing of the orchestra, and then even her heart seemed silenced. She moved as if in a wanton dream, conscious only of him. Yes, she did want him to go that far, she wanted to know the warmth of his lips upon hers . . . Suddenly they were right beneath the mistletoe, and she felt him take her hand for the last forfeit. He pulled her close, and the entire ballroom gasped as Megan Mortimer, a mere lady's companion, instinctively raised her lips to meet those of one of the *beau monde*'s most sought-after and eligible gentlemen.

Greville was a man of considerable experience, but was still unprepared for the sensations that engulfed him as he kissed her. Desire ignited through him like a flame, catching him unawares with its intensity, and searing his heart with its heat. He already knew that his loathing for Megan had turned to liking; now liking had in turn become something much more. Her perfume filled his nostrils, subtle, inviting, gentle, and he longed to crush her soft contours against his body and feel the warmth of her nut-brown hair spilling over his hands; longed to make passionate, exquisite love to her. He had never known anything like this before, it was mistletoe mischief indeed . . .

The orchestra died away and silence hung over the ball. Greville was shaken by the wonderful sensations that were still washing through him, and Megan felt as if the brilliant beam of light from Evangeline's *Laterna Magica* were directed solely upon Greville and her, except that there was nothing phantasmagoric about the mortifying blush that illuminated her face! Please let it be a dream, for she couldn't have *really* been so unprincipled as to . . . ! But she knew she had. No wonder everyone was speechless!

Not quite everyone, for on the Radcliffe House sofa, Evangeline gave a satisfied smile. "I should be outraged and disapproving of such impropriety, but I am too smugly delighted for such airs. Jocelyn, plan one has just come up trumps, or is it plan two?"

"Does it matter, my darling?"

"No." Evangeline smiled again, and her glance moved to Rupert and Chloe, who were as stunned as everyone else by what had just taken place under the kissing bough. "Now, then, Rupert," she murmured, "if you could just get on with things as well . . ."

To the relief of both Greville and Megan, the silence was suddenly broken by the sound of Sybil Garsington's raised voice coming from the entrance hall. "Oh, you beatht, you beatht! Thith ith what I think of you!" There came the thwack of a female fist striking a male chin, then a thud as someone fell to the floor.

Everyone turned toward the new interruption. Lady Garsington did not dare to look, for she shuddered to think what her daughter had done now, but Lord Garsington and Sigismund made all haste to the entrance hall, where they found Sybil standing over Oliver's prone body.

Mr. Mellish, who had witnessed everything, dashed back into the ballroom. "She's laid March out! As neat a bunch of fives as I ever saw!" he cried, and a babble of conversation broke out as everyone began to surge forward to see. This year's Christmas *bal masqué* was by far the most memorable anyone could remember; indeed, when it came to scandal Brighton society found itself spoiled for choice!

Chapter 27

Brighton lay beneath a carpet of white, and street-lamps cast pools of warmth around the Steine as Evangeline's carriage drove back to Radcliffe House in the early hours of Sunday morning. Greville and Megan were avoiding each other's eyes, both feeling a little awkward now that the spur of the moment had passed. Neither of them quite knew how to proceed from here, and Megan feared that come the cold light of day he would rue choosing that particular way of proving all the whispers wrong. Evangeline, however, was well pleased with things, although she paid belated lip service to the rules of society by delivering them both a mild lecture on what was and was not an acceptable way of going on.

Rupert was in another world of happiness, because as far as he was concerned the night could not have gone better. The Old Ship's annual *bal masqué* had finally degenerated into so many sparks and shocks that it resembled a fireworks display, but fortunately for Megan and Greville it was all due to Oliver and the Garsingtons. After giving Oliver a bruised chain and broken tooth, to go with the grazed forehead he had already received from the falling ladder, Sybil sobbed to her outraged family that he *must* marry her. She said she had succumbed to complete temptation in his arms, and therefore he *must* be persuaded to do the honorable thing. Lady Garsington had the vapors, and Lord Garsington shrieked to a footman to bring cognac, which when brought he drank himself, such consideration being a male trait in the family.

Oliver hotly denied everything, and accused Sybil of

wishful thinking, for which insult Sigismund Garsington promptly gave him a bloody nose as well. By then Oliver looked so like a casualty from Trafalgar that Megan could almost have felt sorry for him—almost, but not quite. Besides, Oliver foolishly insisted on protesting his innocence, even though Sigismund Garsington looked on the point of tearing him limb from limb. To be fair to Oliver, there were a number of people who thought he was probably telling the truth. After all, they all knew that until tonight Sybil had been pursuing Greville; now, all of a sudden, she hinted of being in an interesting condition by Oliver? Everyone knew that Oliver had been the first man she had fallen head over heels in love with, and that tonight was the first time she had come face-to-face with him again since he ended matters with her in order to pursue Chloe. Perhaps seeing him again had made Sybil realize she was still in love with him. Whatever the truth, her claims smacked of female wiles; not that anyone would have dared suggest as much in front of Sigismund, who was only with great difficulty restrained from issuing a challenge. Sybil's brother confined himself to warning Oliver that his second *would* call if a proposal of marriage were not forthcoming by the stroke of midnight on Christmas Eve. He also warned him not to leave Brighton if he knew what was healthy for his hide. With that he grabbed Oliver's lapels, propelled him backward to the main entrance, and threw him out into the snow, where a sore rear end was added to the catalog.

Greville would dearly have liked to deal out Oliver's punishment himself, but he had promised Megan he would not do anything, and he was a man of his word. So he had to content himself with watching someone else do the honors, and at least had the comfort of knowing that Sigismund Garsington was a very thorough fellow!

Rupert was delighted to see his rival routed, but then his cup almost overflowed with exultation when Oliver received a very curt congé from Chloe. Oliver begged her to believe in his innocence, but Sir Jocelyn told him that if he ever spoke to his daughter again, Sigismund's would not be the only second to call!

The ball had eventually come to an end. There had been carol-singing by the light of the Yule logs, then mulled wine had been served, and at last everyone had departed. There was much intrigued murmuring concerning the following night's planned musical entertainment at Garsington House, and human nature being what it was, many of those who had previously done their utmost to avoid an invitation, now decided to attend after all, the hope being that Sybil might treat them all to another of her shocking displays. On the other hand, there were certain guests who had now decided that on no account would they be going after all; the names Radcliffe, Holcroft, and Seton would definitely not be announced at Garsington House, because by the next night Oliver might have "come to heel" and be in dutiful future-son-in-law attendance.

As Evangeline's carriage drew up at Radcliffe House, and she looked up at the house that had been her home for such a long time, she knew the moment had come to tell Greville and Rupert of her decision. They heard the news with dismay, but did not attempt to change her mind because they knew there was no point. Once Aunt E had decided a certain course of action was the right and sensible thing to do, there was no budging her. She clearly felt that it was time to move on from Radcliffe House, and that was that. Little was said when they entered the house, which they all, even Megan, now saw with different eyes. This was its last Christmas before being signed away to a royal doom. Nothing would ever be the same again, either for the family or this corner of the Steine. Everyone went to the drawing room to talk a little before retiring, but Megan was still too embarrassed and awkward to join them for long. She excused herself at the first opportunity, but as she reached the staircase, Greville came out of the drawing room behind her.

"Megan?"

She paused with a hand on the garlanded newel post, then turned reluctantly. "Sir Greville?"

"Are we to be formal again?" he asked as he came toward her.

"I-I think it best."

"Why?"

She looked into his eyes. "Because you were merely making a point tonight, Sir Greville."

"I concede that is how it commenced, but—"

"And it is also best, because I am Lady Evangeline's paid companion whereas you are a titled gentleman of considerable fortune," she interrupted quietly.

"A titled gentleman of considerable fortune who is well able to decide for himself what is best."

"Yes, and I am sure that in the morning you will decide very differently from now."

Suddenly he put his hand over hers on the newel post. "You seem sure of how I will feel, Megan, but what of you? How do *you* feel?" he asked softly.

The warmth of his touch made the blood pulse more wildly through her veins, but she strove to appear calm. "I feel embarrassed," she said, trying to slide her hand away.

He would not let her escape. "Embarrassed? Is that all?"

She looked away. "Please, sir . . ."

"My name is Greville, Megan, and after the kiss we shared tonight, I rather think it appropriate if you address me by it, don't you?"

Her gaze fled to his again. "I can't! I am Lady Evangeline's employee, and you—"

He broke in. "I know, I'm a titled gentleman of considerable fortune who was only making a point, but I am also a man who found something wonderful beneath the mistletoe tonight. Do you imagine that such kisses are easy to come by? If you do, you are wrong."

"What are you saying?"

He smiled. "Simply that I do not *wish* to feel any differently in the morning," he replied, and stepped close enough to put an arm around her waist and pull her to him. His lips caressed hers for a long moment—long enough for him to know by the reeling of his senses that what had happened at the ball had not been a transient thing—then he released her. "Good, night, and the sweetest of dreams, Megan," he said huskily, then returned to the drawing room.

Heart pounding, she fled up the stairs.

The sweetest of dreams did indeed come Megan's way that night, dreams of lying in Greville's arms, his lips to hers; his body to hers . . . There was no propriety in what she dreamt, no inhibitions or rules, nothing to hold back the tide of desire that overwhelmed them both. In her sleep they shared the passion that convention expected only the married to enjoy, and when she awoke the next morning she knew that her feelings for Sir Greville Seton had passed all boundaries. She loved him, and there was no going back. But was there to be any going forward? Did he really still feel the same this morning as he did last night? She would only know that when she faced him at breakfast—if she had the courage to go downstairs.

She got out of bed, and opened the curtains and shutters to gaze out on a white world. The overnight clouds had completely vanished, the sun was shining, and because it was Sunday the remains of Great East Street were devoid of workmen. Today was December 21, the midwinter solstice, but with so much light and snow it did not seem possible that it could be the shortest day of the year. The sounds of Christmas drifted from the front of the house, children's laughter as they played in the snow on the Steine, street calls announcing hand-gilded candles and seasonal wreaths, and the inevitable carol playing of the German band outside the Pavilion. It was a perfect day for Evangeline's excursion in the royal sleigh. Mrs. Fosdyke's bunion had been truly vindicated.

The door opened and closed, and ghostly footsteps came to stand next to her. "Yuletide is at hand, mistress."

"And I am only in my nightdress!" Megan replied hastily, and dashed to put on her wrap. "Please knock if you wish to come in, for I might have been completely undressed," she said as she returned to the window.

"Forgive me, lady, for I did not think."

"You certainly didn't."

"How went the ball?" he asked.

"Oh, well enough."

"Is that all thou hast to say? Shame on thee, mistress, for I saw thee at the foot of the stairs with Sir Greville," he chided.

She lowered her eyes awkwardly. "Did you?"

"Aye, and I heard what was said."

"Oh."

The specter was silent for a moment. "And that is still all thou hast to say? Forgive this old shade, mistress, but would not a joyous smile be more appropriate this morning?"

"I am afraid to hope too much, Master Witherspoon." She explained why Greville had kissed her in front of the entire ball.

"And thy fear is that he will have reconsidered?"

"Yes."

"Thou shouldst not anticipate such a calamity, sweet lady, for if I am any judge, his heart throbs for thee even as thine throbs for him."

She managed a smile. "I hope you're right, Master Witherspoon."

There was another short silence, and then he spoke again. "I have a boon to beg of thee, mistress."

"A boon? What sort of boon?" Megan inquired.

"I wish thee to coax the Lady Evangeline to visit St. Nicholas's. I fear she hath become a little lax over such things and that she usually attends another church entirely, but pray ask her all the same, mistress."

Megan was puzzled. "Why?"

"For the good of her soul, sweet lady, for the good of her soul."

Somehow Megan did not think Evangeline's soul had much to do with it. Rollo's interest in the church could only have to do with Belle Bevington, she decided, and then remembered that he had said he could only go where Evangeline went. "It's you who needs to go to the church, isn't it, sir?"

Silence. She smiled. "An eloquent response. I will do what I can for you, but I am only Lady Evangeline's employee, and cannot *make* her go anywhere. And morning service will be the very last thing on her mind this morning. She will be all royal sleigh, I promise you."

"Ah, yes, the royal sleigh," the specter replied with a sigh. "I vow yon cursed contraption has become a grail to her! Nothing would suffice but Master Fosdyke be dispatched to the Marine Pavilion as soon as the sun was up." He sighed again. "Well, I have bided my time this one hundred and forty years, mistress, so I suppose a few more days will not prove my undoing. But if her ladyship could be persuaded to go to yon church before Christmas Day itself is over, I would be most obliged."

She detected a certain note in his voice. "You really mean that, don't you? It *has* to be done before the end of Christmas Day."

He hesitated, as if wanting to answer, but then decided against it. "I durst not to say anything more, mistress, for I have transgressed by asking this much." His steps crossed to the door, which opened and closed again, and Megan was alone once more. One hundred and forty years? She counted back mentally. That would be 1666, she thought, and recalled that all she knew of that year was that in September the great fire of London had occurred.

She remained by the window, her thoughts returning to Greville, but then she saw Evangeline picking her way through the snow toward the summerhouse. She wore a warm rose-colored cloak, and when she turned to glance back for a moment, Megan saw that she had on a royal blue gown beneath. On reaching the summerhouse, she brushed the snow from the bench then sat down and tossed back her hood. Her face looked thoughtful and withdrawn—oddly so, Megan thought, unable to help lingering by the window. Was something wrong? As she watched, Evangeline reached up to undo the gold chain around her neck, then opened the locket to gaze at what lay within. She raised it tenderly to her lips, at which point Megan drew back quickly from the window; such moments were not to be intruded upon.

Chapter 28

Evangeline's quiet mood of the summerhouse had quite lifted when she took her seat at the breakfast table, although Megan noticed that she wasn't wearing the locket. Her royal blue morning gown suited her, and the choice of such a regal color seemed singularly appropriate on a day when she would sally forth in a royal conveyance. Fosdyke had returned from the Marine Pavilion to say that the sleigh would be at her disposal from noon onward, and she was so excited that she couldn't talk about anything else. At least, this was the impression she gave, but Megan suspected she was using constant babble to gloss over any awkwardness resulting from the momentous cotillion.

Rupert's head was in the clouds this morning. Chloe had given him a good night kiss at the end of the ball, Oliver March had been trounced with a vengeance, and all was well in Lord Rupert Radcliffe's world. Greville and Megan could not have been farther from his thoughts, and the advent of the royal sleigh meant not a single jot, unless it meant that he and Chloe could enjoy a romantic and intimate drive in it. He gazed out of the window toward her house, and hummed to himself as he spooned salt into his coffee instead of over his deviled kidneys, forgot to butter his toast, remembered, spread it with strawberry jam instead, and then placed the jam spoon in the mustard pot. His eyes were dreamily happy, and his aunt's chatter went completely over his lovesick head.

Greville came late to breakfast because he had been out somewhere, and he greeted everyone in a genial tone. Megan felt his eyes upon her as he took his place at the table, but she could not bring herself to look into them. She was aware of the door standing open to the hall, and the kissing bough turning slowly upon its rope. Oh, the mischief that could be wrought by mistletoe, aided and abetted by treacherous desires that had lurked in the shadows of acknowledgment, only to step into the full light of open revelation when defenses were down . . . At last she met his gaze. He smiled, and her foolish heart almost turned over with joy. He didn't feel differently this morning!

Evangeline suddenly tapped her cup with her spoon to draw attention. "Now, then, *mes enfants,* I think you should know that I have taken the liberty of sending apologies to Garsington House regarding tonight's, er, concert. Sir Jocelyn is to send a similar message, so we may all be assured of not having to face that wretched Mr. March person."

Greville caught Megan's glance, but said nothing as Evangeline went on, "To pass the time between now and noon I was going to insist upon rehearsals, but I don't think I have the patience." At this she tossed a reproachful glance at Greville, and for a moment Malvolio's cross-gartered yellow stockings seemed to shimmer above the arrangement of holly and tall slender candles newly placed in the center of the table, then she went on. "So, instead I shall busy myself with the costumes and scenery. I do not require any help from anyone, so please do not offer."

Rupert continued to stare out of the window, not having heard a single word, but Greville smiled. "Help with things theatrical? Heaven forfend," he murmured.

"Such facetiousness does not surprise me in the least," Evangeline replied tersely, "but there is time aplenty between now and *Twelfth Night* for you to master Malvolio." She turned to Megan. "My dear, I shall not require you this morning."

Again? Megan had begun to marvel over being employed, for the one thing Lady Evangeline Radcliffe did not seem to require was a companion! The duties required of her so far could almost have been counted on one hand. Megan's conscience pricked. "But, Lady Evangeline, are you quite sure you would not prefer me to help you with the costumes and scenery?"

"I'm absolutely certain, my dear. The morning is yours to do with as you please. Is there anything you particularly wish to do?"

"Well, I-I thought maybe I would walk to St. Nicholas's, and—" Megan was hoping to lead up to Rollo's request, but Evangeline broke in.

"Why, what a happy coincidence!"

"Coincidence?"

"Yes, because Greville mentioned last night that he is also going there this morning. Didn't you, Greville?"

"Mm? Oh, yes, I believe I did," he replied.

"Now you can go there together. You will be too late for morning service, but the walk will do you both good," Evangeline declared, and reached for a warm bread roll from the napkin-covered dish. "Just be back for midday, so that you may see the sleigh."

Megan and Greville set off shortly afterward. She wore her new cloak over her morning gown, and was glad of the honey-colored fur around her face. Her ankle boots were warm and comfortable, as was the muff Evangeline had once again insisted she borrow. He wore his braided charcoal greatcoat and top hat, and there were golden tassels on his Hessian boots. He carried a cane with which he dashed snow from some branches overhanging the Radcliffe House garden wall.

They walked apart, feeling suddenly awkward with each other, and neither of them spoke as they approached Church Street. The snow crunched pleasingly underfoot, and behind them the German band by the Marine Pavilion had been joined by choirboys singing "I Saw Three Ships," which made Christmas now very imminent indeed. Soldiers were clearing snow in front of the barracks at the foot of the hill, and the sound of shovels soon drowned the sweet music from the Steine.

Still nothing was said as they began the climb toward the church, but then Greville suddenly took Megan's hand and drew it over his arm. She glanced up at him, and saw warmth in his eyes. The air itself seemed to sing around her, and she remembered very little of the rest of the ascent to the church, just that suddenly they seemed to be outside it but could not go in because morning service was not quite over.

At last the congregation departed; then the vicar and the choir left as well. The studded door groaned on its hinges as Greville pushed it open. Inside there was the cloying smell of recently extinguished candles, and the sunlight glanced through tendrils of gently curling smoke as they began to walk slowly down the aisle. The carols that had so recently been sung still seemed to ring in the old stonework, as did memories of Christmastides long gone. Megan found herself thinking of the centuries of worshipers who had trodden these same stone flags, countless generations of Sussex folk, right back to medieval times.

Halfway down the aisle Greville suddenly stopped, draped his top hat on the end of a pew, and took her in his arms to kiss her. Her hood fell back from her hair as they stood together, heart beating to heart, lips clinging to lips; it was a sweet stolen moment that neither of them wished to end. But at last they drew apart, and he cupped her face in his hands to look down into her soft brown eyes, so large and dark with happy emotion.

"Oh, Megan, I cannot believe that you have completely changed my existence in so short a time."

"Do you forgive me now for being a companion?" she whispered.

"Do you forgive me for being disagreeably and arrogantly prejudiced against you?"

"You know that I do."

He bent his head to brush his lips gently over hers again, then smiled at her. "I do not begin to understand why my aunt decided to employ a companion, for no lady was ever less in need of one, but I *do* know I'm glad with all my heart that she did."

She put her hands over his. "There is something behind what she has done, isn't there? I know you are right when you say she has no need of me, and yet she still went to great lengths to engage me. Can you think of any reason why she might do such a thing?"

"No. Rupert and I have talked about it, but neither of us has any idea."

Megan moved away. "All I know is that she asked me some rather strange questions when she interviewed me at Wells. She seemed interested in my parents."

Greville spread his hands. "The name Mortimer conveys nothing to me. I have never heard her mention it in any connection, not even vaguely. I suppose, well . . ."

"Yes?"

"It *is* your surname? I mean, your father wasn't your stepfather, or some such thing?"

"No, I am definitely a Mortimer, and there are no former marriages on either side."

"Then, I am at a loss."

Megan lowered her eyes. "Can you imagine any other companion being kept on after kissing her employer's eligible nephew beneath the mistletoe in front of all Brighton? Yet far from being angry, Lady Evangeline seems to approve. She even made certain we walked here together this morning."

"Yes, she did rather, didn't she? No doubt she will admit us all into her confidence when she is ready. Alternatively, of course, we could ask her before then."

"Oh, no, please! What if there isn't anything at all, and she really did decide to employ me simply because she wanted a companion? She would think me very presumptuous indeed for wondering if there is more to it."

He smiled at that. "Then, you *are* very presumptuous indeed, Miss Mortimer, for you *do* wonder," he said teasingly.

She gave him a rather bashful smile. "I know, but so does everyone else, including Miss Holcroft. Anyway, it is one thing to wonder privately, quite another to ask Lady Evangeline outright, so curiosity will have to remain unsatisfied." She glanced down the nave toward his mother's tomb. "Come on, for you have a very particular purpose in coming here, do you not?"

"How—? Ah, yes, I was forgetting the spy in the gallery," he replied, and caught her hand to walk on.

They stood in front of Lady Seton's tomb with their heads bowed, but although Greville was paying due respect to his late mother, Megan could not help glancing down at Belle Bevington's brass memorial in the floor. Now that she looked at it property she could see that it was beautifully engraved with a design of what appeared to be joined rings, one containing a honeybee, the other a spoon. There was an inscription, quaintly spelt with f's instead of s's. Ye final refting place of Belle Bevington, aged six and twenty years, Pearl of Brightelmfton, Diamond of Ye Theatre Royal, Emerald of All Hearts. Died piteoufly as ye refult of injuries from ye great fire of London, buried ye twenty-fifth day of December, Anno Domini 1666. May she find joy with ye angels, and one day be reunited with R.W., Whofe love will never fade.

She stared at those last initials. R.W.? What else could they stand for but Rollo Witherspoon? Yes, of course, the bee for Belle Bevington, the spoon for Rollo Witherspoon, and the rings must be betrothal or wedding rings! The great fire had been in September, yet Belle had not been laid to rest here until Christmas Day. Had she lingered for three long months? Poor Belle. And poor Rollo, to watch his love die in such a tragic way. Then Megan remembered the ghost's parting entreaty that Evangeline should come here to St. Nicholas's "before Christmas Day itself is over." Was that his quest? To be reunited with Belle on the anniversary of the day she was laid to rest one hundred and forty years ago?

Chapter 29

Megan wasn't able to think more about Rollo and Belle for the time being, because Greville turned away from his mother's tomb to go to the altar, and she followed. Once again he took out the snuffbox, removed a sprig of mistletoe, and hid it in the wall. Then he turned to face her. "I think perhaps I should tell you why I do this."

"There is no need."

"I think there is, for I want you to know, to understand . . . Well, to understand me, if nothing else." He put his gloved hand softly to her cheek for a moment, then looked at his mother's tomb again. "You already know that my father left my mother for her companion, but you do *not* know that my parents first met through just such a sprig of mistletoe. The then vicar was a stuffy fellow whose sermons were interminable, and a group of young gentlemen, my father being one, delighted in playing tricks on him. My father's turn happened to fall at Christmas, so he hid some mistletoe behind the altar, knowing the vicar had expressly forbidden it anywhere in the church. My mother happened to see what he did, and went to remove the offending pagan article. Unfortunately, the vicar caught her in the act and accused her of *putting* it there. My father gallantly confessed and was duly castigated, but he fell in love with my mother, and she with him.

My parents were married within the year, I was born eighteen months after that, and every Christmas they hid a sprig of mistletoe on each of the twelve days of the festival. They were happy together until I was about five, but then my mother's health began to fail. My father could not abide illness, and in order to avoid spending too much time with her, he salved his conscience by employing a companion for her. The woman he selected was too much to his liking, and just after my sixth birthday he decamped with her. That Christmas my mother came here alone with the mistletoe. She brought me with her, and I sat in that pew over there, watching as she sobbed her heart out for what she had lost. She continued to come here every Christmas until her death, and I have carried on the tradition ever since. This would have been the first year I had missed because I originally intended to stay in London, but my plans changed at the last moment, and I have been able to place the mistletoe as always."

Megan gazed at him with tear-filled eyes. "It is a very sad story."

"Aunt E doesn't know I come here like this, and since she and I do not view my mother's situation in the same light, I would rather she did not hear of it."

"I won't tell her."

He took both her hands. "Well, now you know my reason for coming here today, but what of yours?"

"Oh, just the walk and the view," Megan replied.

"Indeed? So your intense interest in Belle Bevington's memorial has nothing to do with it?"

Her lips parted. "How—?"

"I saw how closely you were examining it."

Her cheeks warmed. "I-I'm sorry, I didn't mean any disrespect to your mother."

"Nor was any perceived. Why are you interested in Belle?"

The warming increased. "You will think me mad if I tell you."

"Will I?"

She nodded. "Yes, because you already think Lady Evangeline slightly, er, eccentric."

His lips parted. "You aren't going to mention that wretched ghost of hers, are you?"

"Yes, because Master Rollo Witherspoon really does

haunt Radcliffe House. I have seen him, heard him, and spoken to him. I believe he is unable to leave because of Belle Bevington." She led him over to the brass. "I think the bee and the spoon inside the rings are their badges, and that the initials at the end of the inscription refer to him."

"But the initials could stand for anything. Ronald Worthington, Robert Walters, Reginald Wycliffe, Raymond Wibblefarthing . . ."

"Wibblefarthing?" she repeated with a laugh, then shook her head firmly. "Indeed not, for I am sure it's Rollo Witherspoon." She told him everything that had happened since she met his aunt, including the fact that Rollo could not go anywhere except with Evangeline.

When she had finished, Greville was silent for such a long time that she felt quite foolish, but then he exhaled slowly. "I *think* I can furnish an explanation for his adherence to my aunt."

"You can?"

"Yes, but it is only an informed guess. Forgive me if it is also a little indelicate, but it concerns Charles II's, er, prowess, which resulted in offspring who were granted surnames such as FitzCharles and Fitzroy. Another such name was Charrel, which is based upon the Anglo-Saxon pronunciation of Charles, and the lady upon whom he sired this line was called Isabella Beaventon, whom I now have to wonder was Belle Bevington, spelling being somewhat random in those days. Aunt E is a Charrel on her mother's side."

Megan's lips parted with growing excitement. "That would certainly explain Rollo's interest in her." She sighed. "But how am I going to persuade her to come here? It isn't her church." A thought struck her. "Rollo says she must perform the task without knowing what it is about, and he has also forbidden me to speak to her about it. But he didn't tell me I couldn't tell anyone else, so what is there to stop *you* informing her that he needs her to come here to the church?"

"It's worth a try," he answered with a smile, then glanced at his fob watch. "We must go, for it is more than our lives are worth to miss the grand unveiling of the royal sleigh."

They kissed for a last time before emerging into the sunshine and snow, and as they walked back down Church Hill toward Radcliffe House, Megan felt happier than she had done since her parents were alive.

The appearance of the royal sleigh soon attracted an admiring crowd on the Steine. It was an elegant little vehicle, exquisitely lacquered in purple with gilded embellishments, and its curved, flowing runners became the horses' shafts. Two gleaming black Arab horses, jingling with bells, were in harness, and they had Prince of Wales plumes on their backs and heads. There was a front-facing bench seat inside, richly upholstered in velvet, and the sleigh was driven by someone seated on a raised dickey seat at the rear. At first that someone was Rupert, and his passenger was Evangeline, who was thoroughly enjoying the envious stir she was causing among Brighton's elite. The bells tinkled rhythmically and the plumes streamed as the sleigh skimmed over the snow, and to it all was added the Christmas music from the Marine Pavilion. Several snowmen had now been built by excited children, a snowball fight was in progress, chestnuts roasted on glowing braziers, and there were cheers and clapping as Rupert tooled the sleigh expertly around the Steine. It was a wonderful scene, and very conducive to Yuletide spirit.

After a while Evangeline surrendered her place in the sleigh to Chloe, whom Rupert conveyed away at a spanking pace. Today Chloe wore mulberry wool trimmed with black fur, and she was positively brimming with exuberance as Rupert urged the horses past Donaldson's, which was closed because it was Sunday. Chloe's eyes danced with delight, her cheeks were pink, and her lips were parted in laughter as she waved to two ladies who were observing from a chariot that had halted on the corner of St. James's Street. But then her smile vanished as she suddenly saw Oliver in his curricle behind the chariot. He was bruised and battered from his drubbing at the hands of the Garsington siblings, and he winced as he shifted his posterior on the curricle seat. Chloe felt nothing for him now, not a wish to forgive and forget, nor even any compassion for his very public misfortune. He had shattered all her illusions when he walked away from Megan at the ball, and the subsequent scene with Sybil had been the final straw. Today Chloe could not believe she had ever been taken in by him, and when Rupert leaned over to smile down at her as the sleigh skimmed through the snow, it was as if the past few months had never been. All was right in both their worlds again, and she knew that by this time next year she would be Lady Rupert Radcliffe.

Oliver knew it too. He gazed after the sleigh, his face twisted with bitterness. Chloe was the woman he wanted, but she was now denied to him forever because of Sybil Garsington. If ever a man rued something, it was Oliver March, because if he hadn't made the salutary mistake of using his charm and subtleties upon Sybil, her mother, and Mellish, in order to make trouble for Cousin Megan, Sybil's interest in him might never have been reawakened. Now it had come to this! Success had been handed to Rupert on a veritable platter of gold, and he, Oliver, was going to find it very difficult indeed—if not impossible—to wriggle out of marrying Sybil, whom he had certainly never bedded! He had only paid court to the awful creature because Ralph Strickland had wagered him he wouldn't dare! Dear God, Oliver wished he had just paid up cravenly, for if there was one thing he didn't dare now, it was to defy Sigismund Garsington! Even thinking the fellow's name made his knees tremble, so he looked nervously across to Garsington House on the other side of the Steine. To his dismay he saw Sybil standing at an upstairs window. She had seen him, and was waving and beckoning. He could see her lips moving, and did not need to hear her to know what she was saying.

"Cooee, Oliver! Cooee! COOEE!"

He shuddered, and imagined being awakened by her of a morning. No doubt she would put her lips to his slumbering ear in the marriage bed, and send him into a state of witless shock with just such a shrill squeal. A nerve flickered at his temple. He had to have someone to blame, and one person sprang instantly to mind. His eyes swung toward Megan as she stood with Greville, Evangeline, and Sir Jocelyn. It was *her* fault, he thought with savage illogicality, and he would see that she reaped the consequences! Then he flung the curricle forward around the chariot, and away down the Steine toward the seafront.

Evangeline observed his departure, and tilted her head close to Sir Jocelyn. "Behold, one very sulky bear," she murmured.

"One very sulky, very self-pitying bear," Sir Jocelyn replied shrewdly.

The sleigh was returning, and as Megan hurried to speak to Chloe, Evangeline turned quickly to Greville. "Now you must take Miss Mortimer out, sir," she said with a smile. "I am sure you would like to do that, would you not?"

He met her eyes. "You know so, Aunt E."

She nodded. "Well, after that, er, kiss beneath the mistletoe last night, I would be very surprised if you did *not*."

"I trust you mean to soon allow us all into your secret?"

"Secret?" She played the innocent.

"You know exactly what I mean, Aunt E," he chided. "There is something going on that concerns Megan, and since I have very obligingly done as you hoped by forming an attachment for her, I think the very least you can do is explain yourself."

Evangeline looked at him for a long moment. "You have seen through me, I fancy."

"I think so."

She nodded. "Very well, I think you are right to expect an explanation. I promise I will tell you everything when we are back at the house, but for the time being I mean to enjoy the social glory of the sleigh. It is not every day that one can be assured of being the undisputed queen of Brighton. But first I wish you and Miss Mortimer to enjoy it."

There were murmurs as Greville handed Megan into the sleigh, for Oliver's contretemps with the Garsingtons had not entirely banished Lady Evangeline Radcliffe's impudent companion from the *beau monde*'s mind. Megan was hardly aware of anything, she was too speechless with delight to be seated in the Prince of Wales's sleigh. Just over a week ago she had been Lady Jane Strickland's nobody of a companion, now she was about to be driven around the Steine like royalty. She turned to smile up at Greville as he stepped up behind her and took the reins. The black Arabs sprang forward, their plumes dancing, and the sleigh sped away over the snow as if upon air. The runners sang, the bells jingled, and it seemed that the horses trotted in time to the Marine Pavilion band, which was now playing "God rest you merry, gentlemen!"

Megan expected to simply navigate the Steine, but suddenly Greville turned the team toward the Castle Inn, then down Ship Street, where everyone turned to gaze open-mouthed as it passed. On reaching the foot of the street, Greville turned west to drive along the undulating cliff top, where very few people were to be found on a Sunday. The sea was blue to match the sky, and the horses' breath stood out in clouds as Greville brought them up to a canter. At the western edge of the town, he turned the vehicle, and then drove back again at the same brisk speed, but instead of driving up Ship Street again, he followed the track on toward the Star and Garter and Mahomed's Baths, where it swung inland again toward the Steine.

A stagecoach was just leaving the inn, and as Greville reined in to allow it to pass, a woman called to him from the roadside in a broad Sussex accent. "Some mistletoe for your lady, sir?" It was a red-cloaked countrywoman with an enormous basket of carefully tied mistletoe posies, one of which she held out hopefully to Greville.

He laughed and tossed her a coin, which she caught deftly and tested with her teeth before stepping from the curb to give him the posy. "Give the lady a kiss for Christmas, sir, for 'tis not only lucky, 'tis expected!"

"Expected, eh? Well, I must not disappoint," he replied, and to the delight of onlookers he held the mistletoe above Megan's head. "Madam, your lips are needed," he said softly.

She blushed as she turned and tilted her face to meet him. Their lips joined in a warm kiss that drew a rousing cheer from some men who had just emerged from the Star and Garter. The countrywoman gave a satisfied cackle of laughter. "May you both have the finest Christmas ever!" she cried as Greville pressed the mistletoe into Megan's hands, then urged the team on again.

Chapter 30

As Megan and Greville glided along the low cliff top in the sleigh, Ralph Strickland's travel-stained carriage was descending wearily from the Downs toward Brighton. He had left London at noon the previous day, but had been benighted by the weather at the village of Clayton. After setting out once more at daybreak, the carriage had taken until now to labor the final few miles through the snow, and as the first houses of the town appeared by the roadside, Ralph lowered the blinds in order not to be seen, for he sported a black eye that might have been dealt by Tom Belcher himself. The eye wasn't the work of a professional pugilist, however, but of Ralph's wife Sophia, whose build and right hook were every bit as fearsome as her sister Sybil's.

Ralph might have succeeded initially in convincing his better half that he'd been trying to fend off Megan's unwelcome advances when apparently caught in the act in Bath, but doubts had soon begun to trouble Sophia, who knew him rather too well. There had been arguments, some of them very fiery indeed, and she had finally resorted to fisticuffs. Humiliated at being so visibly damaged at a woman's hands, and annoyed at having ultimately failed to pull the wool over that same woman's eyes, Ralph was teaching Sophia a lesson by disappearing for Christmas. Brighton might have seemed a strange choice of hiding place, given that it was a stronghold of Garsingtons and was where he and Sophia were to spend the holiday anyway, but Ralph's plan was to impose himself upon his good friend Oliver. Sophia could go to Hades; he was going to enjoy himself! He imagined an excellent Yuletide, with just the two of them skulking secretly in Oliver's lodgings, imbibing to their hearts' content, and no irritating females to spoil their fun. With luck, there would be a few furtive visits to a certain house of ill repute in Lewes, where the wenches, oh, the wenches . . . He sighed with anticipation.

Lady Jane Strickland's only son and heir was a slightly built man whose elegant good looks would have been spoiled by his tiny button of a nose even without his spouse's handiwork. His dark hair was very curly and short, he possessed sensuously full lips, and his green eyes were fringed by long, almost girlish lashes. Dandified clothing was very much to his taste, as witness the blue-and-cream-striped coat he wore beneath his sweeping navy blue cloak, and there was a bright silver buckle on the wide blue band of his tapered top hat. He considered himself a very stylish fellow, and believed that Sophia should be eternally grateful to have such a paragon for a husband. The fact that she was not had always rankled with him, and he chose to use her lack of appreciation as an excuse to philander. Sophia *deserved* his unfaithfulness!

However, there was very little of the swaggering peacock about him now. He skulked behind the carriage blinds, and kept his head well down as the vehicle drove around the crowded Steine past Garsington House, for it would not have surprised him if—like Sophia—the rest of the family could see through everything as well! At last the coachman reined in at Duchess Place, and Ralph peered cautiously out before alighting. No one he knew was around, so he flung his voluminous cloak around himself and stepped stealthily down. A moment later he had been admitted by Oliver's man, although Oliver himself was not at home.

Hardly had Ralph gone safely inside than there was a cheer from the Steine as Greville drove the sleigh back. Evangeline was now impatient to enjoy it for herself again, but just as she took Megan's place, and Greville was handing the reins to Sir Jocelyn, Evangeline realized her locket was missing. She had reached up to finger it in her usual absentminded way, only to find nothing there.

"My locket has gone! Oh, it must have fallen somewhere in the snow!"

Megan put a quick hand upon the other woman's arm. "Lady Evangeline, did you put it on after breakfast?"

"I never take it off."

"But you did this morning, when you went to the summerhouse. I noticed when I glanced out of my window."

Evangeline's eyes cleared. "Of course! I must have left it there!"

"Shall I go to look for it?"

Evangeline hesitated, then smiled. "Would you, my dear?"

"Of course." Megan turned and immediately hurried away toward Radcliffe House, the posy of mistletoe still in her hand.

Evangeline watched her go, then turned a little uneasily to Sir Jocelyn. "I pray I remembered to close the locket," she murmured.

"It's too late now," he replied. "Besides, you regret not telling her the truth from the outset, so maybe the time has come to put that right."

"I think the time has come for everything, Jocelyn."

Greville glanced curiously from one of them to the other, but said nothing. The fact that Sir Jocelyn was party to the secret, whatever it was, seemed to prove that Megan was right about Evangeline's warm regard for that gentleman. And if Greville himself was any judge, Sir Jocelyn viewed Evangeline in the same light. Lovers were lovers, whatever the generation. The sleigh sprang away again, and Greville turned to look at Megan as she disappeared around the corner of Radcliffe House. The mystery surrounding her was as impenetrable as ever, but his aunt had promised an explanation when they all returned to the house, and he knew she would abide by that.

As Megan went into Radcliffe House, she did not notice Oliver's curricle emerging from the foot of Church Street. He saw her, however, and carefully maneuvered the curricle to a quiet corner by the remains of Great East Street. A mirthless smile animated his lips as he climbed down and tied the horses to an old railing, then he tugged his top hat on firmly and began to walk toward Radcliffe House. His experiences with flying gravel had slipped his mind, so intent was he upon making Megan suffer for the indignities that had been heaped upon him.

There was no one around as Megan hurried out into the walled garden behind the house. Evangeline had given the servants time off to go out in the snow, and those few who remained were sitting warmly around the kitchen fire with cups of tea. Rollo was still around, however, for he had never liked snow. He was in the theater, making holly and mistletoe berries dance in the air, when he heard Megan open the front door. He recognized her footsteps, and came out to speak to her, but she had already disappeared toward the gardens. Rollo was about to follow her snowy footprints when he heard the front door open again, but very stealthily this time. The hairs stirred unpleasantly at the nape of the specter's neck as he watched Oliver slip slyly in. "Beware the ides of March," Rollo breathed, falling in behind as Oliver followed the marks Megan had left on the floor.

Megan had now reached the summerhouse, and was relieved to see the locket lying on the bench. It was open, and as she picked it up she could not fail to see the miniature portrait inside. Her eyes widened with shock, for it was of her father! There was no doubt about it, because the scene painted behind him depicted a very tiny but unmistakable Berengers. Greville's words about Evangeline echoed in her head. *". . . There was someone once, but he broke her heart . . . she carries his likeness in her locket . . ."* Shaken to the very core, Megan gazed at the painted face. Her father and Evangeline? But when? While he was still married to her mother? Oh, no, please don't let that be so . . .

Suddenly someone laid rough hands upon her from behind. Her scream was stopped by a harsh hand, and she was thrust against the side of the summerhouse. "If you think I'm going to let you get away with ruining my life, you're very much mistaken, my dear!" Oliver breathed through gritted teeth.

She was terrified, and bewildered. How could he possibly blame her for what happened? She tried to struggle, but stood no chance against his strength, so she gave up. Perhaps if she pretended to faint . . . ? It was all she could think of, so she went limp in his grasp. His grip relaxed, and she immediately made a dash for it, but the edge of the summerhouse lay in wait. With a scream she lost her footing and fell, striking her head on the step. The mistletoe posy and the locket slipped from her hand. Everything went hazy, then black, and she knew no more as her winter solstice came to a very sudden close indeed.

Oliver neither heard nor saw anything as he stood in frozen shock. She was dead, and the law would judge that he had killed her! He took a hesitant step forward, then panicked as he thought he heard a sound from the house. The ladder still lay by the wall, and he hobbled as fast as his bruises would permit to raise it.

Everything had happened so swiftly that Rollo was caught off guard, but on seeing Oliver making a getaway, the ghost erupted after him across the snowy lawn. "Oh, what hast thou done, March, thou barbarous tick?" he bellowed, then fixed his concentration upon the ladder, which Oliver had now begun to climb as quickly as he could. The ladder swayed like a pendulum, and Oliver gave a shriek and held on for grim death. Rollo concentrated still more, and to Oliver's terror, the ladder began to rise from the ground, still swaying wildly. Higher and higher it went, and an ashen-faced Oliver wrapped his arms and legs tightly around it as he stared down in dread at the garden, where all he could see was Megan lying by the summerhouse. Who was doing this? *How* were they doing it? He closed his eyes as the world lurched sickeningly from side to side.

Greville's voice called suddenly from inside the house. "Megan?"

Rollo's concentration was interrupted, and the ladder dove to the ground like an unsteady arrow, striking earth on the other side of the wall. Oliver gave a loud wail as he was catapulted through the layer of snow and ice covering some deep muddy water by one of the derelict buildings of Great Eastern Street. The water was so cold that it snatched his breath away, and all he could think of was somehow hauling himself out. For a moment he floundered about, but then his clawing hands closed upon a jagged piece of old floorboard. Panic lent him superhuman strength, and he scrambled out, then hobbled as fast as he could for his curricle. His teeth were chattering as much from terror as the cold, and his face was as white as a sheet as he climbed aboard, then drove like the wind for his lodgings.

Meanwhile Rollo had run to kneel in the snow beside Megan. "Open thy eyes, mistress! Please, I beg of thee!" he cried.

Greville appeared from the house. "Megan?" he called again, not able to see her lying by the summerhouse because some shrubs obscured the view.

Rollo stood urgently. "Make haste, master! Make haste!" he implored.

The supernatural plea was so intense that it pierced Greville's consciousness. He turned sharply, and glimpsed a fold of Megan's cloak on the snow. With a cry of dismay, he began to run toward her. He was not alone in the house, for Evangeline and Rupert had just returned as well, bringing Chloe and her father with them. They all heard Greville cry out, but Evangeline had heard Rollo's voice as well.

"Oh, my sainted lord!" she breathed, and caught up her skirts to run out into the garden, where Greville was now kneeling beside Megan. Everyone else followed her, and Chloe gave a horrified gasp as she saw Megan.

"Oh, no! Please, no!" she sobbed, and turned tearfully into Rupert's sheltering embrace.

Rollo had been hopping up and down in anguish, but rushed forward when he saw Evangeline. "Oh, lady, lady! Come quickly! Mistress Megan has been killed!"

Greville felt for Megan's pulse. "She's still alive!" he cried.

"Oh, thank God, thank God," Evangeline whispered, leaning weakly on Sir Jocelyn's arm.

Greville lifted Megan from the snow, and gazed down at her pale face for a long moment before raising her head a little so he could put his lips to hers. "Whoever did this will not get away with it, I promise you, my darling. When I have finished with him, he will wish he had never been born," he whispered, then began to carry her into the house.

Rollo was quite overcome to know Megan was alive after all. "She lives? Oh, praise be! Oh, I vow that I will be avenged upon her murderous cousin. He did it! I saw it all!"

Evangeline's lips parted. "Cousin? What do you mean, Master Witherspoon? What cousin?" she demanded as everyone followed Greville toward the house.

Rupert, Chloe, and Sir Jocelyn exchanged dismayed glances, thinking that this was definitely not the time for such things.

Rollo answered Evangeline. "Why, lady, I refer to that spawn of Beelzebub, Master March! He is Mistress Megan's cousin, the very one who threw her penniless from her home!"

Evangeline was astonished. "Mr. *March* is her cousin?"

Greville turned in the doorway. "Yes, he is," he said calmly, "and if he is the one who did this, I will tear out his evil heart with my bare hands." Then he looked at the other three. "Perhaps you should also know that Master Rollo Witherspoon is very much with us, and is definitely *not* a figment of Aunt E's imagination."

They all stared at him, Rollo included. Then the ghost murmured, "By all the saints and demons, he knows of me!"

Chapter 31

On entering his lodgings, Oliver was startled to find Ralph waiting for him. The two friends looked bemusedly at each other's appearance. Oliver was taken aback by Ralph's colorful chin, and Ralph was astonished to see Oliver's soaking, muddy clothes, grazed forehead, battered nose, bruised chin, ashen face, and limping walk. To say nothing of the way he trembled from head to toe as if he had just seen a ghost.

"Oliver, what in God's own name has happened to you?" Ralph gasped.

Oliver's man had entered the room with him, intending to divest him of his wet clothes, but now Oliver waved him away. "Give us five minutes," he said.

"Sir." The man withdrew, and closed the door.

Oliver went over to the decanter of cognac and poured himself a very large measure, which he drained in one gulp. Then he poured another, and closed his eyes as he tried to quiet the terror that still pounded through him. The cognac burned its way down his throat, and he began to master himself. He had imagined it all! Yes, of course he had. Ladders were inanimate objects! It was all the fault of Ralph's eastern tincture, a little of which he had found in his valise and had foolishly sampled before going out. What happened to Megan was the fault of the tincture as well. It certainly wasn't *his* fault . . .

"What happened?" Ralph asked again as he helped himself to the decanter.

"I might ask the same question of you," Oliver replied, and flung himself on a sofa.

"Sophia happened to me," Ralph said.

"And an overturn in the curricle happened to me," Oliver murmured. "When did you and Sophia arrive?"

"Ah, well, that's a vexing point," Ralph replied. "I'm here, but she isn't. I have decided she needs a little punishment."

"More than the mere fact of being your wife? What *can* she have done?" Oliver remarked dryly.

Ralph colored a little. "If you must know, it's about that business in Bath. Sophia thinks I pounced upon my dear mama's damned companion!"

"As if you would be guilty of such a heinous crime," Oliver murmured.

"I can't believe I gave her a second glance, for she is a very drab piece."

"A drab piece who just happens to be my cousin," Oliver said.

Ralph stared at him. "Your *what?*"

"My cousin. Oh, don't fear I will call you out on her behalf, for nothing could be farther from my mind. Indeed, I wish now that you had succeeded in having your way with her, for it is no more than she warrants. The little viper has caused me a great deal of trouble."

"I-I had no idea she was your kinswoman."

"Nor did I at first. When you originally told me about events in Bath, you didn't mention her name. I soon realized, however, when Lady Jane Strickland's former companion turned up here in Brighton, having been employed by Lady Evangeline Radcliffe, that she was in fact my cousin."

Ralph's jaw dropped. "Here in Brighton, you say?"

"I fear so, and doing very nicely, for she appears to have caught the eye of no less a fellow than Sir Greville Seton."

"*Seton?* But he could have his pick!"

"I know. Quaint, is it not?" Oliver murmured, and shook his glass at Ralph to refill it. "However, perhaps it would be prudent of you to keep out of his way for the foreseeable future, because one simply never knows what he might have been told."

Ralph was liberal with the cognac, and then went to

the window to look out. "I intend to keep well out of everyone's way while I'm here, not just his. I wish him well of her."

"My sentiments precisely," Oliver said, swirling his cognac and thinking about Megan lying so very still in the snow. He didn't know if she was alive or dead, and now that the cognac was giving him courage, he didn't care. No one had seen him at Radcliffe House, so no one would connect him with what befell Megan Mortimer.

Ralph drew a long breath. "Anyway, I've come here secretly, in the hope that you and I could enjoy an idle Christmas together. Unless, of course, you intend to mope around after that Holcroft wench to the detriment of all else?"

"My association with Chloe Holcroft is very definitely over. She has decided she wishes to be Lady Rupert Radcliffe after all."

Ralph was pleased to hear it. "So you are at a loose end?"

"Er, not quite." Sybil's voice seemed to echo in Oliver's head. *Cooee, cooee . . . !*

"There is someone new?"

Oliver got up. "In a manner of speaking. Oh, I'll tell you by and by, I'm not in the mood to stomach talking about her now."

Ralph looked at him in surprise, but said nothing more.

Oliver grinned suddenly. "I have an excellent notion to cheer you up. What do you say to a little visit to Lewes, followed by a shampoo at Mahomed's Baths?"

"I'd say it sounds like an excellent notion."

"Good. I'll clean up and change now, then we can leave immediately. I'll have my man go around to the baths to see that they expect us later."

Fifteen minutes after that, they set off for Lewes in the curricle.

More than an hour had passed, and Megan lay very still in her bed. Her eyes were closed, and her nut-brown hair was brushed loose over the lavender-scented pillow.

A footman had earlier been sent to those same baths that Oliver and Ralph later intended to grace with their dubious presence.

Sheikh Deen Mahomed was renowned for his skills with medicine because he had trained as a surgeon with the East India Company, and he hurried to Radcliffe House the moment the message arrived. He was a short, dark-skinned, dark-eyed man of fifty-seven, who always wore an embroidered blue satin robe, sleeveless emerald velvet coat, and golden turban. After attending to the wound at the back of Megan's head, he administered laudanum to make her more comfortable, and then declared that nothing more could be done except to wait. He was hopeful, however, and reassured everyone that he did not think Megan had come to any lasting harm.

Only when this had been announced did Greville leave to find Oliver, intending to exact full retribution for what had been done. He refused to permit either Rupert or Sir Jocelyn to accompany him, for this was something he needed to do alone. A chilling fury beset him as he strode through the snow in the fading afternoon light. The Steine was almost deserted now, except for a lamplighter and his boy going about their business, and a post chaise that had just arrived outside Garsington House. Tonight was the occasion of the *soirée musicale,* and the sound of Sigismund's hautbois could be heard because the door of the house stood open, the occupant of the post chaise having clearly just gone inside.

Suddenly Sybil's shrill voice shuddered out on to the quiet Steine. "Cooee, Mama! Come quickly! And you, Thigithmund!"

The hautbois broke off mid note, and then there came a wailing female voice that was so like Sybil's as to be virtually indistinguishable. "Oh, Mama! Mama! Walph hath left me!"

Greville recognized it as belonging to Sophia Strickland. So Ralph had upped and gone, eh? It was as well for him, because after Oliver he was next on the list of those due for reprisals. Megan had suffered greatly at both men's hands, and the time for just deserts had arrived! Greville strode on, his eyes hard with determination.

But when he reached Oliver's lodgings, he found his prey was not at home. Oliver's man, who was used to covering up, pretended at first that he knew nothing of his master's whereabouts, but when pinned to the wall by the throat with a fist of iron, he quickly divulged the visit to the Lewes bordello and the booking for Mahomed's Baths. Greville was pleased to learn that Ralph Strickland had descended upon Oliver. Two vile birds to be dealt with by a single stone, he thought. He decided to wait until the visit to the baths. Why endure the discomfort of a ride through the snow to Lewes when his quarries were going to obligingly return to Brighton? So, after warning Oliver's man not to mention his visit, Greville returned to Radcliffe House.

During his absence, Megan had stirred briefly out of unconsciousness. She saw the locket shining at Evangeline's throat as she leaned in concern over the bed, and the mistletoe posy lying upon the bedside table with the unfinished volume of *The Castle of Otranto,* but then the darkness returned.

Evangeline wasn't alone in the room, for Rupert, Chloe, and Sir Jocelyn were there too, as well as Rollo, of course, but only Evangeline knew he was there. Sir Jocelyn was furious that he had not only permitted Oliver to pay court to Chloe, but had actually offered him the hospitality of his house. With hindsight, Chloe's father was hugely sorry that he had not paid more attention to his instincts where Mr. Oliver March was concerned.

Chloe was very upset by the full extent of Oliver's misdeeds. "Oh, how could I *ever* have been so naive as to actually think I loved him! Not even Sybil Garsington deserves such a monster!" she said, wiping her tears with her lace-edged handkerchief as she stood by the window, looking out into the gathering darkness.

Rupert went to her. "You weren't to know, sweetheart," he whispered, pulling her close and putting his lips to her short golden curls.

"How he must have laughed when he found me so easy to humbug!"

"Laughed? Chloe, the villain is in love with you!" Rupert replied, taking her face in his hands. "The only good thing I can say of March is that he lost his black heart to a veritable jewel of womanhood."

"Would that he had never set eyes upon me," she whispered, and slipped her arms around his waist.

"Greville will make him pay his dues," Rupert promised.

Chloe drew back at that. "Violence is not the answer, we have only to look at Megan to know that!"

"Yes, but—"

"No, Rupert. I hope Greville does not find Oliver, and that when he returns here I will be able to dissuade him from further action." She glanced tearfully toward the bed. "Oh, please let Megan recover soon! Please let all be well again!" She hid her face against Rupert's shoulder.

Evangeline straightened from the bedside, and turned to Sir Jocelyn. "I too am most unhappy that Greville has gone off after Mr. March as he has, Jocelyn."

"He was impossible to hold back, my dear," he reminded her.

"I know. I have never seen him in such an icy fury before. He was so controlled it was really quite frightening."

"I hope he thrashes March within an inch of his miserable life," Sir Jocelyn declared calmly.

"And be dragged before a court? What good will *that* do, pray?"

Rollo had been listening. " 'Frailty thy name is woman,' " he murmured, being in full agreement with Sir Jocelyn.

Evangeline rounded upon the sound of his voice. "Better to be a frail but living woman than a rash but dead man!" she cried. "Or an extinct Restoration actor!" she added.

Everyone turned to look at her, but this time without question, for they all accepted that Master Rollo Witherspoon was there after all. Before leaving to beard Oliver in his den, Greville had briefly told them all that

Megan had been talking to the ghost as well, but he made no mention of Belle Bevington because Evangeline still had to perform her task without knowing why. However, he *had* informed Evangeline that the specter required her presence at the church.

Rollo was offended to be termed an extinct Restoration actor. "Mistress, it ill behooves you to heap scorn upon my predicament."

She was a little contrite. "Well, maybe so, but you are a very annoying spirit at times. However, Greville has informed me that you need me to go to St. Nicholas's before Christmas Day is over, and I hereby give you my word that I will do so. Will that serve as recompense for my sharp tongue?"

Joy was evident in Rollo's reply. "Oh, *yes,* mistress! A thousand times yes!"

Evangeline returned her attention to the bed, and put a tender hand to Megan's face. "And when you are better, my dear, I will tell you all about your dear father and me," she whispered, then looked at the others and added, "But it is time to tell the rest of you now."

Chapter 32

It was well into the evening, and guests had begun to arrive for Lord and Lady Garsington's *soirée musicale*. The family was in disarray, not only because Sophia had sobbed constantly since she arrived, but because Sigismund had disappeared. He had gone out earlier without saying where he was going, and had yet to return. His parents and sisters could only console themselves that he had not taken a carriage or saddle horse, and was therefore still in Brighton. There was hope yet that at the appointed hour the Garsington ensemble would be complete.

The arriving guests were agog to see how Sybil went on today after treating them to such a pantomime the night before. Brighton opinion had now generally settled into apportioning equal blame between Sybil and Oliver, deeming them to richly deserve each other. The trouble was that Sybil was simply not the sort of young woman with whom one could sympathize, for she seemed to go out of her way to make an exhibition of herself. She hadn't seemed in the least concerned by what had happened at the ball and, after her loud remarks about succumbing to complete temptation, had escaped her family's clutches to gleefully gallop her way through a boisterous country-dance. Then she had drunk several glasses of champagne in quick succession before her exasperated father and brother seized her. It was a sad but true fact that Ralph Strickland's eastern tincture was only the partial cause of all this embarrassing behavior, because Sybil Garsington was quite simply an awful young woman, and tonight she was still unabashed. She took Oliver's submission for granted, and spoke of him as if he would arrive at any moment.

Sophia was just as awful, and wore a puce taffeta gown that clashed most horribly with Sybil's vermilion satin. The sisters looked very alike, sounded alike, and shared a propensity for indiscretion. Sophia frequently sank into a chair or sofa, flapping her fan for a glass of lemonade, and sighing tearfully that Ralph was the very tragedy of her life, which meant that her marital difficulties were soon common knowledge.

The omnipresent Mr. Mellish—as ever first with the best tidbits of gossip—*swore* he had seen Ralph Strickland in Brighton that very day, driving toward Lewes with Oliver March. And, of course, with a little help from that same Mr. Mellish, everyone was soon hazarding an educated guess as to *why* those two gentlemen were en route for that particular destination!

It was as well that neither Sophia nor Sybil heard these gleeful whispers. Sybil stayed close to her sister, and from time to time could be heard above the babble of conversation. "Cooee, Mama! Papa! Thofia ith in a decline again!" At which Lord Garsington's suppressed winces and Lady Garsington's fixed smiles were absolute models of silent fortitude. Not that *they* were due any sympathy either, because at the same time that whispers concerning their daughters were circulating in one direction, Garsington *mère et père* were being exceedingly busy in the other direction with scurrilous comments about the denizens of Radcliffe House and the Holcrofts. And they pressed on throughout with their dreadful evening, keeping their fingers crossed that their daughters would not disgrace themselves too much, and their son would remember his duty and come home to his hautbois!

While all this was going on, Greville left Radcliffe House to make his way to Mahomed's Baths for his denouement with Oliver and Ralph. Neither Chloe nor his aunt had been able to dissuade him, for when he saw Megan lying so pale and still in the bed, his anger and thirst for revenge was too much to contain. His boots crunched through the ice-crusted snow, and his breath was white as he walked briskly down the Steine. He thought himself alone in his purpose, having strictly forbidden Rupert and Sir Jocelyn to come with him, but unbeknown to him they were following at a discreet distance. They had also defied Chloe and Evangeline, for they determined not to let Greville tackle the tricky likes of Oliver March and Ralph Strickland single-handed. Sir Jocelyn carried a bundle of things tied in a blanket, the exact nature of which he refused to divulge to Rupert.

The plain three-story baths building stood directly on the beach in sight of the old battery. Its pedimented main entrance was at street level, and at the windows there were green roller blinds that were always half lowered for the sake of propriety, although steam and condensation usually made peering in impossible anyway. A line of fly-by-nights was drawn up nearby, their crews stamping their feet and holding their hands out to a lighted brazier.

At the side of the building, below a painted name board that could be seen all along the shore, there was a two-story wrought-iron balcony that projected above the beach, from where it was possible to lean over and touch the masts and rigging of fishing boats that had been hauled close in by the capstans on the cliff. In the darkness the sea was audible if not visible, and as Greville crossed the road from the corner by the Star and Garter, the only people around were the fly-by-night men. He was briefly illuminated by the lighted lamp above the baths entrance, and then he went into the candlelit black-and-white tiled vestibule, where the walls were painted a deep masculine green and the herb-scented air was warm and humid.

A dark staircase led up to the next floor, and the only items of furniture were two Windsor chairs, a table upon which lay the open booking ledger and an array of colognes, and some fine shelves piled high with beautifully laundered white towels. The murmur of male voices drifted from upstairs, together with the splash of water and hiss of steam. Sheikh Deen Mohamed himself happened to be coming down the staircase, and recognized Greville immediately.

He paused at the bottom to put his hands together and bow, and the jeweled brooch in his turban glittered as he straightened in concern "Why, Sir Greville sahib, I trust your call does not signify a deterioration in Miss Mortimer?" His accent was a peculiar mixture of his native Patna, and the Donegal of his Irish wife.

"No, there has not been any change," Greville reassured him quickly.

"Nor should there be, sahib, for the laudanum should be most sedative. You should not fear for her, Sir Greville sahib, because she will soon recover."

"I have faith in your judgment, sir," Greville replied, removing his top hat and gloves.

"Then, may I ask why you are here? I hope you have not made a booking that has been overlooked?"

"I'm not expected, nor on this occasion do I wish to partake of your excellent facilities."

The sheikh was puzzled. "No? Then, how may I be of assistance?"

"I believe Mr. March and Mr. Strickland are here?"

"Oh, yes, indeed."

Greville glanced up the staircase. "What point have they reached in their treatment?"

"They have had vapor baths and now await in their tents for their shampooing. I am just about to take some fresh towels up to them."

"Are you indeed? What perfect timing. And which tents might they be in? The ones at the far end, I hope?"

"That happens to be so, Sir Greville sahib, for they particularly requested the rough flannels."

"This gets better by the moment," Greville declared, and began to unbutton his greatcoat. "I must insist that you allow *me* to shampoo them both."

"You, sahib?" The sheikh was a little taken aback, and clearly wondered if the reason for Sir Greville Seton's unmarried state lay in his sexual preferences!

Greville smiled. "Oh, it's nothing like *that,* I assure you, for no beings on this earth could be less to my liking than those two."

The sheikh's expression changed again, this time to apprehension. "I trust you do not mean to cause trouble, Sir Greville sahib?"

"Not anything that will reflect upon your establishment."

"Do I have your word, sahib?"

"You do." Greville spread his hands. "Would I be less than truthful with you?"

The sheikh bowed. "Oh, undoubtedly, Sir Greville sahib, but on this occasion I will trust you."

The door opened and closed softly behind them as Rupert and Sir Jocelyn came in. Greville turned quickly, and sighed with annoyance. "I thought I made myself clear—" he began, but Sir Jocelyn interrupted quickly.

"We didn't want to be left out, dear boy; after all we too have bones to pick with March and Strickland," he said, placing his blanket bundle on the floor.

"Three against two is hardly cricket," Greville pointed out, looking curiously at the bundle.

Rupert grinned. "It will be two against two, because Sir Jocelyn is only here to umpire the proceedings."

Greville gave in. "Oh, all right, I don't suppose I have any real choice in the matter."

"None whatsoever, dear fellow," Rupert agreed, then rubbed his hands together eagerly. "What's the plan?"

"I haven't got one," Greville admitted. "My only thought was to get here and get my hands on those two reptiles."

Sir Jocelyn gave a chuckle. "Very laudable, I'm sure, but not the answer if we wish to be able to face our women-folk again. So, sirs, allow me to make a few suggestions." He turned to the sheikh and pointed at the cologne bottles on the table. "Which of those smells most like civet cat?" he inquired.

The sheikh was offended. "Civet cat? I stock only the finest—!"

Sir Jocelyn wagged a reproving finger at him. "Come,

now, sir. As I recall, you once dowsed me from that small yellow bottle, and I stank for two days."

"Well, I suppose that one *may* be a little strong," the sheikh conceded reluctantly.

"It's foul, and therefore ideal," Sir Jocelyn said, and pocketed the bottle. Then he looked at Greville and Rupert again. "Thrashing March and Strickland to within an inch of their miserable lives will make you both feel good in the meantime, but our dear ladies will not like it at all. The fair sex is of an inherently tender disposition, abhorring brutish behavior, and indeed that is why we adore them. But they do like to be able to giggle at their vanquished foes."

"Giggle?" Greville repeated in puzzlement.

Sir Jocelyn nodded. "March suffered considerable humiliation last night, but tonight you can make him a complete laughing stock. And Strickland too. Public ridicule is an excellent weapon. So, after giving them both the most bracing shampooing they've ever had, and sprinkling them with the essence of polecat, I suggest you resort to these." He pushed the bundle with his foot.

Greville bent to untie the blanket, and to his astonishment found that Sir Jocelyn had raided Evangeline's theater wardrobe for Malvolio's awful yellow stockings, Feste's jingling jester's hat, a pair of hose, party-colored in pink and silver and cut off at the knees, and the fearsome *Henry VIII* codpiece.

Sir Jocelyn chuckled again. "Just *imagine* the effect these will have on the Garsingtons' *soirée musicale!*"

Greville began to grin. "I think your plan is excellent, Sir Jocelyn. What do you say, Rupert?"

Rupert's eyes shone wickedly. "I say it is a splendid notion."

"I'm glad you think so." Sir Jocelyn tied the bundle again and lifted it from the floor, then he turned to the sheikh. " 'Lead on, Macduff!' " he said.

The sheikh raised an eyebrow. "I know my Shakespeare, Sir Jocelyn," he corrected. "The actual quotation is 'Lay on, Macduff.' "

"Is it, be damned? I didn't realize that," replied Sir Jocelyn. "Well, whatever, just do it."

The sheikh bowed, took some towels from the shelves, and led them upstairs.

Oliver and Ralph were relaxed and unguarded, and did not sense their imminent fate. After enjoying vapor baths, they were now languishing naked in their flannel tents, which were not anything like those that might be found at an army encampment, but were bags that were tied at the throat and had inward-facing "sleeves" into which the masseur slipped his arms in order to apply Oriental unguents. The room was very steamy indeed, with half a dozen tents, only two of which were occupied. While encased to the throat in flannel, Oliver and Ralph were very vulnerable indeed, and as bad luck would have it, their conversation had just turned to Sybil and Sophia, about whom they guffawed with laughter.

The door of the adjacent room burst open behind them, and Sigismund Garsington strode in with a towel tied around his plump middle. He was brandishing a pistol in either hand, and there was a wild expression on his round pink face. "So you find my sisters amusing, eh?" he bellowed, and leveled the pistols at the two men, whose laughter broke off in two squeaks of terror. But they couldn't escape, for they were too well tied in.

At that moment the sheikh ushered the others in as well, and Sigismund rounded upon them, barrels at the ready. The sheikh dropped the towels with shock and scuttled out, but Sir Jocelyn was equal to the moment, and stepped forward with an affable smile.

"Don't be hasty, there's a good chap, sir," he said to Sigismund.

"Hasty? *Hasty?*" cried Sigismund. "I am about to blast these two to kingdom come!"

Oliver and Ralph squeaked again, and their flannel tents trembled visibly.

Sir Jocelyn glanced at them. "They have offended you, sir?" he inquired of Sigismund.

"I heard them poking fun at my sisters."

"Ah. Well, sir, it may interest you to know that we have come here to, er, acquaint these same fellows with the extent of our disapproval."

"You have?" The pistols were lowered, but Oliver and Ralph still looked fit to expire of fright.

Sir Jocelyn came to put a tactful arm around Sigismund's pudgy shoulders. "Yes, we have," he said urbanely, "but our notion of suitable punishment differs a little from yours. Allow me to explain." He whispered what he had said to Greville and Rupert in the vestibule, and the held up the blanket bundle.

Sigismund's rage began to disappear, and his face lit up with a broad grin. "By *gad,* I like it!" he declared.

Sir Jocelyn cleared his throat a little awkwardly. "I haven't quite finished, sir. You see, we thought we would impose our victims upon the *soirée musicale* at Garsington House." He held his breath, wondering what the reaction would be. To his huge relief, Sigismund gave a grunt of approval.

"I see nothing wrong in *that!* I've been wriggling like a damned worm on a hook for years now because I'm expected to play that damned hautbois."

"You have?" Sir Jocelyn said in surprise, for he had always believed Sigismund to be a dedicated musician.

"Yes. That's why I came here this evening. I didn't mean to fall asleep, but I'm glad I did because they'll be chasing around like headless chickens wondering where I am."

"I had no idea," Sir Jocelyn murmured.

"To be honest, I've always wanted to play Sybil's harp, but the old pater and mater won't have it. They think I'll look like a prize daisy."

Sir Jocelyn choked back his laughter. "Indeed? How very fortunate," he managed to say.

Sigismund smiled again. "So it will serve them right if we, er, brighten things up a little, eh? Right, I'll take my dear brother-in-law, and leave you three to toss a coin for March!"

Greville insisted upon the right to deal with Oliver, and soon he and Sigismund went to work. Never had there been two less gentle masseurs, and never had there been two more cowardly victims. Oliver and Ralph squealed and yelled as the rough flannel showed no mercy to their recently steamed bodies. The squeals became howls when Sir Jocelyn poured the odoriferous cologne in around their necks, and the rubbing began all over again.

The craven pair were permitted out of the tents after five minutes, but if they thought they would be permitted to don their own clothes again, they were in error. Soon Oliver was togged in Feste's bell-bedecked hat, Malvolio's yellow stockings, and a towel to hide his modesty, and Ralph wore the knee-length hose and Henry VIII codpiece. They both looked utterly ridiculous, and Sigismund delightedly likened their aroma to that of a Newgate privy. Then, when he had dressed again, they all went downstairs.

The sheikh's eyes widened as he saw the strange procession, and two of his assistants sniggered from a doorway as Oliver and Ralph were herded out into the icy night. There some fly-by-nights were engaged, and the prisoners conveyed to Garsington House, each with a pistol to his head to deter him from any notion of escape.

Astonished footmen did not dare to refuse entry, and Oliver's bells jingled foolishly as he shuffled unwillingly across the gleaming entrance hall toward the double doors of the music room, from beyond which issued the twanging of Sybil's harp as she sang "Where the bee thuckth, there thuck I." Her racket bore off as Sigismund flung the doors open and strode in. "Ladies and gentlemen, pray silence for a very different kind of entertainment!" he announced, and everyone turned with gasps as Greville and Rupert pushed Oliver and Ralph into the glittering room.

"Dance, my good morris men," Greville breathed, and prodded Oliver warningly in the back. Oliver hastily began to leap about, and Ralph followed suit.

Lord and Lady Garsington gaped, Sybil looked as if she needed to hold on to the harp for support, and Sophia slipped from her chair in a dead faint. The rest of the room fell about, helpless with laughter.

Chapter 33

As the Garsingtons' *soiré* disintegrated into farce, Megan was experiencing a very different world. She could see Rollo, and he was as real as any living man as she stood next to him by the porch of St. Nicholas's. The wind was blustery, and there wasn't any snow. Nor were there any outside steps up to the church galleries, and when she looked at some of the old tombstones, they seemed oddly new and freshly inscribed. She glanced toward Brighton, and saw with a start that it had shrunk. It was without the Marine Pavilion and the fine new streets, and was just a small fishing village that ended where the wide-open grass of the Steine began. The church bell was tolling, and a funeral procession was wending its slow way from the lychgate. The black-draped coffin was carried shoulder high by four men, and a long column of mourners followed behind it, many of them sobbing unashamedly. Like Rollo, all were dressed in the fashion of the mid-seventeenth century.

Rollo's cheeks were wet with tears. He wore black plumes in his hat, black ribbons around his elbows, and black lace upon his clothes. He was very tall and handsome, and his grief was palpable as he removed his left glove to kiss the betrothal ring that shone on his fourth finger. Then he donned the glove again and took his place immediately behind the coffin as the procession entered the church. Megan knew why the old tombstones no longer seemed old, for this was Christmas Day, 1666, and the funeral was Belle Bevington's.

She lingered at the door to watch the simple service. Tribute was paid to Brightelmston's most famous daughter, whose beauty and talent was lost to the world forever. She had been trapped as the great fire of London burned all around, and although Rollo had rescued her, she had never recovered. Now she had come home to be laid to rest in the church where she and Rollo were to have been married. The congregation watched as the coffin was lowered beneath the flagstones, then the bell tolled again as everyone except Rollo left the church.

When the church was empty, he again removed his glove in order to take a sprig of mistletoe from inside his coat. Carefully he dropped it down the side of the coffin, where it would not be seen by the men who would come shortly to complete the burial. "For thee, my beloved, in memory of our first kiss," he said softly, the words carrying in spite of the booming of the bell. It was then that Megan saw his betrothal ring had gone.

As he went to don his glove again, something small and golden fell into the grave, and she heard it strike the carved oak. He walked from the church, passing right by her, but although she tried to tell him what had happened, no words would come. She followed him outside, and saw him hurry after the other mourners, who had now gone out through the lychgate and were on their way down the old original road into the town. Open grass, trees, and bushes had replaced the streets and houses of modern Brighton, and where Church Street would one day be, there was only a narrow deserted path that led toward the distant Steine. As she looked, a gang of footpads fell upon Rollo. Some of the mourners ran back to help, but the footpads had already scattered.

She could see Rollo lying dazed on the ground, but suddenly his voice spoke in her ear. "Mistress Megan, Belle and I vowed never to remove our betrothal bands, not even in death. I did not know I had lost mine in the church, believing it to have been stolen by the thieves. Without the ring, my vow was broken, condemning me to a lonely everlasting unless the ring be placed on my finger again. Only now that I have found Lady Evangeline can I be saved. She is my beloved's descendant, blood of her blood, and when she gives me the ring, all will be well once more.

Because Sir Greville hath requested it, she hath promised to go to St. Nicholas's before the end of Christmas Day. When she enters the church, I will receive my redemption."

Everything faded, and there was only the warm coziness of the bed in the blue chamber. Megan felt pleasantly drowsy. Someone was holding her hand. "Canst thou hear me, mistress?"

"Master Witherspoon?"

"Indeed so, sweet lady. How dost thou feel now?"

"Feel?" Her eyes remained closed, but her brows drew together. What a strange question to ask, she thought. She was quite all right; *he* was the one who had been set upon by footpads.

"I think thou dost not recall what thy vile cousin did to thee."

Memory returned with a rush, and with a gasp she opened her eyes. Firelight danced in the hearth, and a candle glowed on the little table, where the mistletoe and book still lay. She could see Rollo sitting on the edge of the bed as he held her hand, but he was only faint again now, not clear and strong as he had been in 1666. "Why is it dark?" she asked. "How long have I been in bed like this?"

"It is almost midnight and still Sunday, mistress. Laudanum has been administered by a strange eastern fellow, and thou hast been asleep since thy encounter with the maggot March at the summerhouse. But we are all assured that thou wilt be as fit as a fiddle in a day or so." He hesitated. "Megan, dost thou recall anything that happened during thy sleep?"

"Yes. I saw Belle's funeral and what happened to your wedding ring," she replied.

"Even if Sir Greville had not told Lady Evangeline she must go to the church, I would still have shown thee my story, for I wish it to be known. I have not broken any rules, Mistress Megan, for I have already told thee that all shades are at liberty to speak to those who are unconscious. On Christmas Day I will be reunited with my beloved Belle."

"I pray so, Master Witherspoon."

"Rollo, please, for I have been most forward with thy given name."

She smiled, but then remembered the locket, and her father's likeness. "Rollo, Lady Evangeline keeps a portrait of my father in her locket . . ."

"Indeed so, Megan. She hath confessed that she loved thy sire greatly, but bowed to her own father's wishes and ended the matter."

Megan's eyes cleared with relief. "So it was over *before* my parents were married?"

"Oh, certes, Megan, thou must not fear otherwise! There was nothing there should not have been; thy sire did not forget his marriage vows, any more than I have forgotten my vow to my beloved Belle. 'Twas enduring love that drove Lady Evangeline to seek thee out when she learned thy parents had both passed on so cruelly, and thy beastly kinsman had ejected thee without a groat to thy name. She wished to take thee into her home as the child she had never had, but feared thy resentment at such presumptuousness."

"How could I possibly resent someone who has been so very kind to me? Someone who brought Sir Greville into my life . . ."

"Ah, yes, Sir Greville." The specter cleared his throat. "That stout fellow is in a veritable lather of anxiety over you. He loves thee dearly, Megan, and hath much to tell thee concerning the exceedingly appropriate humiliation that is now the lot of thy cousin and thy other tormentor, Ralph Strickland."

Megan stared up at him. "Ralph *Strickland?* I-I don't understand . . ."

Rollo got up from the bed. "Sir Greville should tell thee all himself. I will see that he comes directly." He left her.

A few moments later Greville came quickly into the room. He paused for a second or so in the doorway, his anxious eyes resting upon her as if he had feared never to see her again. Then he came to sit on the bed, in order to take her hands, but she sat up to put her arms around his neck, and he held her close.

"Oh, my dearest, dearest Megan, I love you so very much," he whispered, sinking his fingers sensuously into her hair.

"And I love you, Greville, with all my heart," she whispered back.

His arms tightened around her.

Chapter 34

Carol singers came to the door of Radcliffe House on Christmas Eve. Their faces were rosy in the light from their lanterns as they sang "Deck the halls with boughs of holly." More snow had fallen since Sunday, and snowflakes drifted in through the open door. Mrs. Fosdyke had baked spiced biscuits and prepared a silver bowl of mulled wine in which floated clove-pricked oranges, and all the servants were present, except Edward, who had been summarily dismissed the moment Evangeline was acquainted with his dealings with Oliver. Evangeline stood with Sir Jocelyn at the foot of the stairs, and Rupert with Chloe, but of Greville and Megan there was no sign because they were standing in the shadows at the top of the stairs.

It was the first time Megan had been allowed out of bed, and Evangeline had forbidden her to come down. She was in her nightgown, with Evangeline's capacious red plaid shawl over her shoulders and Greville's steadying arm around her waist. Her hair was unpinned, and there was little color in her cheeks, because the effects of the sheikh's laudanum had not quite worn off, but otherwise she was on the mend. If anyone had told her only a week ago that she would be so happy by Christmas Eve, she would have branded them quite mad. But there was bliss in her heart now, and a contentment that she had never dreamed would be hers again. It was so good to have Greville's arm around her, and to know that he loved her as she loved him.

Suddenly he plucked some mistletoe from the greenery twined over the banisters, and held it above her head.

"A kiss, my darling," he whispered, and she raised her lips to his just as the carol singing ended and applause broke out in the hall below.

Rollo watched them from the shadows, and smiled. " 'It was a lover and his lass, With a hey, and a ho and a hey nonino . . .' " he murmured, then sighed. "Oh, Belle, Belle, could it be that by this time tomorrow thou wilt be in these aching arms once more? I pray it be so. I pray it hard indeed." Turning, he walked away, and Megan drew back from Greville's lips as she heard the spectral footsteps.

It was Christmas Day, the sun was shining, and Yuletide greetings were on everyone's lips as the jubilant bells of St. Nicholas's rang out as permitted on this one day of the year, for on every other day the church bells of England were a warning of French invasion. The congregation dispersed at the end of morning service.

As the worshippers departed, the small party from Radcliffe House—Evangeline, Greville, Megan, and Rollo—waited in the carriage in Church Street. Rollo was detectable only by the indentation he made in the seat, and he was all of a fidget because the moment he had been seeking for so long had arrived at last. Evangeline was stylish in emerald-green, and Greville wore his greatcoat. Megan was snug in her new cloak, her feet warmed by a heated brick wrapped in cloth, her hands plunged deep into a cozy muff. She had a little more color today, and felt much better.

The bells continued to peal for ten long minutes, but then fell silent, and as the bell ringers left as well, everyone alighted from the carriage. The church was quiet and so cold that their breath was clearly visible as Greville led them down the aisle toward Belle Bevington's memorial. But when they were only a third of the way, everything suddenly went dark, as if the sun had been extinguished. Evangeline's breath caught uneasily as the dim light of an old-fashioned horn lantern glimmered from behind them, and they turned to see Rollo approaching. He was as clear and real as he had been in Megan's dream.

They all parted instinctively for him to pass, and then they saw Belle. She held an oval vizard mask to her face, and wore a chestnut velvet gown with a divided skirt that revealed a richly laced pink brocade petticoat beneath. Her hair was very dark, and worn in a knot on top of her head, with wispy tendrils around her face and long ringlets over her ears. Three rows of pearls adorned her throat, and diamonds flashed on her fingers as she lowered the vizard to reveal her breathtakingly beautiful face. Her eyes were as blue as forget-me-nots, and there was a small black butterfly patch at the corner of her mouth. Her expression was adoring as she held out her cupped hand to Rollo. In her palm lay the lost betrothal ring. He put the lantern on the floor, then took the ring and slipped it on his finger. Belle stepped into his arms, and as their lips met once more the sunlight of Christmas Day 1806 returned. The ghosts had gone, but the lantern remained where Rollo had left it.

Evangeline's cheeks were wet with tears, and she shook her head as Greville went to her. "No, leave me. I'll be all right, these are tears of happiness. I-I'll just walk on my own in the churchyard for a while, if you don't mind." She bent to retrieve the lantern, then left the church.

Greville turned to Megan. "So, in the words of the Bard, *All's Well that Ends Well.*"

"Yes."

He glanced toward his mother's tomb. "Not all love stories have ended happily in this church," he said softly.

"Ours will," Megan replied, then reached out for his hand. "Come, there's something we must do now."

"Do?"

She caught his hand and led him to the altar. There she took a tiny sprig of mistletoe from inside her muff, and gave it to him. It is *our* tradition now," she said, and reached over to put it in the secret place.

Greville smiled. "And will you still wish to do that when you are a titled lady?" he asked quietly.

Her eyes widened. "Titled lady?"

"I wish you to be my Lady Seton, Megan. Do you accept?"

"Yes, oh, yes," she whispered, and their lips came together in the sort of Christmas kiss that had no business taking place in such a hallowed place.

Rollo's voice sounded distantly. " 'Give me a thousand kisses, then a hundred, then a thousand more . . .' "

Belle's answering laughter, kittenish, provocative, echoed faintly around the ancient stonework, then disappeared.

Postscript

The 1806 production of *Twelfth Night* was a resounding success. It was universally agreed that there had never been a finer Malvolio than Sir Greville Seton, and that Evangeline's phantasmagoric effects were wonderful indeed. Mind you, there was a slight disturbance at one point when several people in the audience cried out that they could see the ghostly and entirely incongruous figures of a Restoration lady and gentleman strolling hand in hand across the stage. Evangeline merely pointed out that her transparencies must have gotten mixed up somehow.

At St. Nicholas's church on St. Valentine's Day 1807, Megan became Lady Seton and Chloe became Lady Rupert Radcliffe. It was a wonderfully happy occasion that was made very grand indeed by the attendance of the Prince of Wales, who had come to Brighton especially to formalize the purchase of Radcliffe House. Evangeline and Sir Jocelyn had their own nuptials planned for May Day, which just happened to be Evangeline's birthday.

After the debacle of their *soirée musicale,* the Garsingtons had decamped abroad, Gibraltar being unfortunate enough to find itself their chosen destination. Only Sigismund stayed in England, and now that he had escaped torture by hautbois, had become a much more tolerant and contented fellow; indeed he, Greville, and Rupert became good friends. Sigismund could no longer abide to even hear an orchestra, and on account of this was one day to find his way into the arms of the Duchess of Oldenburg, who was sister to Czar Alexander II and who shared Sigismund's loathing for music. But that was another story.

As for Oliver and Ralph, their fate was sealed. Sigismund's new tolerance did not extend to letting either of them escape the Garsington marital hook, and at a very hasty wedding on New Year's Eve an ecstatically happy Sybil became Mrs. March. Ralph was forced back to Sophia, who now trusted him less than ever, and nagged him constantly.

It was unfortunate for both Garsington sons-in-law that Gibraltar was a very small rock, with very few places for them to steal a few moments of peace and quiet. Oh, how often did the Pillars of Hercules ring to the clarion calls of their wives. "Cooee, Oliver! Cooee, Walph! COOEE! **COOEE!**"